# A Mark in the Road

## Angelique Burrell

*Enjoy!*

*Angelique Burrell*

*To Walt, Hadyn, and Chase,*
*my favorite road trip companions*

Saturday, May 25, 2019

*Golden Valley News*
Fallon, Nevada

## Woman Missing; Car Found Abandoned Along Route 50

Kenna Cook, 24, of Daly City, Calif., was reported missing Thursday when she failed to arrive in Copper Mountain, Colo., at her new residence.

Her family reported last hearing from her on Wednesday afternoon, when she stopped in Fallon, Nev.

Cook is described as 5'4" with brown hair, fair complexion, brown eyes, and weighs approximately 135 pounds.

Police recovered a gold Honda Accord registered to Cook yesterday on Route 50, east of Valterra, Nev. Although the vehicle showed no signs of an accident, the Sterling County Sheriff's Office reported skid marks near the scene.

A reward has been offered by the family for any information leading to the whereabouts of Cook. Contact the Sterling County Sheriff's Office with information.

# CHAPTER 1

A silver BMW crossed Chicago Avenue, clipping the rear tire of a bicycle. The bike spiraled left as the rider crashed into the curb, and the car skidded to a stop.

The vision was all in Mason's mind. His friend Addie was driving, but she didn't see the accident.

"Mason? Hello? Did you hear me?" Addie's eyes flipped between him and the road as she drove them to school. "Where did you go? Really. We were talking and it's like you disappeared."

"Yeah. Sorry. It's just—" Mason pointed back to the intersection. "I got distracted. There was a new tire track." His light brown hair flopped into his eyes from the wind, and he pushed it back, resting his head in his hand. Thoughts of the accident mingled with the remnants of his conversation with Addie.

"Geez, dude. I mean, it's fun when you make up stories when we're bored and all, but I need you to focus. We're almost to school. This is important."

Mason shook his head clear. The bags under Addie's eyes were a telltale sign that she had spent most of the previous night crying. "I know. I know. I got you."

"What do you know?" Addie challenged.

"To focus. You need me to focus."

"And?"

"And…" A glimmer of what she had said when he was paying attention to the tire tracks flashed in his mind. "And, I won't say anything to anyone."

Addie leaned her head against the headrest and relaxed her shoulders. "I mean, really. Tell no one. Don't say anything about my moving to a soul. No matter what."

"Got it." Mason studied the pale brown freckles that dotted Addie's cheek. They reminded him of their summers as kids. He used to call her "freckle-face" because they darkened so much in the sun. Now, they hinted at how close summer was. "But why not tell anyone?"

Addie glared at him, and her brown eyes, which she always claimed were hazel, pierced through him. "Are you kidding me?"

"No. Really," Mason said. "I mean, it's not like it's a secret you can keep from your friends. They'll find out you're moving. If not from you, then from their parents. All your mom has to do is tell one person, and the news will fly around their cocktail parties. You know how parents gossip."

"I can't tell my friends today. Okay?" she snapped. "I've barely processed it myself. I can't handle their questions. Not yet. I don't have answers."

Mason leaned back against the passenger seat and let the air between them breathe. He'd grown up next door to Addie and knew firsthand how stubborn she was. She named their fort Arendelle the summer he was ten and she was nine because she loved the movie *Frozen*. If she wouldn't budge on a fort name, she wasn't going to budge on this.

"Fair enough," he said.

She waved a hand toward the road behind them. "Fine. Tell me about the skid marks back there. What story did you make up this time? Maybe it'll get my mind off how mad I am about my dad's work transfer."

Mason gazed out the passenger window, not wanting to think about what he had seen but telling her anyway. "A guy on a bicycle, probably a commuter 'cause he wore one of those black crossbody bags, you know, like he was headed to the train. Well, he crossed Chicago Avenue in front of a silver BMW. The driver hit the brakes as soon as she saw him."

Addie and Mason waited at an intersection as runners from the nearby college crossed in front of them, jogging slowly. It was probably the end of their cool-down run, and Mason's eyes followed them as they continued down the side street. He wished he'd gone on a run before school. It would've cleared his mind.

"Well?" Addie asked.

"She just missed him," Mason lied.

Addie's face relaxed a little. "Lucky morning for that guy. Not so lucky for me."

"Yeah," Mason agreed, because there was nothing else he could say.

"What else?" she asked. "Did the commuter guy even know he was almost hit? Or did he just keep riding?"

Mason replayed the image in his mind: The woman skidded to a stop as soon as her front bumper caught the bike's rear tire. Thankfully, the guy was wearing a helmet, but still. The rider's impact with the curb was ugly enough to distract Mason from his conversation with Addie, a conversation that began the night before.

Mason didn't want to think about their conversation or the commuter, so he steered Addie toward something general. "You don't need me to tell you what happened. If you look at the skid marks closely enough, they'll tell you what happened."

"Yeah, yeah. The speed, the pavement temperature, the wheels... all of it tells what happened," Addie mimicked. "You've told me all that. But what I really want to know is how you can make up so many different stories. I mean, really, you're so specific."

"Imagination. I have a great imagination." Right now, though, Mason's imagination wasn't good enough to imagine Addie gone.

Since last night, when she told him that her family was moving to Nevada, he'd been unmoored by the thought that he'd no longer hear music blasting from Addie's Jeep as she pulled into her drive just before curfew or see her running out the front door when her friend Becca picked her up. Ever since she moved in next door, he'd been falling in and out of love with her—depending on the year—and even though she was currently dating Declan Dapko, Mason couldn't get his mind off her.

"Why aren't you doing better in English with that imagination?"

"You got me." Mason shrugged. "Really, though, the tire marks aren't all about imagination if you know the science behind them."

Addie rolled her eyes, and he knew, at least for the moment, she wasn't thinking about her move.

"Actually," he continued. "You should be asking why I'm not doing better in physics."

"Whatever."

"Really, it's a lot about science." He knew the tire marks left by her boyfriend, Declan, were coming up. They were a perfect example because, like Declan, they were typical.

"Nice try. What did you say a minute ago? A silver BMW? A commuter on a bike with a crossbody bag? And the other day, a coyote early in the morning?" Addie smiled, the first smile he'd seen all morning. "A guy in a yellow VW Bug with a blue flower in the vase? Remember that one? That's not science."

"It was a blue hydrangea," he said. "And most VW Bugs have a flower in the vase. That's not creative."

"But a *blue hydrangea*?" Addie raised an eyebrow. "What are you, a florist?"

"They exist. Look them up." He wondered if he was too detailed in his descriptions. It had been easier to narrate most of what he saw, though, like this morning, he often left out the bad parts.

"I don't doubt their existence," she said. "But where did you pull a *blue hydrangea* out of? That's my point. How do you come up with so many details like that?"

"Consider it 'filling in the gaps.'" They'd returned to normal, or at least as close to normal as they could knowing she was moving in less than a month.

"Look." Mason pointed to the mark on the road left by Declan. They'd been driving over it since Monday, and Mason knew it was the car he read about in the newspaper, the one full of the kids responsible for destroying several mailboxes in the neighborhood—batting practice out the window. Even though Mason knew who'd been driving the "unidentified black car," he hadn't shared that bit of information with Addie or the police.

Addie slowed her Jeep slightly.

"Look at that one again," he said. "You can see the slide, the trailed mark, and then the slight ridge, the darkening at the edge. It's faded, but do you remember how dark it was a couple days ago? Can you tell me how it was made?"

"Are you seriously quizzing me?" Addie asked.

Mason put his arm out the window and played with the cool morning wind as she drove. "I'm waiting."

"Well, Mr. Henley..." she teased as she took the same corner. "The driver took the turn too fast because..."

*Because he's an egotistical douche who needs to beat down others to make himself feel big.*

"...he was in a hurry to get some coffee," Addie said.

"See, you're filling in the gaps."

"Sure, just not as specific as your blue flower," she said, coming to a stop at another intersection and waiting for a blue minivan to cross.

"What if I told you that Declan was the driver that made those tire marks?" Mason watched Addie's face, hoping she didn't light up at the mention of her boyfriend.

She scrunched her eyes, ever so slightly, as if in concentration.

*Not a dreamy look. I'll take that.*

Addie flashed a smile as an idea occurred to her. "I would say that Declan took the corner too fast because he was so anxious to see me."

"See, you do have a good imagination," Mason said with a laugh.

"Not funny." Addie reached to hit him, but he dodged out of the way.

"You're punishing me enough by putting the top down." Mason turned down the heat. "My feet are on fire. Why turn the heat on if you put the top down?"

"You know the rule. Check the temp."

Mason looked at his phone and rolled his eyes. Addie's rule was that the top had to be down if the temperature was sixty or higher. "Sixty-two barely qualifies. What are you? A glutton for punishment? Is that why you decided to go out with Declan?"

"Do we really have to discuss that again? You're like the big brother I never wanted. I told you there's a sensitive side to Declan that people don't see."

"Oh, that's right!" Mason hit his forehead in mock realization. "I forgot that he cried when we watched *Gnomeo and Juliet* in English."

"I know he used to be a player, but he's changed," Addie insisted. "He matured a lot when he did that internship with his dad's law firm last summer too."

Mason sat up a bit straighter. "I see him when you aren't around. He's not as changed as you think."

"You're just jealous because you secretly want to date me."

Mason looked out the window to hide the heat that rose in his cheeks.

"Oh stop; I'm teasing," Addie said with a laugh. "I know you've hated him since you were babies, but until he gives me reason to doubt him, I'm going to believe him."

Declan was also a senior, which means he'd annoyed Mason for most of his life. Declan was arrogant and loud and self-absorbed. If he wasn't concerned about himself, he was concerned about making everyone else concerned about him.

"What happened with that one?" Addie asked as she drove over another skid mark.

"A green Subaru stopped suddenly because the driver thought he missed his turn. Didn't I tell you that yesterday?"

"Don't be salty," she cajoled. "I was checking your memory. Look who's crabby now."

"You're the one who's trying to change the subject."

Mason shifted in his seat to see Addie more clearly. He couldn't fathom how she could believe Declan's "sweetness" act. They'd discussed Declan's breakup with Talia at the end of last year and the rumors that Mason was sure Declan had spread. Addie wasn't clueless about the type of person Declan was.

But if Declan had told Addie that he'd changed, Mason knew she'd give him the benefit of the doubt. That's how nice she was. Mason had to trust that Addie would see the truth eventually.

"Tell me," Addie said. "How do you do it? How do you remember all the stories you make up about the skid marks? I don't think you've ever forgotten a story you've told me."

"Maybe you're the one who's forgotten. And I've been making up new stories, pretending that I told them before."

They inched forward in traffic, and Mason couldn't pry his eyes from her. He followed the wisps of golden-brown hair that escaped her messy bun and floated in the breeze. Those strands of hair convinced him that her rule of putting the Jeep top down whenever the temperature was above sixty was brilliant. She said it made her happy when she drove to school in the open air, and this morning, she definitely needed the open air, and so did he. Everything seemed to be closing in around him.

They'd been carpooling since Mason got his license. But once Addie got her license, there was an unspoken understanding that her Jeep Wrangler was way cooler than his Toyota Prius.

"Really, how do you do it?" she asked, glancing at him.

The morning sun hit Addie's eyes, and Mason almost saw hazel. He fished in the glove compartment for her sunglasses and handed them to her.

"Thanks. Well? How do you keep all the skid marks straight?"

She was still trying to prevent him from asking the real questions, either about Declan or her impending move. She was in avoidance mode, something he'd seen before. He was too. He fought to keep from asking what he really wanted to know or from saying what he really wanted to say.

"I guess I have a good memory."

"Well, use that good memory to remember not to say anything to anyone at school," Addie said. "I'm so glad it's Friday. And Monday's Memorial Day. No school."

Mason nodded and gazed at the kids walking on the sidewalk, moving faster than their line of cars. His thoughts returned to the night before, to Addie sitting on the old wooden swing in his backyard. She hadn't sat on the swing in years, not since her parents' near-divorce over her father's increased interest in some woman at work.

Last night, when Mason looked out the back door and saw Addie sitting on the swing, he knew something was very wrong.

# CHAPTER 2

Addie inched the Jeep forward in the morning progression into the high school parking lot while Mason replayed the previous night in his mind, seeing her swaying slowly on the swing in his backyard. He'd stepped onto his back porch and whispered, "Olly Olly Oxen."

Her cheeks were shiny with tears when she looked up and finished the phrase, "Free, Free, Free."

Mason half-expected her to say that she'd broken up with Declan, that he'd cheated on her or something. Instead, Mason was blown away when she said she was moving.

He looked at Addie now as she focused on the line of cars, barely moving, in front of them. Her head rested against the headrest, a posture that hid the reality behind her sunglasses. The pool of tears in her eyes glistened in the sun.

Mason rubbed his own eyes, which were burning from his sleepless night. After talking with Addie by the swing, he'd lain in bed and rehashed all the questions he should've asked her, all the things he might've said, all the things he never had the courage to say to her.

Last night, she told him that the swing was the first place she thought to go when her parents told her they were moving. It had been

"Safe" for all the neighborhood games, and she wanted to feel that sense of comfort again.

Mason longed to tell her that he felt that way whenever he was with her, but he didn't have the nerve. After lying in bed all night thinking about her leaving, he wished he could tell her, but she wasn't ready to hear it. Not yet.

"Wednesday's my last day, and finals start next week," he said instead. He wanted to relish the fact that seniors didn't have to take second semester finals, but it only meant fewer days driving with Addie.

"A countdown to the end of the school year isn't going to help me cope with today, okay?"

"Sorry." Mason focused on the taillights in front of them and kept his mouth shut. He was leaving in August, going two-and-a-half hours away to the University of Illinois Urbana-Champaign, but he hadn't thought she would ever leave. He imagined coming home during break and hanging out with her, helping her plan college visits—even inviting her to U of I to visit him.

Loose strands of her hair danced in the wind and settled on her cheeks, blending into her freckles.

"You know, I'm really going to miss you," he said.

"Don't."

"But—"

"No." She held her palm up, blocking his words.

Mason's hair flopped over his eyes again, but he left it. It hid what he didn't want to give away.

"I can't." She waited a moment, then reached over and ruffled his hair. "You know, if you don't cut your hair soon, it'll be as long as mine."

Mason shagged his hair over his eyes. "I like it long. I think I look like I'm twelve with short hair."

"It looks good long." Addie reached for his hair again, but he ducked. "I think I heard Grace say something about how cute you look when you're running. Your hair goes flying."

He half-smiled and winked. "How about Sophie? Did she say anything?"

"Nice try." Addie pulled into the parking lot, and her tone sharpened. "Remember, don't tell anyone about my move to Ta-hoax."

"Don't you mean Tahoe?

"No. Ta-hoax. I've renamed it."

"You do know that's dorky, right? Did it take you all night to come up with that?"

"I refuse to believe this is my reality. It has to be a sick joke my parents are playing on me."

"It's not like you're moving to the middle of Wyoming or something. I'm sure there's an actual population there."

"Are you kidding? Really?" Addie sped over the final speed bump.

Mason was sure it was to punish him.

"I *don't* want to move. It might be a great place to live, but it's not the place *I* want to live. How do you not get that? I'm a junior. Next year is my senior year. It's easy for you to think like my parents; you're graduating and leaving."

Her move was too new to see any other way than totally devastating, which was exactly how he saw it. "I'm not thinking like your parents. I'm just trying to find something positive. It doesn't have to be the end of the world."

"Well, it is. Understand this—" Addie hit her hand against the steering wheel to punctuate each word. "There. Are. No. Positives."

Mason wanted to be strong, to be supportive, to be positive, but her words vibrated in his chest. She was moving thousands of miles away, out of his life.

"University of Illinois is nowhere near Nevada," he blurted.

Addie's jaw unclenched and her mouth opened as if she might speak, but she snapped it shut.

Mason didn't know what to make of his comment either. What was his problem? They weren't dating; they had never dated. He never even told Addie that he wanted to date her. And yet, they'd been friends since she was eight and he was nine.

He had been in shock since the moment she told him that her father had been transferred to Nevada. His stomach seemed to have stopped working, and, apparently, so had his mind.

"Thanks for the geography lesson." Addie locked eyes with him, and Mason couldn't tell if there was anger or pity in her stare. Or, he hoped, affection? Even after all these years living next door to her, he still couldn't read her looks.

Addie got out of the Jeep without saying a word, slammed the door, and walked toward the school.

*Anger. It must be anger.*

He grabbed his backpack and jogged to catch up to her. "Look, I haven't processed what you told me. We've been neighbors since I was in third grade. I like having you around—or knowing you're around, even if I'm not."

"Really?" Addie glared at him over her shoulder and kept walking.

"That didn't come out right." Mason snagged Addie's sleeve. "I'm a dork, remember?"

When she faced him, her cheeks were streaked with tears.

He grasped her arms and longed to pull her to him. Tears weaved paths over her freckles, and his heart broke because she was so beautiful, even in her sadness. Everything was wrong.

The sun highlighted the green flecks in her brown eyes, and the girl that fell off the swing in his backyard when they were kids stared back at him. Back then, he had grabbed her outstretched hand and helped her stand up out of the dirt, with her knees scraped and bloodied. When she stared up at him now, as she did then, he still didn't know what to say.

Addie broke free from Mason and pointed at the yellow brick building. "You at least get to finish high school here. You went to your prom with all your friends. You wore a toga and that dorky superhero outfit." She cracked a smile despite her tears. "What *were* you supposed to be?"

Mason shrugged. He had worked hard to repress that embarrassing memory. "Super Marathon Man. Bad idea, I know, but better than Nick. He was Captain Fartlek."

"Well, you got to dress like a dork. And go to bonfires, and the senior tailgate, and play pretend beer pong with the principal. What an idiot. Him, not you. You even got to wear these." She hit the "University of Illinois XC" logo on his chest. "For 'commitment day' or whatever it's called. And my senior year? It'll be in a school I don't know, with kids I don't know, with teachers I don't know, in a town I don't know. Everything, I don't know. How much will that suck?"

Mason couldn't resist the urge any longer and pulled her to him, hugging her. It was the only thing he could do and exactly what he longed to do.

She drew in a deep breath and sobbed into his chest. "I'm finally going to be a senior, and it'll be nothing like I thought it would be, nothing like I wanted...."

Mason rested his forehead on Addie's bun and let his own tears disappear into it.

They hadn't just been neighbors since he was in the third grade; they had terrorized the neighborhood on Razors together, they had captured tadpoles and toads and turtles, they had raced each other on bikes, they had had lemonade stands and toy stands, they had competed over who could do the most consecutive backflips on his family's trampoline—ending in his broken arm and a loss—and they had helped each other navigate middle school and high school. Carpooling wasn't a convenience; it was part of their friendship.

Since neither of them had a sibling, they had become each other's. When he didn't understand girls—actually, he still didn't understand girls—Addie explained to him why saying "that P.E. uniform looks like it was made for you" wasn't a compliment. And when Addie didn't understand boys, or at least what boys really wanted, Mason explained that they weren't referring to her Jeep when they said "nice rack." She had argued that point with him until he showed her a Jeep that *did* have a rack. That shut her up, then made her laugh.

And now, with her family moving to Incline Village, Nevada, so her dad could manage a Harlan Hotel in Lake Tahoe, Mason was losing a part of himself.

"Look," he said, still holding her and breathing in the strawberry scent of her shampoo. "You have the rest of this year and a couple weeks of summer. Trust me, at your new school, you will be the mysterious, cool, new girl that everyone will want to be friends with. Come on, I've seen videos of you on a snowboard. From the Midwest or not, you can ride the rail."

"You really are a dork. That's skateboarding." She broke from his hug and dug a finger into his sternum. "Seriously. Say nothing."

Mason raised his hands in surrender. "I know. You told me a million times." His thoughts flashed to the night before, sitting in the grass, occasionally catching her legs as she swayed on the swing and told him everything. "Plus, it's your news to tell, not mine."

She held his gaze for a moment, as if gauging his sincerity, and then nodded before heading toward the school.

"I'm sure I've seen a snowboarder ride the rail." Mason chased after her. "Don't you watch X Sports?"

"Again, you're a dork. Really." She nudged him with her shoulder as he came up alongside her. "Thanks."

He nudged her back, and they walked to the side entrance of the building. "Do you have anything after school?"

"Nothing. All my clubs ended last week. More time to study for finals, I guess."

"I have track practice, unless you want to talk after your day of secret-keeping."

"I'll be fine. Go to practice. The team needs you. Maybe Sophie will finally notice you."

Mason nodded toward Sophie, who was already weaving past people in the hall, headed in their direction. "Looks like she's noticed you. I'll never understand her need to wave so enthusiastically."

"I hope I can keep it together." Addie looked at Mason and wiped away the remnants of her tears.

If Addie broke during school and said anything about her move, the news would ripple through the students like an earthquake.

"Stay strong," he whispered just before Sophie wrapped an arm around Addie.

# CHAPTER 3

Mason dropped his bag in Addie's Jeep after school and headed to the track to warm up. She hadn't responded to any of the five texts he sent during the day, and his Snap was left on read. He was anxious to know how her day went, but he also knew that she'd have contacted him if she needed to. And what he needed right now was a long run. For him, the school day had been exactly as expected. Days from graduation, the teachers had given up trying to teach anything and the general atmosphere was a blend of giddy anxiety and cool nostalgia. Nothing made sense.

A tangible hippie-esque love oozed over the entire senior class. It was so unlike anything he had felt in the halls all year—or all of high school, for that matter—that he didn't trust the sentiment. Uninhibited expression ruled the halls. Girls randomly approached him between classes and gave him a hug or patted him on the arm and said, "I never told you, but I always thought you were cute." School felt like the intersection between a funeral and an AA meeting.

At its most alluring moments, the feeling sucked him in and bathed him in its warm glow, making him almost like some of his long-standing nemeses. Darren, who said the most repulsive things in the lunchroom. Jay, who never seemed to wear deodorant. Olivia, who told him to "screw off" for trying to help her when she'd tripped on the stairs. Everyone was beginning to seem wonderful, and the closer graduation got, the more they seemed like people he would miss.

Everyone except Declan. Nothing about Declan took on the rosy hue of graduation. When he pretended to endear himself to a teacher and then mocked her behind her back or when he laughed about copying someone's homework and getting a better grade, Mason was as repulsed as ever. Today, though, even after weeks of such sentimentality, Mason felt the finality of senior year. Addie said she was leaving and reality hit hard.

MASON JOGGED SLOWLY AROUND THE TRACK WITH HIS teammates after their workout, thinking about when he saw Addie on the way to fourth-period Psych. Her dark circles broadcasted her sleepless night, and her puffy eyes and red nose told him that her hope of holding it together at school had failed. The day must have been exhausting for her, especially if she avoided answering her ever-questioning friends.

When he passed her in the hall before seventh period, he held up two fingers—two more periods. Her slight nod indicated that she didn't want to say so much as "hi" for fear of crying again. But she did try to smile. It was brief and small, but it was there.

Maybe his own senior-year sentimentality had caused his resurgence of feeling for Addie. Whatever it was, Mason knew he needed a good long run.

He shot a wave to his teammates and left the track.

He didn't think about anything as he followed the path along the river. That's what he loved most about running—his mind's ability to turn off. He ran hard until the path curved away from the river and headed toward Mud Lake. Running had saved him in high school. It had given him a family when he didn't know many people, and it had kept popularity, and all its requirements, at a comfortable arm's length.

He couldn't party on weekends when he had to run ten miles in the morning. When he started XC, he thought it was a fall sport. He quickly learned that winter indoor track and spring outdoor track were required training for cross country runners, with a state meet attached. That state meet was going to be held a week after graduation. Mason needed to be prepared. As a distance runner, his eight mindless laps around the track had to be at a solid pace if he wanted to make All-State.

He circled the dam and started the five miles back, heading toward home. The air was warm. Summer hadn't fully begun, but he was dripping in sweat. Stride after stride, Mason focused on the sound of each foot hitting the gravel path.

Ground squirrels scampered off the path as he approached, and the brush occasionally opened to show the river, running alongside him. Mason went through his periodic check of form: keep the left arm tight —it liked to flap out—land on the flat of the foot to keep momentum, relax the shoulders, run tall. But as he got closer to home, images of Addie flipped through his mind.

Laughing with the wind whipping her hair. Singing "Something Beautiful" with her left leg up on the seat while she drove. Crying when he held her that morning. These images invaded the blank space that running created, and he couldn't shake free of them.

Mason wanted to turn off his mind again, but it was useless. He was too close to home and too close to Addie. Carpooling with her had been exactly what he needed, he now understood. Sure, he'd been annoyed when she was perpetually late because she couldn't figure out what configuration of leggings and sweatshirt to wear. But talking with her had always felt natural. He didn't hyper-analyze every word or phrase and second-guess himself for hours after conversations with Addie like he did with other girls. With her, he laughed with ease, and he just as easily sat in silence. She was low-drama and genuine, and Mason couldn't figure out what she saw in Declan.

Mason left the path and followed the road toward home. His feet rhythmically padded the asphalt as his mind drifted to a memory from years ago, of teaching Addie how to shoot a basket. How he had stood behind her in his driveway and put his hand over hers to demonstrate how to roll the basketball off her palm. Her hand, cool and soft, was tiny under his.

The memory was interrupted by an SUV slamming on its brakes. The driver's body lurched forward with the momentum and slammed back when her seatbelt engaged. In front of the SUV, a blur of dark brown hair disappeared.

Mason came to an abrupt stop on the side of the road and bent over, hands on knees, gasping for air. The vision, visceral and real, sucked the air from him. He had crossed Douglas Avenue and didn't notice the new tire marks until he ran over them.

He stood and looked back at the tire tracks.

*Had the child been hit?*

The road would give him clues if he could only focus.

# CHAPTER 4

Mason examined the skid marks. Short, staccato marks. The brakes didn't lock. That was a good sign.

Reluctantly, he jogged back across Douglas Avenue and focused on the vision as it filled his mind. The driver, probably in her early thirties, was watching the road; she wasn't fiddling with her phone or Chapstick. She was simply driving down the side street when the child ran out from between two parked cars after a soccer ball. The woman braked in time, only running over the soccer ball, which lodged in the undercarriage of her Highlander.

Mason squatted in the grass, his head in his hands, thankful that the child hadn't been hit. He wanted to vomit. The too-familiar mix of fear and panic gripped his stomach. Addie was the only person who listened to him when he talked about the tire marks, even if she thought it was a joke. She'd been an outlet for all the stress the visions caused, and the tire marks gave them something to talk about when her world seemed far from his. Now, he realized, their worlds were actually going to be far from each other. And when she left, he'd once again have no one to talk to about the skid marks.

For the rest of the run, Mason fixated on his regular mental rant.

*What's the purpose of all these visions? They've haunted my mind since I was a child, and they do nothing but derail my thoughts and terrorize me.*

If they were supposed to be some type of learning experience, Mason had learned enough. He didn't need to see children almost getting hit by vehicles to know he should keep his eyes on the road. And he most certainly didn't need to see Declan's reckless driving to know he was a jerk.

Mason reached home to find Addie sitting on the steps of his front porch, talking on the phone. He smiled and waved as he pulled his backpack from her Jeep, happy to have his thoughts focused back on her. She held up a finger and motioned for him to wait. He stretched out on the grass and strained to hear if she was talking to one of her friends, if she told them about her move.

"You suck at eavesdropping; did you know that?" she said when she hung up.

"What are you talking about?" he said with a smirk. "You're sitting on my stairs. I'm just stretching in my yard."

"Your neck. A dead giveaway. You couldn't have stretched that more if you tried." Addie patted the step next to her. "How was your run? You look like crap."

"Thanks. Typically, I try not to break a sweat. I don't know what got into me."

Addie pointed toward the Jeep. "You got all your stuff?"

"Yeah. Who were you talking to?" Mason asked again as he sat across from her.

"Sophie—she wanted to get together tonight. She's dying to know what's going on."

"Are you going to see her?"

"No. I told her I had to visit my—" Addie held out a hand, inviting Mason to finish her sentence.

"Grandmother." He smiled. "Thought I heard something about that. Did you tell her that I'm free?"

"You wish!" Addie leaned over and smacked Mason on the arm, then wiped the sweat off her palm. "Gross."

"How did you hold up today?" Mason asked.

"It was hard. I couldn't focus on anything long enough to even register how much the day sucked." Addie shook her head. "I'm glad it's the weekend."

"I don't know how you did it. Grace stalked me in P.E. and demanded I tell her what was going on with you. She's ruthless, but don't worry. I didn't cave, even when she threatened to spike the volley-ball in my face."

Mason hoped the joke would make Addie laugh, but it didn't.

"Yeah, I think she was kind of pissed that I wouldn't tell her what's going on."

"Hey, let's go around back," Mason said. "This cement is too uncomfortable to sit on."

"If you wore longer shorts, you wouldn't have a problem. What's with running shorts anyway?"

"Have you ever chaffed? Then you'd know."

"TMI, Mason!"

They walked around back, and Mason dropped his backpack on his deck before they headed to the swing.

"You know, I think I finally figured out why the drama group keeps breaking into tears every time they see each other," he said. "Have you listened to people in the halls?"

"Please don't try to explain why the drama kids act the way they do," Addie said. "That's going too far."

"I think I've been brainwashed by all the end-of-the-year-love," he joked.

Addie sat on the swing, and Mason pushed her lightly from behind.

"Really, though. Thanks for covering for me today. I'll tell them tomorrow. Right now, I can't talk about it or even think about it without crying."

Mason could tell by the slight quaver in her voice that her eyes were already filling.

"How did you not tell them today?" he asked. "All they had to do was look at you to know something was up."

Mason sat on the ground near Addie's feet, just as he had the night before.

"They asked, sure." Addie wiped the tears from her cheeks and sniffled. "I told them I wasn't ready to talk. I mean, I don't want to tell them at school. They probably think my parents are fighting again or something."

That was all she was probably capable of explaining. The day had to have been hard. Mason figured Declan hadn't pushed Addie—he would've let it go and moved on to thinking about himself—but Sophie, Becca, and Grace weren't people to let things go. Addie's puffy eyes would've been an invitation to probe, and if they hunted Mason down in P.E., they definitely drilled her.

"How am I even going to tell them?" Addie finally said. "They'll freak. Do you think they'll be mad that I didn't tell them right away?"

"Depends. Are you talking about your friends or Declan?"

"Please!" Addie kicked him, but he caught her foot and used it to swing her side-to-side. "Of course, I'm talking about my friends."

"Then maybe you shouldn't tell them that you told me," Mason said. "They might be hurt by that."

"True."

"But feel free to tell Declan that you told me," he added.

"Ha!" Addie leaned back, holding on to the ropes, and looked at the cloud puffs floating by. "What happened between you two? You used to be friends."

"The more interesting question is why do you like him?"

"I told you. He's changed. He's not perfect, but he's trying to figure himself out. He was super bummed when he didn't get scouted to play D1, and that humbled him."

Mason snorted.

Addie sat up abruptly and her hair tumbled into her face as she looked at him. "How can you not see it?"

"Humility and Declan have never been friends. He's as arrogant as ever. And his laugh? It's a guffaw! Who laughs like that?"

"Who says *guffaw*?"

"It's like he wants everyone to hear him laughing."

"You've never liked him, not since you were kids."

"There's a reason I haven't liked him since we were kids. I've never looked at him the same since he intentionally hit Ethan in the face with a baseball."

Mason leaned back against the tree, remembering all the blood when the baseball shattered the kid's nose. Declan hadn't looked surprised that he'd hit Ethan. Instead, he smirked.

"Sure, Declan said it was an accident," Mason said, the image still running through his head. "But Ethan was a better pitcher than Declan, and Declan doesn't like it when people are better at something than he is."

"That was so long ago," Addie said. "He's not that jealous now. And he doesn't act like he does around everyone else when it's just the two of us."

"I bet he doesn't. Please don't tell me he's romantic. I'd know you're full of it."

Addie leaned back again, lifting her feet into the air and pumping her legs. "You only see one side of him. He can be really sweet."

"I'm sure... when he wants something."

"Don't be a pig," Addie said. "I think the end of senior year is getting to you. That or this whole Tahoe-pocalypse is."

"Tahoe-pocalypse? I thought it was Ta-hoax." Mason chuckled. "I won't try to understand what you see in Declan if you promise not to talk like the school newspaper staff."

Addie dragged her feet on the ground to stop herself and leaned toward him, lips pursed. "I spent the whole day trying to think of that one after you shot down Ta-hoax. I need a name for this disaster my parents have created."

Mason couldn't help but laugh at her serious tone.

"Really, though," she said, lightening up. "Doesn't it sound catchy? Tahoe-pocalypse. Say it."

"Sounds overly dramatic."

"And *guffaw* isn't?" Addie kicked dirt toward him. "I don't think I've ever heard anyone actually use that word."

"Just listen the next time he laughs," Mason said, rolling his eyes. "When other people are around, not when it's just the two of you and he's being all 'sweet and romantic.' Listen to him laugh. Then you'll be saying *guffaw*, too."

The back porch light came on at Addie's house. Her mom stood at the door, cupped her hands over her eyes, and peered out. Addie didn't say anything, but her back noticeably tensed.

"You could tell your friends tonight," Mason said. "I'm sure you could still get together with Sophie."

Before Addie could respond, her mom opened the back door, and the jangle of Indy's collar rang out as she ran from Addie's yard to Mason's.

"Come here, Indy," Addie called. She turned back to Mason. "I'm too exhausted to see Sophie tonight. Maybe tomorrow. I don't know."

Indy, a black lab mix, ran up and poked Addie's leg with her nose, her way of demanding Addie scratch behind her ears. When Addie got the dog as a birthday present when she was ten, Indy became the leader of Mason and Addie's summer adventures. Even now, Addie joked about Indy trying to herd her to bed or pushing the bathroom door open to find her.

After checking on Addie, Indy turned her attention to Mason. She licked his face, and when he tried to push her away, she started licking his legs.

"I think Indy missed you," Addie joked.

"I think Indy likes dried sweat." Mason stood to escape the dog. "Scoot over. You need to save me from this beast."

Addie made room for him on the wooden seat. "She's harmless. Aren't you, girl?" Addie leaned down and patted Indy on the head.

Mason thought, a bit too late, about how bad he must smell. Sitting so close to Addie was not a good idea. When he was younger and his feet didn't touch the ground, sitting side-by-side wasn't a problem.

"I know it doesn't make sense," Addie went on, ignoring Mason's shifting in the seat. "I should've texted my friends as soon as my dad made his little declaration. But I just couldn't. I don't know. It seemed like if I did, then it would be real. Like I would be letting it happen."

"But there isn't anything you can do."

"I know. I just didn't want to believe it was going to happen. I still don't want to believe it."

"Maybe it isn't," Mason offered and immediately regretted it.

"You think?" The pitch of Addie's voice raised in hope.

"Yeah." He looked at his running shoes as he toed the dirt. "Maybe your dad is zombie-possessed, and he wants to lure you and your mom away from civilization."

Addie nudged him with her elbow, and he pretended that she knocked him off the swing. He stood, happy for a reason to get his smelly self away from her.

"He's totally zombie-possessed," Addie said. "But I don't think that'll stop him. I'll tell my friends tomorrow. Today was hard enough."

"I can't believe Sophie didn't drive right over here after school."

"She knows me better than that," Addie said. "She's giving me space."

"The longer you wait, the harder it'll be."

"Yeah, I know. What's that saying about pulling off a Band-Aid?"

Mason sat down and petted Indy as she licked his legs. "I have no clue. I'm too tough for Band-Aids," he joked.

"Yeah, right. Well, I'll get it over with tomorrow."

"Look, I know you know." Mason leaned his back against the tree and looked at Addie. "But you can text me anytime."

"Thanks," Addie said. "You've been a lifesaver."

"After you tell your friends, you'll all hang out for the rest of the weekend and cry together. And, if you feel like it, you can tell them how cool and supportive I've been. Maybe Sophie'll want to go on a date with me after all."

Addie got up and tousled Mason's hair. "In your dreams. You are so not her type."

Mason grabbed his heart in mock agony. "Don't crush my hopes. I'm fragile."

"Fragile." Addie laughed. "And too tough for Band-Aids?"

"You might as well give them plenty of time to plan your going-away party," Mason said.

A slight smile tugged at the corners of Addie's mouth, and it probably wasn't because she wanted a going-away party or even liked to party. She was most likely thinking the same thing Mason was—that her friends would go overboard planning her going-away party. Sophie and Becca, in particular, were iconic at West High for hyper-planning decorations for the homecoming dances and the Varsity Club parade floats.

"It will all be okay, right?" With this question, with her gaze, Addie seemed to mean more than just telling her friends. She meant the entire move.

"Yes," Mason said, trying to sound like he believed it.

"Thanks."

Mason pushed Indy away from him. "I don't think I need a shower now. Your dog has cleaned me."

"Not quite. You definitely stink." Addie flashed a smile and walked back to her house, Indy loping behind her.

# KENNA

*The throbbing in my head jars me awake. I lay there with my eyes closed and will my head to stop pounding. My whole being wants nothing more than to melt into the bed and fall back asleep. Why do I have such a headache? I search my mind for memories of the night before.*

*What did I do?*

*Was I out with my friends?*

*Did we do too many tequila shots?*

*Thoughts of standing on the side of the road next to my stalled car emerge from the fog of my mind.*

*I open my eyes and jerk upright.*

*"What the heck?" My voice disappears into the air around me.*

*My eyes are open, but the room is dark. Is it still night? My head spins, and my stomach lurches. I stand to run to the bathroom, but my head crashes into something hard.*

*I crumple to the floor and wretch.*

*Spitting the sour taste from my mouth, I look around, letting my eyes adjust to the darkness. A faint light seeps through cracks of what must be a door, and I lunge toward it. I grasp the edges of what feels like wood, searching for a handle or knob, but there's nothing. When my fingers brush against a soft loop of fabric, I grasp it and yank, throwing my body into my effort. My head crashes into the ceiling again, and the throbbing forces me to my knees.*

*"Hello?" I call.*

*My words sink into the silence and disappear into the walls.*

*Where am I?*

*I focus on the faint light rimming the door and stand slowly, holding my hand above my head to protect my throbbing skull. My fingers skim rough wood and small circles of wire.*

*Is that chicken wire?*

*What's happened?*

*I reach for the outline of a door and grope for the soft loop of the handle. When nothing budges, I throw my shoulder against the door hoping to shove it open.*

*I dig my fingers into the patches of light to get ahold of freedom, not caring that my fingernails bend and break.*

*I bang my fist against wood and scream.*

# CHAPTER 5

Sharing the visions he had when they crossed over skid marks—even if Addie didn't know they were real—had relieved a burden that weighed on Mason. But more than that, Addie was his friend, his neighbor, someone who had always been there for him. And now she was leaving.

Long ago, he'd tried to talk to his parents about the visions. At six, he thought everyone saw them. He regularly narrated what he saw when they drove over skid marks, and after a particularly gruesome accident between a car and a dog, his mom told him to stop making up stories. He remembered the look she gave him, like she was trying to put together a puzzle, her head tilted to the side, eyes squinched, mouth open. Six-year-old Mason tried to tell her that he wasn't making the stories up. He desperately wanted to understand what he saw: the look on the driver's face, the young girl who'd been chasing the dog falling to her knees and crumpling to the ground. He needed to talk through it. But his mom wouldn't listen. She couldn't hear what he was telling her, the incomprehensible truth Mason had yet to realize—that he saw events that had already happened and were no longer there. Events that no one else could see.

His mother's imagination didn't expand in the ways Mason needed it to. She told him not to make up stories about accidents, that it wasn't funny, and he listened to her. He even began to think that the visions were all make-believe. He repeated to himself what his mother told him: the visions were all in his mind, figments of his overactive imagination.

Mason stopped talking about the visions he saw, even when he learned that the stories weren't figments of his imagination after all.

He was eight when he walked past the TV during the six o'clock news and heard the reporter say, "Deadly car accident in Elmhurst...." A picture of the car accident, captured by an onlooker, filled the screen. In the center of the picture, amidst the broken glass, shattered taillights, and charred roadway, barely visible unless you knew it was there, sat a hot pink eyeglass case. Mason stopped on his way to the kitchen and stared at the image. He knew that hot pink eyeglass case. He'd seen it when his family drove home from Elmhurst just a few hours earlier.

They'd been stuck in traffic after leaving his grandparents' house. By the time they made it through the accident scene, three vehicles had been towed, two ambulances were en route to the hospital, and glass and debris littered the roadway. Mason didn't have to look at the only vehicle that remained, so badly burned that it was hardly recognizable as a car, to know what had happened. He closed his eyes, and the accident unfolded in one fluid motion.

A dark blue car, not aware that the white car ahead had slowed, changed lanes and caught the tail end of the white car, whose driver felt the hit but didn't register the magnitude of it. The momentum of the hit went unchecked until she lost control of her car and slammed on the brakes.

Mason, sitting in the backseat of his parent's Lexus, eyes closed, watched as the driver of the white car whipped her head around to track the movement of her now-spinning car. A hot pink eyeglass case bounced from her center console into the windshield and then ricocheted to the side window. At the moment the eyeglass case hit the passenger window, the glass shattered. To Mason, it seemed like the pink case had smashed the window, but it didn't. A black SUV did. In the space of time it took for the hot pink case to hover, then drop, the impact of the SUV forced the white car into another car, which collided with a lamppost. Glass, plastic shards of taillights, part of a fender, and the hot pink eyeglass case came to rest in the road. All of it, a violently choreographed dance.

When the news showed the scene as it had been shortly after the accident, and when Mason matched that image with the one he'd seen earlier, with the pink case encrusted in shattered glass, he fell to his knees in his living room.

"I saw that," Mason said to his dad. "I saw those cars."

His dad, like his mom, couldn't hear what he was telling him, not the incomprehensible truth of what Mason now realized: he could see visions of accidents after they had happened. His father's imagination, like his mother's, could not expand in the ways Mason needed it to. Instead, Mason's dad assumed that his son's reaction was another example of his sensitive nature.

"I know, kiddo," he said. "It's sad. I didn't know how bad the accident was either."

Mason stared at his dad but said nothing. He felt deserted. Neither his father nor his mother, and possibly no one, could see what he did. At the age of eight, on the floor of his living room, he learned that his parents could not always understand him, that things could not always be explained, and that life did not always end happily.

Two people had died in that accident. One of them had been a teenager in the passenger seat of the white car. Mason had seen his face when the SUV hit him, all the panic, confusion, and fear in his wide eyes, his mouth open in a soundless scream.

Mason went to his room when the news ended, and *60 Minutes* began. Silence filled his new reality, and he needed to process the fact that the images he had seen for as long as he could remember were not in his imagination after all. Since he couldn't talk about this new realization with his parents, he curled on his bed and cried.

After years of silence, of thinking of himself as a freak, of running miles to escape his own mind, Mason started driving Addie to school when he got his license. By then, Mason had grown accustomed to suppressing the stories he saw on the road along with his questions about why he saw the visions. Sure, he could've tried to talk to his mom again about the visions. When he was older, he could better articulate what was happening in his mind. But how do you start a conversation like that?

Silence was easier. That is, silence was easier until Addie asked a simple question, and then the silence was broken.

They had just started carpooling when Addie noticed skid marks in the road.

She pointed to them and asked, "Think someone didn't see the light change colors and slammed on their brakes?"

Without thinking, Mason said, "No. A souped-up Honda and red Mustang raced when the light turned green. Those marks were caused during acceleration, not braking." He hadn't really meant to say it out loud, but no one had asked him what had caused a tire mark before.

A beat passed before Addie asked, "Who won?"

"Sadly, the Honda."

Her simple question about even, dark skid marks at the intersection of Charles and Chicago avenues released, slightly, the hold Mason had over his mind. If she had ignored his comment or told him he was ridiculous, he wouldn't have said anything more. But she didn't. She asked about another small set of tire marks on Jackson Avenue.

"A goose in the road that almost got hit."

Addie began looking for tire marks nearly as much as he did. She did it for entertainment, and he did it to be prepared for whatever vision would overwhelm his mind.

In Addie, Mason found an outlet for the reality he had hidden since he was a child. He didn't care that she thought he was making it all up. Talking about the tire marks became fun. She asked questions. She wondered about unusual-looking marks. She made up details to add to his stories. And after a few months, it became their thing.

He didn't tell her that he obsessively looked for news about traffic accidents on any roads he might be traveling in order to prepare himself for tragic shocks. He didn't tell her that he read newspaper articles about neighboring areas, especially if his family was driving to see relatives. He didn't tell her that a deep fear overcame him when they drove over tire tracks that hadn't been there the day before.

But he did tell her enough details about the visions he saw to give him comfort in the illusion that he was sharing the burden of truth with someone. Sometimes he would tease her when she made up a new story for a tire track he had already explained but, most times, he just listened to the new tale she told. She would never know how deeply he appreciated those times. The emptiness that had entered his heart when he saw the hot pink eyeglass case was filled by the illusion that she understood him and he wasn't alone.

# CHAPTER 6

"I'm not flying to Tahoe."

"What?" It was May 29, the last day of school for seniors, but the fact that this was also the last day Mason would carpool with Addie dampened the excitement of the end of high school. He was half-tempted to drive her to school for her three remaining days of finals.

"I told my parents that I wasn't going to fly to Tahoe."

"How are you going to get there, then?" Mason saw a new skid mark up ahead and didn't want to deal with it.

*Why couldn't people drive like they're supposed to?*

"Drive," Addie said.

"Drive to Tahoe?" Mason asked as they rolled over the marks. "What'd they say?"

His mind flooded with the vision of a small girl, maybe four or five, breaking free from her mom's hand and running across the street to meet a man who must have been her dad, probably walking home from the train.

"I know this is a lot to ask," Addie said, unaware of the image that occupied Mason's thoughts. "But I told them I want to drive the Jeep."

Mason was too caught up in the vision of the little girl to pay attention to Addie.

"Indy can't fly," she continued. "It's too hot in the summer in

Reno, which is where we'd have to land. The temperature in Reno could be over ninety degrees. I mean, it could even be over one hundred. And that's totally unsafe for a dog. I don't think the airline would let Indy fly. Plus, she's too big. Not to mention she has anxiety and would probably have a heart attack if she flew."

The words "Reno" and "Indy" tangled with the vision of the little girl's brown pigtails swinging in circles as she ran, oblivious to the Escalade headed for her. It swerved left as it skidded to a stop, just missing the little girl. Simultaneously, Mason and the driver sighed in relief as the girl bounded into her father's arms. Mason understood the fear of the open-mouthed, wide-eyed mother standing on the sidewalk, arms outstretched.

"My parents said Indy would have to go with a pet courier. Can you believe that? They would ship my dog with strangers? She's almost seven. That makes her an old lady in dog years. I told them no, I wouldn't allow that. How do we know some random courier would treat her right? It's not like Indy can talk. So, Indy and I are going to drive to Tahoe. What do you think?"

Addie didn't register Mason's mental absence or his tight grip on the armrest.

"You're going to drive? To Tahoe?" Mason took a deep breath and focused on Addie.

She returned his gaze. "Yes. That's what I said."

"Why? That seems dangerous. Any number of accidents could happen. Someone could fall asleep while driving or a deer could jump in front of the car. There are a ton of deer out there—"

"Weren't you listening? I just told you why."

"I mean..." Mason shook his head. "That's like, I don't even know how many miles. Your parents are willing to do that?"

He wished he had followed her train of thought. He cursed the vision and the pointlessness of seeing it. The little girl was fine. Why did he need to feel their terror?

Addie's fingers uncurled and curled around the steering wheel, and she kept her eyes on the road.

"You didn't talk to them about it?" Mason asked.

"I did." She checked her blind spot and stole a glance at Mason. "They can't drive."

"Bummer. I guess that's out then." Mason scanned the road ahead hoping there were no more surprises.

"They said driving could be an option..." She bit her lower lip, then rushed through the words. "But they want me to go with someone who's eighteen. Declan's eighteen..."

Mason bristled at the thought of Declan driving to Tahoe with Addie. Forget the potential accidents that could happen during days of driving; it was the nights that unsettled him.

"What about the girls? Why not drive with them?" he asked. "You'd have a blast."

"My dad said I can't drive to Tahoe with a group of girls. He doesn't think it'd be safe."

They rolled over the faded remnants of Declan's tire mark, and Mason saw Declan and his friends laughing after rearranging the neighborhood mailboxes yet again. It was obvious that Addie would be safer with a group of her friends than with Declan.

"That's sexist," Mason said.

"I know, that's what I said." Addie slumped in her seat. "They said they'd ask my uncle Louis to drive with me. Can you believe that? I finally got them to agree to me driving and then they put all these restrictions on it, making it impossible."

"Are you sure your parents can't drive? You have three cars. You can caravan."

Addie shook her head. "The movers are loading Mom's car. And dad's is a company car, so he's leaving that and getting a new one in Nevada."

"That leaves your Jeep."

"And the dog."

Mason ran his fingers through his hair, suddenly nervous that her parents might agree to let Declan drive with her. "Your parents aren't going to let your boyfriend drive you across the country, right?"

"I know. If I asked, I'm sure it would be a hard no. It's just, this is the only thing I can look forward to about this move. I think it'd be fun —but not with my uncle."

Mason exhaled slowly and before he could change his mind, he blurted, "How about me? Would they let me drive with you?"

A sly smile escaped her lips. "Your name might've come up last night."

"What? You already thought of that?" He tried to sound offended, but, secretly, he was thrilled that Addie would want to drive across the country with him. "You were waiting for me to volunteer!"

"My parents and I discussed it, and after going through all the options, they specifically said that I can only drive to Tahoe with *you*. Or Uncle Louis."

"Are you sure they said me? I'm a male." Mason had second thoughts about his offer when he realized the number of skid marks he would see over days of driving. "That seems like reason enough for them to say no. I mean, what if I attacked you?"

"You? Please!" Addie broke into laughter.

Mason should have been offended, but his energy was focused on trying to understand what he'd just volunteered for.

"Look, I went back and forth with my parents for hours about all the different possibilities. You are the one they trust the most."

"Why?"

"Really?" Addie said. "Have you met yourself? Look, if they won't let me stay here for my senior year, I at least want to approach Tahoe on my own terms, not in some rental car from the Reno Airport."

"But the girls..." Mason said. "No would-be attacker would stand a chance. Have you seen Grace spike a volleyball? And look at my arms. I'm sure Becca can bench more than me."

"Are you done?" she asked. "You're an Eagle Scout. Beat that when it comes to camping across the country."

Addie pulled onto their street. If she'd spent a night arguing with her parents and they conceded, he knew he would be driving with her to Tahoe.

"And you?" he asked. "Are you okay driving with me?"

"Are you kidding? Of course! I've practically known you my entire life. I've kicked your butt in most games we've played since I was, what? Eight? Including trampoline backflips. Remember that?"

"How could I forget?" Mason rubbed his left forearm.

Addie's face softened. "We'll have fun on a road trip together. Look at how much fun we've had driving to school over the past two years."

"I think Declan will want to smash my face in."

"Please!" Addie pulled into her driveway.

"Well, that was our last official carpool," Mason said when the Jeep stopped.

"I know."

Addie's whispered response reminded him that this *last* was the beginning of a string of *lasts*.

"Look." Addie turned to face him, eyes pleading. "I know it's a lot to ask, but you were the one who offered."

Mason smiled. "You know me so well. You played me with that Declan comment."

"Sorry." She batted her eyes and clasped her hands under her chin. "You'd be giving up at least a week of your summer. I know it's a huge favor to ask, and I'll owe you one. But I need you. I really need you to do this. Will you do it? Please."

Mason relished the thought of a road trip with Addie. What could be more enticing than that? It could be the actual start of something, or, as dorky as it sounded, it would be their final carpool. And how much fun would the freedom of a road trip be before his freshman year of college? He wanted to plan where they could stop, what they could do. He wanted to spend time with Addie, to laugh with her, to help make her move easier, to keep her safe.

He wanted to do anything but feel his chest tightening and his stomach hollowing out at the thought of all the skid marks he would have to endure.

# CHAPTER 7

"Please?" Addie whispered, and the word nudged Mason from his fear.

His suburb had shown him more marks on the road than he wanted to ever experience. This latest tire mark—revealing the girl's pigtails swinging past the front grille of an Escalade—reinforced his terror. Mason had gotten used to the Peterson's dog running loose and almost getting hit by Mrs. Walsh's Honda. He had gotten used to Richie Benstein in his black Camaro squealing out of the school parking lot; the Zalk's blue Explorer skidding to a stop at most stop signs around town. He had even gotten used to Declan's loose turns and donuts in whatever empty parking lot he found. Mason didn't need today's tire marks to remind him of how terrifying new marks could be or how useless they made him feel. He couldn't stop the Escalade from almost hitting that girl. He could only watch, a spectator in someone else's nightmare.

The thought of traveling thousands of miles, over all new marks, each one a new experience, a new sensation, a new nightmare to re-live, terrified him.

But his desire to be with Addie was greater.

"Of course," Mason said.

A cross-country road trip—correction, an unsupervised cross-country road trip—was cool, way cool. And he told himself that he could shake the thought of how many tire tracks he might see in the course of 2,000-plus miles for her, to be with her even for a few more days.

"Great. I knew I could count on you!" Addie bounced in her seat. "This is going to be awesome."

Her smile was radiant, and he loved that he was the reason it lit up her face.

Addie grabbed his hand and squeezed. "It's the only thing I can look forward to about this whole Tahoe-nado. I feel like I'm finally making a—"

"Tahoe-nado?" Mason laughed. "No. Not there yet. Still a work in progress."

Addie's face fell. "But I worked on that one for days! You know, it's like *Sharknado*..."

"I know. I get it," he said. "And it's just as cheesy, but I guess we've got a few thousand miles to figure it out."

With that, Addie's smile returned, and her eyes sparkled. "Thanks! I really mean it! I owe you the world."

"When do we need to leave?"

"The moving van comes on June 18. I want to leave a couple days before it gets here. I don't want to see the house all emptied out."

"Wow. Not a lot of time." His smile faded as he mentally calculated the number of days that remained with Addie as his neighbor.

"Your parents will be okay with you driving, right?" she asked.

"Sure. Why not?" He could already hear his dad losing it. Dinner tonight was going to be intense.

"I mean, like you mentioned ... you're a guy. I'm a girl."

"Oh you think they'll worry that you might attack me?" Mason joked, and Addie's cheeks flushed. A flicker of hope danced in his chest. "They know you have a boyfriend, and you don't think of me like that."

Addie broke his stare and looked toward Mason's house. "Totally."

The flicker remained alive.

*Yes, I can handle any tire marks I'll see for this chance with Addie.*

"Camping, huh?" Mason said. "I didn't peg you for a camper. I guess we need a tent."

"You have a tent, don't you? I told my parents you have a tent."

"It's small," he said. "I mean, I guess it technically fits two, but it's tight."

"It'll work. We're two. And Indy."

Mason was already afraid that when it came down to it, her parents would change their minds. When they had a couple of days to think about it, they'd realize letting Addie camp across the country with a dog and the boy next door was a b-rated horror movie waiting to happen.

"Really," he said, "your dad is okay with this? He'll actually let us camp across the country together?"

"He already said yes."

"He might change his mind, you know. Or your mom will." Mason thought it only fair to warn her.

"No. Not possible. I will make their lives miserable if they do, and they know it. If they said yes, it's yes." Addie started talking faster. "Besides, my dad is too busy with his promotion at work, and Mom with all the packing at home. Neither of them will have time to worry about me. I mean, my dad'll make sure the Jeep is ready for the drive and that we have everything we need and all, but he's going to be busy with his new position."

Mason's mind returned to all the unknown tire marks he would have to endure. He told himself that it couldn't be as bad as he imagined. Plus, he could share them with Addie, just like he had been doing. That would help.

Addie continued, "As long as we tell my parents where we are each day, they'll be fine. Plus, Indy can protect us. I told them that she'd probably like to sleep outside. She loves being outside."

She was definitely rambling now, and, if it wasn't for the tire marks staining the whole idea, Mason would've found her excitement contagious.

"Maybe she'll scare raccoons away or something." Addie's eyebrows knitted together. "Will there be bears? Maybe we'll keep her inside the tent, and she can keep watch at the door. Wait, the opening in a tent isn't called a 'door,' is it? I don't know what it's called. Wait, it's a flap, right?"

She seemed giddy with the thought of the trip, and he couldn't blame her. It was something in the whole messed-up situation for her to be excited about, even if it was a one-way trip.

Mason cracked a smile. "I guess this is going to happen, huh? But what if I can't get off work?" He knew he'd be able to. Plenty of life-guards at Centennial Beach, the local-quarry-turned-swimming-spot, would happily take his hours.

"You'll figure it out." Addie got out of the Jeep. "Just talk to your parents before mine do."

"I'll ask them tonight."

"I'm dying to know what they say. Text me when you talk to them." Addie gave him a quick hug. "Thanks."

"You better not do that," Mason joked. "Your mom might see us hugging and think there's something going on. Remember, I am a male, after all."

Addie hit her forehead with the palm of her hand. "How could I forget? Text me as soon as you talk to them!"

# KENNA

I wake again, thankful that my head isn't pounding as much. I feel foggy, like a dream still clings to me, begging me to return. I want to stay in its embrace, free from reality. I reach for my glass of water, the one I always set on my nightstand when I go to bed because I know I'll wake up thirsty in the middle of the night. I grope for the glass, but my nightstand is gone. My fingers run over grit and find a plastic water bottle. I grab it and take a long drink. It tastes bitter, and I remember where I'm at. I open my eyes in the darkness, and the light outlining the door taunts me.

I sit up, slowly, remembering my collision the last time I moved too quickly. When was that? Hours ago? Yesterday? Days ago?

My mouth is dry, and I can't help but drink the rest of the water in the bottle, despite its bitter taste.

Where am I? How did I get here? I sort through my memories for snatches of anything that can ground me in reality. I was driving to Colorado to live with my friend Rachel. My car broke down. I couldn't get a cell signal. A pickup screeched to a stop near me, and two guys got out.

This is all very wrong. I lunge for the door. I shouldn't be here. I claw at the door and stumble backward. The door tilts—or I do.

I crash into the wall, and a shower of dirt falls to the ground with me. My head spins even when my eyes are closed. I reach out to steady the *rotating earth, but my fingers only graze the dirt. The bitter taste of the water fills my mouth as I fight sleep.*

*The water was drugged. I'm being drugged. My head feels like a weight as I lie in the dirt. I strain to lift my head, but it doesn't budge.*

*Fight. I have to fight. My arms are logs, but I drag them under me. I prop myself up on my elbows and rest my head in my hands. It's so heavy; my head is too heavy to hold. I slump into the ground.*

*I envision myself moving, struggling for the mattress, pulling myself up, but I know it's a fantasy. My cheek rests on the dirt floor, and I no longer care about the drool that slides from my open mouth and disappears into the ground.*

# CHAPTER 8

M ason walked into his house through the garage and smelled the sweet vanilla scent of cookies before he heard the familiar clanking of pans and banging of cabinet doors. He figured his mom, who was usually making something in the kitchen, was baking. He didn't complain because it was usually good, even if it was healthy. In middle school, he'd wised up to her putting vegetables into food that shouldn't have vegetables in it. She made fudgesicles with kale and fried rice with cauliflower. For the most part, his dad was oblivious.

"Happy last day of school!" Mom slid a pan into the oven and turned to Mason, her brown-gray hair swept back in a clip. "How does it feel?"

"Weird," he said. He grabbed a cookie from the cooling rack. It was still warm, and he inspected it for signs of zucchini before taking a bite.

She gave him a quick squeeze around the waist. "I feel like I should've taken a picture of you leaving this morning, you know, to put next to the picture of your first day of kindergarten. Bookends."

"No crying," Mason said and returned her hug. Lately, she cried whenever she talked about him leaving for college, declaring that the house would be too lonely and too quiet without him.

"These aren't bad." He held the last bit of cookie up before popping it into his mouth. "What did you put in them this time?"

"Chickpeas. Good, aren't they?" She broke off a piece and ate it. "And they have a lot of protein."

"Don't tell Dad."

"Do I ever?" Mom opened the oven and peered at the batch on the cookie sheet. "I forgot to set the timer. When did I put those in?"

"Maybe two minutes ago." He gestured to his backpack. "I'm going to my room to unpack high school. Call me if you need another taste test."

Mason took the stairs two at a time, not ready to talk about the road trip. He knew his mom would be the first to agree to it, but the idea of driving thousands of miles was a bit too unnerving to talk about just yet.

In his room, he dropped his backpack by his desk and opened the blinds, cringing at the Pokémon stickers still in the corner of his window from his elementary school obsession. He should probably get a razor blade and peel those off before he left for college. Beyond them, Addie's Jeep sat in her driveway promising fun. The top-down-sun-flooding-the-Jeep type of fun while he drove across the country with Addie.

*This is going to be okay.*

What could be better than a few more days with her? He fidgeted with his blinds as he considered how the days would lead into nights. The thought of sleeping next to Addie in his tent, the tent he'd slept in by himself or with his dad for all those Boy Scout trips, made him nervous. He needed to focus on practical matters.

When was the last time he even used his tent? He'd have to air it out and make sure he had all the stakes. He'd have to find the sleeping bags and wash them. He went to his desk to make a list. When he turned on his computer, an article about a car accident in Oswego that he'd read that morning lit up his screen. He clicked it closed, but his mind had already returned to the thought of all the new tire marks he would see on the trip with Addie.

Day after day, driving thousands of miles, they would encounter accidents much worse than the five-car pile-up that created rush-hour havoc on Route 30. How many times would Mason experience the terror of crashing into another car, an animal—or worse, a person—

when they drove to Nevada? He didn't want the unexpected shock of a car swerving into the wrong lane, barreling into oncoming traffic while texting, driving under the influence, scrolling through Facebook, dropping French fries, falling asleep, spilling coffee, swatting bees...There were so many ways things could go wrong.

For every tire track he drove over, he felt each moment as he saw it. He saw the screams, the wide eyes, the white knuckles. He felt the fear, the confusion, the shock. Those moments were real, a part of someone's life, someone's history, and they became part of his.

This trip would confirm all his fears and push all his boundaries.

But he told Addie he would do it, and she was worth it.

---

MASON GOOGLED TRAFFIC ACCIDENTS ON I-88, A ROAD they'd have to drive, even though he knew he shouldn't. The first link was to a news article from the day before. A photo of a middle-aged man smiling into the camera sat next to a headline that read, "Man Killed on I-88."

Mason scanned the article. A man had been pinned between his pickup and a trailer when another pickup skidded into him. Mason looked at the photo again. The man was smiling, his eyes bright with life. But after this accident, an accident that Mason might have to relive, he would be dead.

Great. The worst possible accident.

*I cannot handle this drive.*

Maybe he could convince Addie to fly to Tahoe and get there before her parents. They could camp somewhere in the Tahoe area. But Mason knew the idea was ridiculous. Addie wouldn't even consider it, and there was Indy. Addie needed to drive for the dog.

Mason went to the window again and looked at her Jeep, at the seat he'd occupied all of senior year. He couldn't envision anyone but him in that seat. She needed his help, and she trusted he'd be there for her.

His heart tugged at him, begging him to be who she needed him to be, to embrace all the possibilities this trip offered. And yet, the photograph of the dead man lingered in his peripheral vision, preventing him from shaking off his doubt.

That was only one death-stained section of road. How many other deaths would proclaim themselves on the highway?

The smell of burning cookies brought him back from his thoughts. He leaned out his door and called to his mom, "I think they're done."

She often forgot about food in the oven, especially if she didn't set a timer.

"Crap!" A book thudded on the table and, within seconds, the cookie tray clattered on the stove.

Mason returned to his computer, clicked off the article, and Googled the route. It was 1,930 miles from Naperville, Illinois, to Incline Village, Nevada. Most of that drive was on I-80, a road that averaged 160,000 vehicles each day. Even worse, it ranked as one of the deadliest interstates in the U.S.

The less time he spent on that road, the better. He zoomed in on the route. There were any number of alternatives. Who cared if it took a little longer to get to Nevada? That would mean more time with Addie, which would be even better if there were fewer car accidents.

They could drop south a bit and go through Colorado. That drive would probably be prettier. Then Mason found Route 50, "The Loneliest Road in America."

The Travel Nevada website said it offered "plenty of space at your own pace." Perfect. Lonely was good. Fewer people crashed into each other on lonely roads. Mason searched for the average number of travelers on Route 50 and found nothing. That could only mean one thing: not enough people traveled on the road to warrant counting.

The only recent information Mason found was from four days earlier. A missing woman. He scanned the article. No accident, but "the Sterling County Sheriff's Office reported skid marks near the scene."

Mason leaned back in his chair. Skid marks near the scene. That could mean any number of things. It could be a coincidence. Maybe where she stopped her car happened to be next to skid marks that were made days earlier. Or the skid marks could've been made after her car was abandoned. Mason scratched his head and looked at the article again.

What if this woman pulled over and someone driving past skidded to a stop near her? And what if that person was responsible for whatever happened to her? Would Mason be able to see what happened to this woman if he drove over the skid marks?

Mason reread the article, this time more carefully. The woman was headed to Colorado, driving in the opposite direction than Mason and Addie would be going. What side of the road were the skid marks on? The article didn't say.

Mason zoomed in on the picture of the woman. Her dark brown hair fell behind her back in slight waves as she smiled up at the camera, eyes bright. A memory tugged at his heart. Had he seen this woman before? Maybe in a different accident? But that didn't make sense. She was from California, and Mason had never been to California. He reread her name. Kenna Cook. A memory rushed from the past and punched him in the gut.

*"Hi Kenna!" Mason waved at his neighbor as she rode her bike on the street past his house. He returned to his toy dump truck, running it up the driveway toward the small pile of mulch he'd been building.*

*The loud screech of tires made Mason jump. His mother was immediately at the front door, then running out. Instead of stopping at him like he thought she would, she ran past him to the street. Mason whirled around and froze.*

*Kenna's bike was under a blue pickup truck. At the sight of her white basket crushed under the tire of the pickup, everything went silent for Mason, just like when he was underwater and could only hear his own heart beating. Kenna's mother ran past him, her mouth open, but Mason did not hear her screams.*

It wasn't that he forgot about Kenna Sadler and the family that lived next door. It was more like he repressed the entire memory. He was five when that accident happened. Kenna was ten, which was why she was allowed to ride her bike in the street and Mason wasn't. At least, that was what Mason's dad had said when Mason asked to ride his bike in the street too. "Maybe when you're older," his dad said. After the accident, though, Mason lost all interest in his bike.

Mason focused his attention on the picture of Kenna Cook. Her dark brown hair was similar to the coloring of his old neighbor, but longer and more angular, not the round full face he remembered seeing in the picture that sat on top of Kenna Sadler's coffin.

For years, Mason had felt immense guilt about Kenna's death. He'd blamed himself for waving at her and saying hi. He thought he'd distracted her and that's why she didn't see the pickup truck barreling into her. Even though his parents told him he wasn't to blame, that the driver had been drunk, that Mason was lucky he hadn't been hit as well, he still felt responsible.

And now, a woman who was only slightly younger than what Kenna Sadler would've been if she lived, a woman whose name *was* Kenna, was missing. Mason Googled Kenna Cook leaving off the word "missing." Multiple images flooded Mason's screen. Kenna clutched a snowboard and stuck her tongue out. Kenna stood on a surfboard, arms spread wide. Kenna, smiling cheek-to-cheek with a friend.

Mason switched to videos and clicked on a Youtube link. Kenna was with friends, contemplating jumping off a bridge into the water below. Mason laughed along with them as they built the courage to jump. Then, without warning, Kenna climbed the rail and launched herself into the air. Her screams were eclipsed by her friend's as she recorded Kenna's plummet into the lake. This Kenna was vibrant and alive.

Mason sat back in his chair. He could imagine what her mother was thinking. He thought about Mrs. Sadler when she saw her daughter's bike, broken under the wheel of the pickup, which was only a mirror of her daughter's body. Mrs. Sadler's face had been contorted in anguish, mouth wide in a scream, but Mason's own terror had blocked out all sound.

Another neighbor, Mason didn't remember who, had scooped him up and hurried him into his house, but not before the look of Mrs. Sadler's silent scream embedded itself into his mind. Mason's parents brought him to counseling, especially after his nightmares persisted for months after the accident. He sat in the doctor's office and drew pictures and played with toy cars, talking through what he remembered, trying to get the images of Kenna's broken bike and her mother's contorted face out of his head.

When did those images stop haunting him? Was that when the silent images of other accidents started to fill his mind? Were his visions some sort of reaction to the trauma of Kenna's death? He'd heard of soldiers seeing people and enemies who weren't really there when they returned from war. Could these visions be some sort of PTSD?

Mason tried to remember if he saw the visions before Kenna's death. He didn't think so, especially since the shock of that accident had filled his nightmares for so long. If he'd seen visions before that, would her accident have been so traumatic?

He reread the article. What if the skid marks near this woman's car were connected to her disappearance? According to the date of the article, it would be almost a month before they would drive over this road. The skid marks would probably fade into the pavement and out of his sight before he and Addie ever got there.

He looked at Kenna's photograph and thought about his neighbor, how full of life she had been too. An overwhelming feeling came over Mason that he had to go on this road trip, not just for Addie, but for this missing Kenna. If there was a chance that he could do something to help her, he needed to try.

SUNDAY, MAY 26, 2019

*Golden Valley News*
Fallon, Nevada

## Search Continues for Missing Woman

Valterra County and Sterling County Police, with the help of local volunteers, searched the desert along Route 50 for the driver of an abandoned gold Honda Accord. Kenna Cook, 24, was last heard from on Wednesday and reported missing on Thursday when she failed to arrive in Copper Mountain, Colo., at her new residence.

A room under Cook's name was reserved at the Days Inn in Delta, Utah, for Wednesday night, but she never checked in, according to the hotel manager.

Police and volunteers conducted a grid search of the area at 7 A.M. yesterday but suspended the search at nightfall. "We will reconvene the search at first light," Deputy Stan Burke of the Valterra Police Department said. "Thanks to all the community members who have come out to assist. Please remember to bring plenty of water tomorrow and protect yourself from the sun. No one should search alone. The desert is dangerous."

The police believe Cook may have tried to walk to get assistance after her car broke down.

Cook is described as 5'4" with long brown hair and approximately 135 pounds. She called her mother on Wednesday afternoon from Fallon, where she reportedly stopped for gas.

Contact the Sterling County Sheriff's Office if you have any information.

# CHAPTER 9

The rope creaked under Mason's weight as he sat on the swing and texted Addie. The dinner discussion with his parents had gone as he imagined. He looked up through the leaves at the darkening sky, letting the swing sway slightly. Eighteen used to seem like a world away, and now it was here.

He barely sensed Addie's approach. She simply brushed his hand and squeezed next to him on the swing seat. When they were little, they could sit side-by-side without touching, but now her thigh pressed into his. This time, he couldn't blame the perspiration gathering on his upper lip on having just finished a run.

Neither of them said a thing. For Mason, the events of the last week —finding out about Addie's move, the memory of Kenna Sadler, learning about the missing woman, the summer ahead—all seemed too much to handle. They swayed in silence as the sky turned a deeper shade of blue. He told himself to take slow, deep breaths and, as he did, he relaxed into the swing, into Addie, into the idea of traveling 2,000 miles.

"Your parents are okay with it, right?" Addie said after a bit, kicking her feet out. "Your text wasn't clear."

"No."

Her legs froze mid-air, and she turned to him. "What do you mean, 'no'?"

"No, as in my dad thinks we're too young to travel that far alone."

"So?" Addie demanded, sitting up straighter.

"So, my mom reminded my dad that she was 17 when she left California—alone—and drove to Illinois in order to start a new life."

"And?"

"And my dad said that that was a very long time ago, and times have changed. To which my mother said, '*Very* long time ago? That *very* long time ago was the reason I met you.' And my dad knew enough to stop talking."

Addie shoved Mason's arm. "How'd it end? You're killing me."

"My mom said it was a good idea, and that it would give me a little independence before leaving for college."

Addie smiled and kicked her legs out again. "Smart woman."

"When my dad said something along the lines of 'Your inner hippie does not need to get involved,' that's when I left the room."

"Oh. Not a smart man."

"Don't worry," Mason said. "My mom will win. My dad was only digging himself deeper when I left."

"Sounds like it."

Mason lifted his feet and relaxed into Addie's swinging. She shivered slightly against the cool breeze. He wished he wore a sweatshirt—so he could give it to her.

"What's going on in your house?" he asked.

"My mom wanted to call your mom about the trip, but I told her not to until I heard from you."

"I'm sure my mom has already called her to complain about my dad."

"Ha. Probably. It would give my mom a break from packing even though I think she's secretly thrilled about this move. She keeps talking about buying a paddleboard."

A few early fireflies twinkled deep in the backyard. Mason pointed to them. "Remember our contests when we were kids?"

"I always caught more than you," Addie said with a laugh. "And I'd get so mad when you insisted we let them go before we went in. I used to think you were getting back at me for winning."

"They'd die if we didn't let them go." Mason looked at Addie, remembering how she used to grab for her jar and thrust out her lower lip in a pout when he untwisted the top.

She stopped their slow swinging and shifted to look at him square in the face. "I never told you, but I brought them in one night. A whole jar of them. Your mom called you, and you left before you opened my jar. They were so pretty in my room, like Christmas lights in July, just for me. But in the morning, they were all dead. I cried."

Her brown eyes glistened, and he knew her tears now were for all that she was about to lose. "I never told you because I thought you'd be mad at me." She leaned toward him, and her face was so close that he held his breath. Her eyes dropped to his lips.

Mason wanted to kiss her, felt a tingling inside that told him she wanted to kiss him too. He was about to lean toward her when Indy barked at Addie's back door. Addie shifted back and looked away. The moment was lost. Once again they were side-by-side, like the kids they used to be.

"Why is your mom packing so much?" Mason hoped his voice didn't betray his longing. "Isn't that what the movers are supposed to do? Pack things?"

"Yeah, but she thinks they won't be careful with all her precious belongings."

"Sounds like someone I know," he said. "What was that about your dog? That annoying one that just barked."

Addie dug her feet into the ground, and Mason lurched forward as the swing came to an abrupt stop.

"Are you accusing me of being like my mother?"

"Defensive much?" he taunted. "I was simply pointing out a similarity."

She smiled and wrapped an arm around his waist. "I'm only teasing."

Again, his heart skipped. He breathed in the strawberry scent of her hair that he'd come to love. This trip was going to be difficult for more than one reason.

"Why aren't you out with your friends tonight?" Addie asked. "Seniors are done."

"Are you kidding? And miss all this drama?" He swept an arm toward his house.

"I'd happily miss all the drama if it meant no move."

"True." Mason reached an arm behind her and held the swing's ropes. "Seniors are done, but track isn't. I have training at 5:30 tomorrow morning. That puts a damper on the end-of-the-year partying. The state meet is still coming up."

"That sucks. I think Declan's going over to Jake's. He's having a party tonight."

"And Declan didn't invite you?"

Mason was fishing, but he wanted to know what was going on between the two of them. Declan was usually hanging out at her house, putting on his fake "I'm a clean, cut kid" smile for her mother, and Mason hadn't seen him in a few days.

"Sure he did, but I still have school," Addie said. "Finals start tomorrow. I'm not lucky enough to be a senior."

That meant Declan was still in the picture, though Mason had no reason to think he wouldn't have been, except for that moment a little bit ago. Unless he imagined the almost kiss. Was that all in his head?

"Did you tell Declan I was driving you to Tahoe?"

"No. I was waiting to hear from you, remember?"

The lights on Mason's back porch turned off, and he and Addie instinctively stopped swaying.

"You don't think they forgot about you and locked you out, do you?" she asked.

"Maybe this is a test of my camping skills."

# CHAPTER 10

With the back porch lights off, darkness settled across the yard. Addie looked at Mason. "You're sure that your parents will say yes?"

"Yeah. Mom already has."

"It'll all be okay, right?"

Mason wanted to be the rock-solid person Addie needed. He knew her question was still about more than the trip. "I know it will be, even if it doesn't feel like it right now."

She let out a long exhale. "I know too. But I definitely don't feel it."

"It's all too new. At least we'll have fun camping. That's the easy part. I'll look into where there are CAAs along the way."

"CAAs?" Addie asked.

"I forgot, you only stay at Harlan Hotels," he teased. "It stands for Campgrounds Across America. It's a chain, so they'll have standard amenities."

Sitting on the swing, with Addie so close, Mason was confident that everything would be okay. It was strange to think her move was somehow bringing them closer, and he hoped that closeness wouldn't be temporary.

"Thanks for doing this," she said. "Driving to Tahoe with me, and all. I know I totally bullied you into it with my Declan comment, and

I'm messing up part of your summer. You didn't have to say you'd do it, but you did. Thanks."

"I think by the time this is all over, I'll be thanking you."

*And hopefully, this missing Kenna will be thanking you too.*

Mason looked across the yard, avoiding the question in her searching looks. "Don't worry, I'm not a creeper," he added. "I just think that I need this trip as much as you do."

She raised an eyebrow. "We'll have a couple thousand miles for you to fill me in; that is, when we aren't too busy singing at the top of our lungs."

Mason nudged her shoulder. "Is that what you imagine? Us belting Ed Sheeran songs with the top down?"

"Not a bad visual. Close. I was thinking Taylor Swift."

"Eww. Smell that?" He fanned the air in front of his face. "I think it's a sign that I should be in charge of the music."

"It's a skunk, not a sign." Addie hit him on the chest. "You worry about the route, and I'll deal with the music."

"Are you afraid of giving up musical power? Afraid of a little punk?"

"Afraid? I'm driving cross-country with you. That hardly qualifies me as afraid." She tucked her nose under her T-shirt. "Since when do you listen to punk? I'm sure it's as bad as this stench."

"You'd like The Menzingers. It's good running music."

"No music for you. Route only. And if you try to argue..." She squinted into the darkness, then pointed. "Look. Over there."

"What?"

"There!" Addie stabbed the air, pointing to the back corner of his yard. "There's something out there. Do you see it?"

The vague outline of an animal skittered through the shadows. Mason stopped the swing from moving.

"Please tell me that's not a—"

Mason raised his hand to silence Addie.

The skunk moved into the light from the moon, and they sat, as taut as the swing's rope, until it moved out of his yard.

"Holy crap," Addie said with a loud exhale. "I'm glad Indy wasn't out here."

"You aren't kidding. How do you even get skunk smell out of dog fur?" Mason made a mental note to Google it before the trip.

"You don't think we'll run into wild animals when we're camping, do you?" Addie asked.

Mason lifted his feet, and the swing began its slow sway again. "No, the wild animals typically stay at Harlan Hotels. We should be fine."

"I deserved that." Addie reached around him, grabbed the rope, and leaned back as far as she could to look up at the sky. As her hair reached toward the ground, her shirt pulled up. Mason wanted to run his fingers along her exposed skin to connect the pale freckles that dotted her stomach.

Instead, he focused on the back corner of his yard and the darkness that the skunk had disappeared into.

"Fine, I'll plan the route. You plan the music," he said.

Addie smiled. Just like naming the fort, she'd won. And Mason didn't mind at all.

"Straight route or scenic route?" He'd already planned for the answer he knew she'd give.

"Is that a philosophical question, Mason?" She pulled herself up and her hair, now messy, framed her face. "You sound like an inspirational poster: 'It's not about the destination, it's about the journey.'"

"Don't you mean, 'I took the road less traveled and that has made all the difference?'"

"And you got a B-minus in English?" Addie teased.

"The poem is hardly unknown. I'm sure it's on an inspirational poster too."

"Yeah. I guess." Her eyes wandered over the yard. "My dad was talking about it being a straight shot on I-80."

"I know. I Google-Mapped it. Super straight. And super boring."

"This is my trip." Addie's eyes took on an intense focus. "And I am *not* going the super-straight, super-boring route."

"*My* trip?"

"*Our* trip." Addie returned his smile. "You know what I mean. Dad's dictated so much already. We're not going on I-80."

"Don't worry. I knew you wouldn't settle for the straight shot. I've already mapped out a route. We'll start on I-80 and then drop down and go through Colorado."

"Do we have to go on I-80 at all?"

"Only for a little bit. It'll still be *your* trip." Mason nudged her again. They could avoid I-80 if they wanted, but that would add too much time. He hoped to get to The Loneliest Road before the skid marks near Kenna's car disappeared.

"Can we stop in Vail? Or Steamboat Springs? I haven't been to either place and would love to check them out."

"We can stop anywhere we want, up to a point," Mason promised. "Your dad did give us a time limit. We only have four days."

"Fair enough. How about food? I've been watching a lot of Food Network lately. We should find as many food trucks as we can. You know, like the ones that serve gourmet sandwiches only on waffles or ones that make grilled cheese sandwiches but in totally bizarre ways."

"You have a weird fascination with food," Mason said. "You know that, right?"

"What's weird about liking food? You should try it sometime—eat something with more flavor than a Pop-Tart."

"Don't hate on the Frosted S'mores Pop-Tarts."

"Maybe we'll find a truck that only serves sandwiches on Pop-Tarts. How about that?" Energy infused Addie's words.

Mason hoped she saw something positive in the move. "That might be a little hard to find in the middle of nowhere," he said.

"Yeah, well, we'll see. Everywhere is somewhere."

"Now *you* sound like an inspirational poster." His eyes followed the slope of her nose down to her slightly parted lips, then he quickly looked away.

*She's a friend. Breathe. She has a boyfriend.*

"I'll plan the route—only on I-80 for a day, at most—and I'll book the campsites."

"Deal. And I'll find the food trucks."

"Good luck finding a gourmet Pop-Tart-Waffle-Grilled-Cheese-Sandwich truck," he said.

"Oh, you wait. I'll find it. And you'll thank me."

The breeze picked up as the energy of their conversation faded. He replayed the vision of Addie's stomach as she leaned back on the swing, her shirt sliding up and catching on her bra.

"I think we should go in," he said. "Shouldn't you be studying for finals?"

"I've done all I can to prepare. Instead, I have food truck research to do."

There was probably a lot more that she had to do, including a lot of packing and goodbyes between now and June 16.

"I'll see you tomorrow," Mason said, getting off the swing and shivering a little, maybe because of the chill of the night or maybe because Addie was no longer so close to him.

Addie took a deep breath and followed. "Thanks."

"Are you kidding? I should be thanking you. I get 2,000 miles of Taylor Swift."

"And food trucks."

"Food poisoning, got it."

"You're going to be a changed man when this trip is over," Addie said with a laugh.

"The way you said that makes it sound like a threat."

"A promise." She gave him a quick hug and turned back to her house. He waited until she entered through the back door before he sat back down on the swing.

*Yes, I will definitely be changed.*

The entire prospect of the road trip scared the crap out of him. And besides the drive, he was leaving for college soon—a new town, new people, new tragedies. He wanted to always look up at the sky from this swing; he was used to this town and the patterns his life had fallen into, even his pattern of falling in and out of love with Addie.

"I hope everything works out—for me, for Addie, and for the missing woman," Mason said to the air.

He'd do more research tonight. There was still a possibility that she'd already been found, and then he could focus on Addie.

He went inside to see if his parents' fight was over or if his dad was asleep on the couch.

*Green River News*
  Green River, Utah

### Woman Still Missing; No Leads in Case

The search continues for Kenna Cook, 24, who has not been heard from since Wednesday and reported missing when she didn't turn up in Copper Mountain, Colo. as scheduled on Thursday. Valterra County and Sterling County Police Departments report no leads in the case. The ground search provided no indication of the direction Cook may have gone and yielded no clues as to her whereabouts.

Cook's car, which was found abandoned along Route 50 between Ely and Valterra, was towed by authorities to a local mechanic to check for mechanical failure.

It is not known if someone stopped to help her or if she decided to leave her vehicle to find help. Authorities hired an accident-reconstruction expert to examine skid marks near the area of her recovered vehicle, but the report was inconclusive.

If you have any information about Cook, please contact local authorities.

# CHAPTER 11

---

**M**ason contemplated not showing up to Addie's going-away party because it was at Declan's, which meant there would be bad music, a lot of drunks and, of course, Declan. Addie probably wouldn't even know most of the people; a handful would be there for the *going-away*, the rest for the *party*.

When Addie told Declan that Mason was driving with her to Nevada, he'd flipped. Mason was working at Centennial Beach when Declan, wearing one of his signature, too-small T-shirts—that he probably wore in the hopes of making his arms look bigger—stormed up to him. He demanded that Mason "step down," that's what he said with his chest puffed out and his finger pointed in Mason's face. He was easy to diffuse, especially since three lifeguards suddenly appeared next to Mason. The fact that Declan thought Addie's parents would trust him enough to let him drive her was further evidence of his self-absorption.

Despite not wanting another confrontation with Declan, Mason was too nervous about the trip to sit at home the night before they left. He decided on the inconspicuous entrance through the back gate of Declan's yard. When they were kids, Declan and Mason used to hang out at each other's houses, but that was when they were on the same Little League team. When Declan joined a travel team, that changed and so did Declan.

The yard, however, hadn't changed, except it felt smaller. Several kids smoked around the fire pit, which was lit even though the weather was warm. Mason knew the bonfire masked the odor of whatever they exhaled.

Mason had avoided most of Declan's parties over the last couple of years, though he often heard about them, either in school on Mondays or through poorly-coded jokes on Snapchat. Declan's parents seemed to be perpetually out of town, what Mason took to be a sort of willful negligence of their son's behavior. Mason entered the house through the kitchen and walked into a swarm of red cups. Beer pong was taking up much of the kitchen table, and the sink was filled with ice and bottles of vodka.

Mason poured a bottle of water into a Solo cup and walked toward the living room in the hopes of finding Addie. He passed two girls curled over a photo album on the dining table, laughing and sighing over pictures before writing notes to Addie. The album must have been the work of Sophie, Grace, and Becca, and it would certainly make for some entertaining reading on the drive. Mason chatted with a few people he knew as he looked for Addie, many of whom didn't even know about the road trip.

He made his way into the basement and stopped on the last step when he saw Addie leaning over the pool table to take a shot in a short white skirt that hugged her curves. He heard the cue ball hit, but he saw nothing but her.

"Hey, Mason," Sophie called, pulling him out of his trance.

"Hi!" He smiled at Sophie. Mason had told Addie that he had a crush on Sophie, and at one point he thought he did, but he could no longer pretend. Addie had stolen his heart years ago.

"Want to play the winner?" Becca asked as he walked up to the table.

"It sounds like my favorite movie is playing in there." He motioned to the theater room where the noise of a car chase vibrated the walls. "It's so creative."

Addie rolled her eyes. "You're such a snob, Mason. It's an action film. They're all supposed to sound alike."

"You want to play, or what?" Becca repeated.

"Of course I do. I'll take down whoever wins this game."

"Make sure you sign the photo album," Sophie said. "I got some great pics from your mom, Mason. Remember Robbie's birthday party when he turned 10? The one at Chuck-E-Cheese? Too funny!"

"My mom didn't tell me she gave you pictures, the traitor," Mason said. "I remember that party, and I looked like a total dork in that Pikachu T-shirt."

"You wore that shirt all the time," Addie said, laughing.

"Not all of us were as fashion-conscious as you at such a young age," he teased.

"The pics are fabulous," Addie said. "You'll laugh. We were so little!"

Mason looked between Becca and Sophie. "Great idea with the book. I saw some girls writing in it upstairs."

"I can't believe we've known each other for as long as we have," Becca said.

"Addie, do you remember when Becca moved here, and I thought she was going to steal you away from me?" Sophie asked.

"Oh my gosh, there's a pic of the three of us, and Sophie's giving me such a stink eye. It's hysterical!" Becca laughed. "She looks like she has a plan to murder me at the next sleepover."

Addie turned to Mason. "You can always look at it when we're driving. We'll have plenty of time."

"And you have to write her a note," Becca said.

"I still can't believe your parents are letting you drive across the country, especially with Mason," Sophie said.

"What do you mean, 'especially with Mason?'" he asked.

"I don't mean it like anything bad," Sophie said. "I mean my parents would never let me drive thousands of miles alone with a boy."

"Well, I'm probably a safer bet than Declan," Mason said as his eyes scanned the basement. "Speaking of him, where is your boyfriend? Shouldn't he be showering you with affection the night before you leave?"

"Funny," Addie said. She leaned over the table, aimed, and sent the yellow ball into the corner pocket.

"Wow. And with such authority," he teased.

"Stick around, and I'll kick your butt next."

As if on cue, Declan bounded down the basement stairs, trailed by his sidekick, Frank, and a group of people.

"There she is!" Declan yelled. "Are you hiding from me down here? You have a going-away beer bong to do!" He let out a laugh and put his arm around Addie's waist. If you counted his spiky blond hair, Declan was a few inches taller than Mason, but Mason met his glare directly.

With his dark eyes still fixed on Mason, Declan spoke to the group that trailed him. "What do you say? Don't you think the chauffeur should do a beer bong too?"

The crowd cheered, and J.D. held the beer bong up to Mason.

Mason raised his Solo cup in a mock toast. Then he leaned close to Declan and whispered in his ear. "Don't worry. I'll look after her for you. She's in good hands."

Mason enjoyed rubbing it in. It was petty of him, sure, but it was the only weapon he had at the moment that mattered.

"If I know this girl, she'll be looking after you," Declan said through gritted teeth. He squeezed his arm around Addie's waist, steering her toward the bar. "Let's go, babe."

"Let me finish my game," Addie said, wriggling free of him.

"Don't be long." Declan's eyes followed Addie back to the pool table before he joined a group of kids doing shots at the bar.

"He's in a rare mood," Mason said.

"Don't worry. I've seen it before. He's fine."

Mason looked over his shoulder at Declan and wondered if he should stay to keep an eye on Addie. "Really?" he asked.

"Really," Addie said.

Becca spent a solid minute lining up her shot, before sinking the cue ball instead.

"Good one," Addie heckled.

"Can you beat her?" Mason asked Sophie.

"Not a chance. She already beat me once tonight."

Addie leaned over and aimed. She attempted to run the three-ball down the rail and into the corner but missed.

"I might have a chance," Mason said.

"Not likely," Addie said with a smile.

"Hey, Addie!" Declan called. "Come here and join us!"

"Almost done." Addie passed the cue stick to Becca.

"Guess I'll have to pass on that game," Mason said. "Your sweetheart over there won't wait for me to beat you in a game."

"Yeah, you're probably right." Addie glanced at Declan pouring another round of shots from a half-empty bottle of Cuervo.

Mason followed her gaze. "If you want me to stay, I will."

"It's all good," she said.

Grace skipped down the stairs and ran up to Becca. "Whatever you do, do *not* go in the backyard. Your ex is out there. Hi, Mason."

Mason nodded a hello to Grace before asking Addie, "Are you going to make a 7 A.M. departure after a night like this?"

"We'll make sure she's there," Sophie said, putting an arm around Addie. "She's staying at my house tonight, and her parents would kill me if we tried to keep her."

"Don't worry," Addie said. "You know I'm not drinking, no matter what Declan thinks he can make me do."

"Why do you have to leave so early tomorrow, anyway?" Grace asked.

"We have a long day of driving," Mason said. "And Addie's dad wants us at the campsite before dark."

"I love that you're camping!" Grace did a little hop as she clapped her hands. "That is totally anti-Harlan Hotel. Way to stick it to your dad, Addie."

Mason turned to Addie. "Wait, we could've stayed at Harlan hotels all the way to Tahoe?"

"He might have told me that he could set it up for us." She grinned sheepishly and then turned on Grace. "Way to go. That wasn't public knowledge."

"Keeping things quiet is not her thing." Becca stuck out her tongue at Grace and then pulled her in for a hug. "But we love her anyway."

"It's my dad. He's trying to control everything, like usual," Addie said. "I wasn't having it. Plus, camping gives us more freedom."

Mason smiled at her. "Totally. Who needs a hotel, and their comfy beds and running water?"

"Exactly," Addie agreed, laughing.

"I'm bummed that I have a club game so far away tomorrow, Addie. I would totally be there if I didn't have soccer," Becca said.

"I know," Addie said. "Don't worry about it."

"If my coach wasn't such a monster…"

"We'll send you a pic before she gets on the road," Grace said. "You'll be there in spirit."

"And you could score a goal in my honor," Addie said.

"Addie, come on!" Declan yelled again, waving her over. He threw back another shot and slammed the shot glass down on the bar. The alcohol only magnified his terrible personality.

"Take care of yourself tonight. Declan looks completely toasted."

"I know. Don't worry. I can handle him." Addie peered into Mason's cup. "I see someone else knows my trick."

They heard Declan laugh at whatever crude joke someone probably made. He was louder than usual—clearly an effect of the alcohol. Mason hoped he'd pass out within the hour.

"That's definitely a guffaw. You have to agree."

Addie laughed. "Maybe a little."

"His girlfriend's last night in town, and he's more concerned about getting wasted."

Addie's smile faded.

Mason mentally kicked himself. "Did I say that out loud?"

Addie shrugged.

"What I meant was, he's clearly so devastated that you're leaving that he's drinking away his sorrows," Mason said. "That, or he's trying to see two of you."

"Hey, Addie. You'll see him all day tomorrow. Come hang with us." Declan stumbled from a standing position, if that was possible.

"Good luck," Mason said to Addie. He turned to Sophie, Becca, and Grace. "Great party, girls. Keep an eye on her."

Addie walked over to Declan and was swallowed in his embrace. So much for the rest of her pool game.

# CHAPTER 12

Mason sat on his bed, trying to remember what he was forgetting when his phone chimed with a text from Addie.

"Done packing? Need to leave by 7 or dad will freak."

Mason had gone for a ten-mile run at five A.M. in an attempt to calm his nerves. It didn't work. He was back in plenty of time to see Sophie and Grace make good on their promise to Addie's parents. They brought her home early, like they said they would. Mason watched their arrival from his bedroom window. This was real. They were leaving.

As for his packing, he was done after his last load of laundry two days ago. They would be on the road for only a few days, and he was a minimalist—training from his Boy Scout days.

Out his window, the Jeep sat in Addie's driveway, top down and ready to go. Mason's worries about all the new tire marks he would see crept into his mind again. "I hope I can do this," he said to himself.

Addie's dad rolled her small suitcase out to the Jeep, and her mom followed with a bin of something. Dog food, maybe? Mason left the window and sat at the end of his bed.

*Deep breaths.*

He repeated the mantra in his mind.

He'd gone over the route countless times in order to prepare himself. He'd examined the number of fatalities, crashes, and car troubles along each stretch of road. He knew the open-range areas where cows might wander onto the road and the size of the towns along Route 50. He knew where the missing woman's Honda had been found—between Ely and Valterra, Nevada—and speculated about the number of travelers who might wear down the tracks found near her car.

And all of this knowledge didn't matter. When it came down to it, the only thing that mattered was how mentally destroyed he would be after miles of surprise skid marks.

Mason dropped his head in his hands and then flopped back on his bed. He thought about all his attempts to prepare himself for this trip. He had spent hours driving farther and farther from home: west to Oswego, east to LaGrange, north to Rosemont. He even drove to Six Flags, practically in Wisconsin, hoping to desensitize himself to all the different skid marks he might see. His parents weren't the cross-country drivers some of his friends' parents were, and most of Mason's extended family lived nearby. There hadn't been much long-distance travel in his childhood, and when their family did go on vacation, they flew. Mason had been thankful for that fact for most of his life, but now he understood how unprepared it left him for this trip. All his recent attempts to prepare for the shock of an unexpected tire mark were as impractical as running a marathon in snow boots. He would never be prepared to face all the accidents he was sure to encounter.

When he first started driving, he struggled to balance the visions that played in his mind with what was actually happening on the road. After only three months, his parents threatened to take his license away because they thought he wasn't focused enough on driving. In reality, he was too focused. Now, on this cross-country road trip, he hoped he could control his reactions if they drove over anything serious.

On one of his training drives, he had burst into tears on I-355 near Schaumburg. As he drove over a skid mark, he saw the driver of a minivan turn sharply to the right. She was young, a teenager, reaching for something under her seat when she jerked the wheel too hard. She over-corrected to the left, now with both hands on the wheel, and slammed on the brakes, steering to the right, too late. She skidded and struck the center divider. Mason saw the panic on her face, her eyes wide and confused. Her passenger, probably her dad, yelled something. The gold minivan rebounded off the divider and skidded. Mason watched, helpless, as the minivan slid. The passenger reached out slowly, as if fighting against air, and laid his hand on the girl's arm. It was the only moment of calm that Mason felt in the swirl of chaos.

Drivers slammed on their brakes to avoid colliding with the minivan as it careened across three lanes of traffic. Its unobstructed momentum recklessly gathered force until it wrapped around a lamppost, flattening the distance between the passenger and the driver. In Mason's mind, he saw the force of the impact hurtle the driver forward until her seat belt yanked her back into place. Her mouth opened in a scream, but Mason heard nothing. Instead, tears sprang from his eyes without warning as the passenger was crushed into the post. Blood and glass and fragments of airbags shattered the air around Mason, burying him under their weight.

He didn't have to read about the accident to know the outcome. Sometimes, when he wasn't sure, he looked up the accidents online to see if the people survived. This accident left no doubt. When he experienced it, the intense clarity of the scene passed over him and left him struggling to focus on his own driving. He had cried out, giving voice to the girl's silent screams, but there was nothing he could do. The accident had happened in the past. Mason didn't understand why he had to witness such a horrific crash.

*What was the point of feeling their pain when there was nothing he could do about it?*

Checking newsfeeds might prepare him for the facts of what was to come, but articles could never prepare him for the reality of each crash, for the truth behind the events, for the expressions on the people's faces. An accident like that was rare, he knew. But not rare enough.

All his attempts to get used to driving unknown roads had only convinced him that driving cross-country was the worst thing he could possibly do to himself. Briefly, he had thought that he needed this trip, that aside from the glorious days he could spend with Addie, the trip would help him grow and understand this odd power he possessed more thoroughly. But he was wrong. He didn't need to understand it. He needed to fly places, take a train. Or stay home.

But there was nothing he could do about it now. He had made a promise to Addie. And he had made an unspoken promise to Kenna to read the skid marks found near her car if he could.

Mason sat up on his bed and scanned his room one more time, trying to remember what he was forgetting. He saw his phone charger plugged in near his computer, grabbed it, and left the room.

He tossed his duffel on the driveway next to the Jeep and headed back toward his garage for the camping gear.

"Is this all you packed?" Addie called after him.

He stole a glance back, then turned when he saw Sophie struggling with a cooler.

Mason helped Sophie lift the cooler into the back. "I'm only going to be gone for a few days, remember?" he said and immediately wished he hadn't. The fact that she was packing for forever was not something she needed to be reminded of.

"Plus," he added to fill the quiet his comment had left, "the camping stuff will take up enough space."

"I packed some water," Addie said. "I know we can buy some on the road, but these will get us started."

"And you have a ton of snacks," Grace said. "We loaded you up with a driving care package."

"More like a car package," Sophie snorted.

Mason was glad Sophie and Grace were there to lighten the mood. He didn't know how late they stayed at the party, but he was thankful Addie was true to her word and didn't look hungover.

"I need to grab the camping stuff," he said and headed toward his garage. "We don't want to be without a tent."

Indy barreled out of the house and chased Mason into his garage. Mason grabbed a Frisbee and tossed it to Indy. She jumped up and caught it, and they returned to the Jeep, each carrying their essentials.

Addie's mom joined them with a blanket in her hands.

"Hi, Mrs. Lynmar," Mason said.

"Hi, Mason. I'm going to put this over the back seat." She spread out the blanket and tucked it around the back seats. "I don't want Indy to destroy the seats. Fix it when it needs it, okay? Will you lift this bag, so I can—thanks."

Mason smiled at Addie as her mom fidgeted with the blanket.

When she finished, she looked at Addie. "Do you want to take another look around your room before you go?"

"No. I'm good," Addie said. "We were just in there."

"Your folks are coming over, right Mason?" Mrs. Lynmar asked.

"Yes, any minute. My mom is probably making sandwiches or something. And Dad is probably making sure I didn't forget any camping equipment."

Right then, Mason's parents walked out of the house. His dad carried a sleeping bag and his mom, a plastic container.

"See?" Mason added with a smile.

Indy jumped into the driver's seat when Addie opened the door. Sophie and Grace crowded around to pet her.

"We won't get far with you driving, Indy," Addie joked. "Out! You have to go in the back."

Indy sat there, tongue hanging out her mouth and tail wagging.

"Let's take a pic for Becca," Sophie said. And the three girls took a selfie next to Indy in the driver's seat.

"Ok, kids," Addie's dad said. "Call if you need anything. Follow Google Maps. Don't stop at big truck stops—stick to gas stations."

"And only eat at places you recognize," Mason's mom added.

Mason raised his eyebrows at Addie, silently asking if food trucks counted as places they recognized. And then there was a flurry of hugs and goodbyes and back pats as their parents unleashed additional reminders.

"Don't stop at any one place for too long."

"Call us every day."

"Text us."

"Wear sunscreen when the top is down."

"Send pictures!"

"Watch your gas gauge."

"Don't stop on the side of the highway."

"Take breaks."

"Get to your campsite before dark."

"We've got it," Addie broke in. "You told us all this already."

Addie scooted Indy into the backseat and hugged Grace and Sophie one last time. She climbed into the driver's seat. "I'll take the first shift," Addie said to Mason, her voice tight.

Mason nodded and climbed in the passenger seat.

Their parents and Sophie and Grace crowded together on the driveway, waving at them as they pulled out.

Addie and Mason waved back, and as easy and as hard as that, they drove off.

# CHAPTER 13

Addie and Mason were silent for some time as Addie drove through the neighborhood, headed west.

No parents. Wild and free.

That might have been Indy's thought as she sat upright on the backseat, stretching her nose toward the open air. Mason knew Addie wasn't thinking about what lay ahead, only what remained behind: the home she had lived in half her life. He imagined her thoughts. No more hanging out on the Riverwalk. No more agonizing over decisions at Naper Candy Corner. No more taking pictures with her friends in front of the Dandelion Fountain. No more playing pick-up sand volleyball games at the park.

Contemplating her heartbreak kept Mason's focus off his own fears of the unknown tire marks. In the silence, he understood the magnitude of this trip, and he was honored that she had picked him to share it. Well, kind of picked him, by default.

Leading up to this trip, his focus had been on himself and the missing Kenna. But now he understood what he'd been overlooking—Addie's sadness. As much as he had planned for the drive, he hadn't been prepared for the emotional weight of her loss once it actually started. And from the silence, he could tell she hadn't been prepared for it either. Only Indy seemed genuinely thrilled, with her tongue flapping in the wind.

Addie navigated them onto the highway. Tears slid down her cheeks, but Mason knew enough to stay silent. They passed the driving range and the outlet mall. The wind whipped around them and dried her tears. When they went through a toll, Mason decided that she needed a diversion from her thoughts.

"I think we should only listen to the radio for this whole trip. No iPhones."

"Why?" Addie wiped any remaining tears from her cheeks.

"We can listen to the local radio stations. You know, get a bit of the local flavor." Of course, if he happened to catch a local traffic report, he wouldn't complain. He slipped into his best teacher voice. "To better understand the people who inhabit this land we call America."

"Why do we want to better understand places we're driving through? It's not like we're stopping?"

"That is such a typical response from a high schooler," Mason taunted.

"Excuse me?"

"I'm speaking from the point of view of a college student. It's important to learn the perspective of others, the world outside the suburbs, to understand rural America."

"I can turn around, you know," Addie said. "We haven't gone far enough for me to be stuck with you."

Mason smiled at her threat.

"Was this my parents' secret plan," Addie continued, "to have you annoy me, so I'll return home and fly with them instead of driving?"

"Your parents aren't that crafty," Mason said. "And they don't see 'annoying' when they look at me. They see tall, tough, and trustworthy."

"Don't you mean tedious and taxing?"

"Talented."

"Tiresome."

"Titillating."

"You win," Addie said with a laugh. "Please don't say that word again. Ever."

They passed a sign for the DeKalb Oasis. He pointed and opened his mouth to speak, but she cut him off.

"We're not stopping to pee yet. Don't even ask."

"I wasn't going to. But they do have a Starbucks," Mason said.

"We've been on the road for all of 35 minutes. We aren't far enough away from my parents yet."

Mason fiddled with the radio to find a station without static. "Let's see what rural America has to offer."

"How long are we on this road?"

"Only across part of Illinois. Then we'll get on I-80 to cross Iowa and Nebraska."

"That sounds long."

"That might be an understatement," Mason said. Since they had gotten on I-88, Mason had been plagued by constant reminders of why tailgating is a bad idea. The repeated visions of people glancing at their phones only to look back at the road in time to slam on their brakes to avoid rear-ending someone annoyed him. As they drove further from the suburbs, he hoped the tire marks would be less frequent.

"How long will it take to cross Iowa?" Addie asked. "I want to mentally prepare myself."

"We haven't even left Illinois. That's awfully ambitious of you." He motioned to the view out the front window. "Don't you want to focus on the beauty around you?"

The road stretched into the cornfields that grew up alongside it.

"So exciting, Look, a cow." Addie pointed out her window.

"Is that sarcasm? From you? Remember, this drive was your idea."

"True."

"You could've simply insisted on first class for the flight to Reno, but no," Mason teased.

"I wanted to drive for the dog, not for my own comfort, remember?"

As if to remind Mason of her presence, Indy wedged her wet nose under his arm as it rested on the center console.

"Oh, this is definitely not comfortable," he said, and he meant it, but didn't. He slowly peeled each thigh off the seat. "Are your thighs sticking to the seat like mine are?"

Addie rolled her eyes and pointed to the side of the road. "Did you see that? It was a gym shoe. Who loses a gym shoe on the highway?"

"You got me," Mason said.

"You don't want to make up a story about it, like you do for the skid marks?" Addie asked.

"My creative powers only go so far," Mason said. "Hey, how was the party?" What he really wanted to know though, was what happened with Declan?

The fact that Declan hadn't shown up at Addie's before they left either meant he was too hungover to say goodbye like a decent boyfriend or something was up between them.

"Fine. It got pretty wild."

"I thought it seemed pretty tame when I left," he teased. "Glad to see it picked up."

"I hate to admit it, but I think you're right."

"Right about what? It being tame when I left? Because I was only joking. It definitely wasn't."

"No," Addie said, then paused. "Declan does guffaw."

Mason waited for her to say more, but she didn't.

"Well?" he probed. "What happened?"

"We broke up."

He felt his heart open. He didn't want to sound too excited by her news, so he focused on the passing cornfields and took a deep breath to control his mounting excitement before asking, "Why? Because you're leaving?"

"No, because he's a pig."

"This, I knew."

"Go ahead, say it," Addie mocked. "I told you so."

Mason didn't laugh. The thought that Declan might've done something truly terrible took root in his brain. "I was hoping he'd pass out early. What'd he do?"

"He wanted me to do shots."

"I saw that starting before I left." Mason cursed himself for leaving the party. He knew he should've stayed.

"Thankfully, he was too drunk to see me pour them out."

"Smart." Mason silently prayed that the road would continue to be clear because he didn't want anything to distract him from listening to her.

"Then he wanted me to go to his room for a going-away present."

Mason tensed. He didn't like where this was headed.

"Don't worry," she said. "I wasn't drunk like he hoped."

Mason had heard stories about Declan, and he'd hoped they were only rumors. His fear that they weren't was part of the reason he hated that Addie was dating him.

"Yeah, I'm sure you can imagine what he wanted," she said. "What a douche. I told him he was supposed to give *me* a going-away present. I'm the one leaving."

"Good point."

"Yeah, well, that didn't work so well. Guess what present he wanted to give me. No, don't." Addie raised her hand as if warding off the memory. "I don't want to think about it."

"He gives males a bad name," Mason said.

"He gives pigs a bad name."

"I'm glad you're okay. I mean, are you okay?"

"Yeah. All good," she said. "Just mad that he turned out to be such a jerk. Isn't that exactly what you said he was?"

"Don't worry. It's not like I have 2,000 miles to rub it in or anything."

"Great."

"I figured something was up when he didn't show up this morning to say goodbye and flex his muscles for my benefit. That, or I figured he was too hungover."

"Oh, I'm sure he's that. And probably passed out with some stupid sophomore who thinks he's amazing."

A vision passed in Mason's mind as they sped over a skid mark, and he couldn't help but blurt out the bizarre scene. "A car braked hard when a bag of onions flew off a truck. It barely missed the front end of the car. Can you imagine a whole truck hauling nothing but bags of onions?"

"What are you talking about?" Addie asked.

"The tire tracks back there. We went over some skid marks."

"Got it." Addie smiled at him. "Thanks. I need to get my mind off that jerk."

Mason felt a pang of guilt because she thought he was changing the subject to help her. But the vision had been so unexpected and unusual that he couldn't help but share it.

"Look, if you want to talk about him, we can," he said, wishing he hadn't shut her down, even if the last thing he wanted was to think about Declan putting his hands anywhere on Addie.

"No, I'm good. Tell me about that one." Addie pointed as they rolled over two short parallel skid marks.

"It's typical. We'll see those all day long. Quick brake in traffic after a college student looked at her phone. We're near the university." Mason motioned to the dorms in the distance.

As they drove, he told her half-truths about skid marks they passed. But eventually, they stopped talking and listened to the radio. Mason found a consistent thread in the visions he saw. Patterns, he learned, were easy to find: drivers not paying attention, cars coming to quick stops in traffic, missed exits, blown tires, deer.

He began to settle into the drive. The visions that regularly danced across his mind were typical, not tragic. There was a good chance that the drive wouldn't be as bad as he feared. He still planned to check the news on his phone, if they weren't in a dead zone, but maybe there wasn't anything to worry about. He briefly thought of the missing woman, but she was miles and days away. He relaxed into his seat and looked more to the horizon than the road.

"Do you think I'm being too hard on my parents?" Addie asked.

"Too hard? Why do you think you're being hard on them?"

"This whole driving thing? I know they're stressed about it. Do you think it was too nasty of me to demand it?"

"Actually," he said, "I think you let them off easy."

"Really?" Addie searched his expression for a smirk.

"Really. You've handled all this pretty calmly—I mean, for a seventeen-year-old."

"For a seventeen-year-old? Are you kidding me?" Indy sat up, sensing the change in Addie's tone, and licked Addie's cheek. "Now you and my parents are in for it."

"I was only joking," he teased. "I mean, you're barely seventeen, more like sixteen."

"I may've let my parents off easy, but I won't let you off easy. We're going sightseeing. Next sign I see, we stop."

"You do not want to make that threat. We're still in Illinois. It'll probably be a president's birthplace or something."

The brown sign designating "Ronald Reagan's Boyhood Home" came into view and Mason pointed. "I told you."

"Not a problem," she said. "We'll learn a little about our history and the people of America. Wasn't that your goal?"

"Yeah, but..."

"Just keep talking, and maybe if you're lucky, you'll get to see a big ball of twine and the biggest wad of gum." Addie took the Dixon exit and followed the signs toward Reagan's childhood home.

"Hey, look!" She pointed to another sign. "We can also see the fake Berlin Wall. Awesome!"

# Chapter 14

"The eight-dollar fee will be worth it—he was a president, after all," Addie said as she dragged Mason up to the bronze bust of Ronald Reagan and took a selfie. "To commemorate our tour."

Her excitement faded quickly as Willard Hardigan, their seventy-something guide, slowly led them through room after room. Their group consisted of a couple who could have passed for Willard's parents, two women in their mid-sixties, and Addie and Mason. Addie, who was once at the front of the tour chatting happily with the elderly couple, soon lagged behind.

After a ten-minute explanation of how the mahogany detail on each dresser and nightstand in the bedrooms was carved, Addie couldn't even muster the plastic smile she wore throughout Mr. Hardigan's speech about the modern convenience of the Detroit Jewel stove that sat in Nelle Reagan's kitchen. When one of the women asked a question about the restoration project, Addie audibly sighed. Only after the guide told the woman not to call him Mr. Hardigan, that his friends call him Willy, did a true grin light across Addie's face.

"What's so funny?" Mason asked her as they followed the group into the living room.

"His last name," she whispered.

Mason repeated the guide's name in his mind a couple times before catching on. "What are you, a sophomore boy?"

Addie giggled until Willy stretched a gnarled finger toward the fireplace and began a story about coins hidden under a loose tile in the hearth. The story started with a nine-year-old Reagan and meandered until Reagan's return to the house at the age of seventy-three.

When they finally made it back to the parlor, with an invitation to sit on a wooden bench to watch a video reviewing Reagan's presidency, Addie insisted she could hear Indy whining and pulled Mason away for their escape.

Indy barked when they approached. "Ok, maybe that wasn't my thing," Addie said. "But that doesn't mean I'm done torturing you. We're just done with guided tours and presidents."

Mason laughed as he untied Indy. "Didn't you find it even the tiniest bit interesting?"

"Heck to the no! What's wrong with you?"

"Does this mean no fake Berlin Wall?" Mason pointed toward the sign.

"It's back to cornfields and highways for you."

"I think you've got this torture thing down."

<hr>

MASON WASN'T THINKING ABOUT POTENTIAL TIRE MARKS AS Addie steered them back toward I-88, and he wasn't thinking about the long drive that was still ahead of them. He was only thinking about how good it felt to tease Addie and hear her laugh. And how beautiful she looked with one leg tucked up and the other stretched toward the pedal as she sang along with the radio.

Then they rolled over a skid mark so intense, it caused Mason to cry out.

"What's wrong?" Addie asked, instinctively slowing the Jeep to look at him.

He couldn't respond as he processed the driver of a midnight blue

Audi, a twenty-something man with dark stubble on his face, looking at his phone and blowing through a stop sign. When his attention returned to driving, it was too late. He slammed on his brakes and turned the wheel, leaving the two tire marks Addie had driven over. An old man walking across the street turned toward the sound as he was struck by the car. Upon impact, the man left his feet, spun in the air, and landed hard on his side. Mason didn't know the outcome, but it couldn't have been good.

"Mason," Addie insisted. "What happened? What's wrong? Did you swallow a bug?"

He returned to the present and fumbled for words. "I don't know. I think...maybe it was a bee. I think I got stung." He reached for his leg and pretended to look at a spot on his right calf.

"Geez! You scared the crap out of me," Addie said, turning onto the ramp. "Your eyes went all wide, and you were like, I don't know, totally frozen. I thought you were going to throw up or something."

"Just startled, that's all," Mason said. The memory of the man's body flying through the air replayed in his mind. The impact with the concrete, the angle of his arm, his stillness—it was on a loop. Even the driver's expression, eyes wide at the realization of what he'd just done.

Mason thought about the miles they still had to go, and the magnitude of the trip returned. He thought about his neighbor Kenna's accident all those years ago. This same sick feeling filled his gut then. He was helpless. He couldn't do anything to save Kenna or this old man. Maybe he could do something to help the missing Kenna but that was still days away.

*There is so much riding on this trip. How did I ever think I could have fun?*

"You're not allergic, are you?" Addie asked. "Do I need to find a hospital?"

"No, all good," he said. He focused on his phone. He needed to know if the man had lived, though he doubted that possibility. And he needed to look for news about the missing woman.

"What are you doing? Trying to find some better music? Because you said no iPhones," Addie reminded him.

"No. Just looking at the route. I want to make sure we didn't eat up too much time with that stop."

Mason had been pretending for years, creating stories to cover his reactions and actions. Was this the purpose of his visions? To perfect his skill at lying? But was he really that good at lying, if no one would have believed the truth anyway?

# KENNA

There's another bottle of water next to me, but now that I know it is drugged, I dump it out. I'm so thirsty, and it will only tempt me. I don't want to be tempted. I want to be awake when whoever has locked me in here opens that door.

Dirt crumbles under my fingertips as I run them along the walls and floor, searching for anything I can use as a weapon. I used to love the slightly sweet scent of soil. Now it's tinged with the stink of ammonia, pressing in on me, suffocating me with the fear that I will forever be buried here.

Don't think like that, I tell myself. I will leave this place. I have to.

My fingers brush against something hard on the ground. I grab it, disappointed by its small size, and fumble for the on/off switch of what must be a plastic flashlight.

"Please work," I gasp.

When I click it on, a narrow beam of light glints off the chicken wire embedded in the dirt walls and ceiling.

Terror grips me tighter, and I drop the flashlight. I knew the wire was there, but seeing it surround me makes everything worse. The flashlight rolls on the ground, and the beam illuminates a worn and filthy mattress in the dirt. I know I'm just as filthy. I can smell urine on me. A sob wells in my chest, but I stifle it.

*I grab the flashlight, desperately wanting to plunge myself back into darkness and escape the sight of my reality, but I force myself to run the beam along the length of the ceiling to gauge the size of my prison. Wood posts, partially buried into the walls, reinforce this claustrophobic cave. I hope the weight of whatever is over me doesn't crash down before I escape.*

*A gray plastic bucket, probably what I'm supposed to use as a toilet, sits in the corner. I grab for it, praying it has a metal handle I can pry off. It doesn't. Whatever handle had been there is gone.*

*I scan the darkness again, searching for anything I can use as a weapon, but there's nothing else—only a mattress, the bucket, an empty plastic bottle, and the tiny flashlight in my hand.*

*Maybe I could dig out one of the wood posts from the wall and use it to ram the door. I'd risk a partial cave-in if I could break down the door. I test all the beams, throwing my body weight at them, digging my fingers around them, searching for weaknesses, but none of them budge.*

*I collapse on the mattress, exhausted and hungry and thankful I poured out the water that I now desperately want to drink. After one more look around, I switch off the flashlight and sink into the darkness.*

*When the door opens, I will run.*

# CHAPTER 15

Mason and Addie stopped in Des Moines for lunch, and true to Addie's word, she led them right to a whole line of food trucks in Sculpture Park.

Mason needed to stretch, and it felt good to walk through the park. He'd never seen anything like Sculpture Park before. Statues of all sorts were situated around the immense lawn —a large metal spider, wire letters shaped into a giant open book, figures that seemed to float as if they were dancing. Mason always thought his hometown was unique, but this was a different level.

"I am definitely hungry," Addie said as they walked along a paved path toward the food trucks.

"Couldn't have planned this better if we tried," Mason said.

Addie's jaw dropped. "What do you mean? You said we were going through Des Moines. I did plan this." She pretended to pout.

He playfully shoved her shoulder. "This is way better than a Pop-Tart truck."

The red-and-orange truck with the name Stuffed with Stuff painted on the side drew their attention. The name illustrated its specialty; a variety of foods spilled out of the "u" in "Stuffed" and "Stuff"—pizza, tacos, chicken, and something that resembled mac and cheese.

Addie pointed to the long line of people. "That's a good sign."

"But their name is sketchy," Mason said. "It's a cornucopia of food."

"Be adventurous." Addie read the menu hanging on the side of the truck while Indy searched the ground for anything that had become unstuffed. "I am definitely getting the lasagna stuffed sandwich."

"I can't even imagine what that will look like. I think I'll go with the meatball stuffed sandwich."

"Boring!"

"Well, the pot roast stuffed sandwich sounds too messy," Mason said.

"How about the enchilada stuffed one?" Addie said. "That one is on cornbread."

They inched closer to the ordering window.

"I think I'll stick with my original," Mason said. "Please, no more suggestions, or I won't be able to eat lunch at all."

Addie looked around the park while they waited. "This place is cool. I love all the sculptures. And it's perfect for Indy." Indy had crawled half under the food truck as she strained to get some elusive piece of food.

"Maybe we can find a spot to sit over by that snowman-looking thing." Mason pointed toward the shade of two large white balls stacked on each other.

"Good idea. This totally beats the VW beetle spider in the middle of a cornfield that I was hoping to stop at. I guess I'll have to find something else."

"That toy train museum we saw was cool. I can't imagine how long it took to put together over a mile of tracks, or how the twenty-six trains didn't crash into each other."

"True," Addie agreed. "Indy looked so cute tied to that big caboose outside the museum though."

The stop in Dixon reminded Mason that he had to get to Nevada before it was too late. Today, though, they could only go as far as the CAA in Grand Island, Nebraska. While Addie was driving, Mason had searched for more information about Kenna but only found articles he'd already read. Nothing new. And nothing that suggested she'd been found.

Mason scratched Indy's head. "This whole trip is dog heaven. You're loving all the new smells, aren't you, girl?"

Indy, chewing something, looked up at Mason.

"And apparently you're loving all the new food," he teased.

When they got their food, they sat on the grass between a seahorse constructed out of what looked like metallic driftwood and a giant bronze sculpture titled "The Vault" that vaguely resembled a capital letter L.

"I'm not sure how that's a vault." Mason eyed the statue. "I must be missing something."

"From the wrong angle, it looks like it should be dedicated to our tour guide at the Reagan home," Addie said, tilting her head to examine it.

"Now that you've said that, I can't look at it." Mason shifted so his back was to the sculpture. "I don't think I understand modern art."

"Maybe it's not a vault like in a bank, but a gymnast on a vault," Addie said, tilting her head to the other side.

"Don't over-analyze. Just eat. Indy is seriously eyeing your sandwich. How does your stuffed mess of lasagna taste?"

Addie took a big bite. "It's on garlic bread," she said, mouth full. "How awesome is that?"

Mason laughed. It was nice to sit and relax. After he ate his meatball sandwich, which he was pleased to learn was also on garlic bread, he leaned back with his hands behind his head. As he let each muscle in his back and legs relax, he felt himself melt into the ground, his tension disappearing into the blades of grass. He didn't realize he'd been clenching his muscles, bracing for another terrible scene since the Dixon accident, until he lay on the lawn. The image of the old man and the picture of the missing woman fought to regain his attention, but he breathed slowly, stilling his thoughts. He wanted to be here with Addie, in the middle of all the statues, together.

"That looks like a snowman, except it only has two parts." Addie pointed toward the white balls towering over them.

Mason rolled on his side to look. "I agree. Aren't snowmen supposed to have three?"

"Oh my gosh! Do you remember making snowmen when we were younger? I almost forgot. What were we? Ten?"

"You seem to forget that I'm a year older than you." Mason leaned on his elbow and propped his head in his hand.

"Whatever. Remember the one we made that was so tall, we had to get a ladder to put the head on?" She got up and ran to the stacked white balls with Indy chasing at her heels. "Come here, Mason. Let's take a pic."

Mason joined her, and they gave up trying to get anything but Indy's butt in the picture.

"I think we took a picture with the butt of the sculpture, too," Mason laughed, pointing to the other side. "They're eyeballs stacked on each other."

"I like the snowman idea better," Addie said, looking at the photo before posting it. "Something to remember our snowman-making days."

"Send me all these pictures, okay?"

Mason looked over her shoulder as she flipped through Snapchat. Her shoulders drooped, and he sensed the levity leaving her face.

"Becs won her soccer game." Addie gave Mason a weak smile. "And Sophie and Grace are hanging out at the beach. Looks like the world goes on without me."

Mason didn't know what to say, so he walked alongside Addie as she followed the path.

"Who's going to build snowmen with me now?" she asked.

"We haven't built a snowman in years," Mason reminded her. "Plus, you'll have no problem finding someone to join you if you ever want to make one."

"Yeah, well, I doubt I'll feel much like making a snowman anyway."

They came upon two huge egg-shaped heads, both with oversized mouths. One egg smiled maniacally, exposing a full set of steel teeth. The other was less enthusiastic, with more of a smirk. "This is the stuff of nightmares," Mason said.

"Definitely picture-worthy." Instinctively, they each stuck out an arm as if caught in the steel teeth as Addie snapped a picture.

"Your mom will be thrilled to see that," he said, laughing at the picture she showed him.

"I'll text it to her. It'll be my check-in."

"Put it on Insta," Mason said. "I'm sure Declan'd love to see me getting eaten by a monster."

Mason was shocked by his own comment. He raised his eyebrows and bit his lower lip in apology.

"I couldn't care less what Declan thinks," Addie said. "I hope he sobered up and realized what he lost."

Mason let out a breath and thought about how long Addie and Declan dated. It was close to three months, hardly an astonishing length of time for high school, but longer than Mason had dated anyone.

Indy tugged Mason after a squirrel that crisscrossed in front of their path, clearly taunting the dog.

"What if he tried to get you back?" Mason couldn't help himself. He had to ask. The park was vast, but not big enough to absorb Mason's worries.

"Not a chance," Addie said. "He guffaws, remember? And now I don't have to worry about a long-distance relationship."

Mason's heart sank.

# CHAPTER 16

Mason was thankful when the green sign announced that they'd finally reached Grand Island, Nebraska. It had been a long day of traveling, and the night before had been a lot longer for Addie. After lunch, they took a quick picture at Freedom Rock to see what was painted on it, drove past a bank that had been robbed by Bonnie and Clyde, circled a tree that grew in the middle of the road, and waved at the Smiley Face Water Tower off I-80. It was technically just under four and a half hours from Des Moines to Grand Island, but it took them an hour longer. They were definitely pushing the boundaries of her father's "Get there before dark" mandate.

But they were seeing America, all the strange fixations, collections, and passions of a variety of people. Mason relished the freedom of the gravel side roads, where cars could slide and skid to a stop without leaving traces of residue on stones. After only one day of traveling, his understanding of how full his life could be outside the walls he built to protect himself had expanded.

Mason was surprised that no neon signs promising gas stations and fast food greeted them when they took the exit off the highway. To the right and left, cornfields beckoned.

"Are you sure this is right?" Addie asked.

Mason looked at the glowing blue line on his map. "Yep. Go left."

Addie turned toward the distant silhouettes of a farmhouse and silo. She nodded toward Mason's phone. "Got a lot of faith in that, don't you?"

"Would Google Maps ever lead you astray?"

Past a line of trees, the green-and-blue CAA sign flickered in the dark horizon.

"Home sweet home," Mason said.

"We're in the middle of a cornfield." Addie's hand swept the surrounding area as she turned into the Campgrounds Across America parking lot.

"Think of our campsite as an oasis in a desert of corn." Mason pointed. "Look, it even has trees."

"Let's hope we can put our tent under one," Addie said. "All that corn creeps me out. Mr. Janik, my biology teacher, said corn sweats. That's totally gross, like it's alive or something."

"It is alive," Mason said. "It's a plant."

"Yeah, well, plants aren't supposed to sweat. You, and all your running friends, I get that. But a plant?"

It was almost eight P.M. when Mason checked in to their reserved camping spot. Thankfully, they still had a little sunlight left. Addie took Indy for a walk, while Mason unloaded their camping equipment.

His stomach flipped at the thought that he would be sleeping next to Addie inside the tent he was unpacking. It was part of the plan, of course, but knowing it would happen was a lot different than having it happen.

"You're not the only thing sweating," he said to the corn.

In the fifteen minutes it took Addie to tour the CAA, Mason had the tent up and was staking it to the ground.

"Wow," she said when she saw his progress. "You really are an Eagle Scout."

"Are you mocking me?"

"No, I'm impressed. I was planning on helping you. I just didn't know you were so fast."

"That's what she ... never mind. Here, help me finish." Mason handed Addie a stake, his cheeks burning from his stale joke. "Will you get the front?"

She snorted and took the stake, eyeing the tent as she walked around to the front. "This is it? Huh."

"What do you mean?" He pointed to the base. "Put the stake through the metal loop under the entrance."

Addie drove the stake in with the heel of her shoe, then unzipped the tent and crawled inside. "It's cozy."

Indy followed her and sniffed around the edges.

"Here." Mason tossed in the sleeping bags and pillows.

"This is serious camping." She moved the rolled-up sleeping bags to the back of the tent, and Indy lay down inside.

Mason handed Addie the electric lantern. "We'll need this soon. It's getting dark." Then he climbed in, pulling the cooler behind him.

"Will that attract animals?" She pointed to the cooler.

"Maybe your dog." He reached in and grabbed a water bottle. "Want one?"

"I'm good," Addie said. "Thanks."

The breeze rippled the sides of the tent.

"This'll be kind of fun," she added.

"Haven't you ever camped before?" Mason rolled up the flaps that covered the mesh openings from the inside.

"Never. My dad works for Harlan Hotels, did you forget?" She gestured to the exposed mesh openings. "Are you going to leave those rolled up like that all night?"

"If we want a breeze. Depends how cold it gets."

"Can people see in our tent?"

"Why? What do you plan to do?" Mason teased.

"Funny." Addie kicked his foot. "I plan to sleep without people watching me."

"Don't worry. No one's interested in watching you sleep. Plus, I don't think Indy will let anyone get near our tent."

At the sound of her name, Indy wagged her tail, and it hit the sides of the tent.

"Don't get too comfy, dog," Mason said. "You might be outside tonight."

"Should we spread those out?" Addie pointed to the sleeping bags.

"Might as well. Here, hand me one."

They unrolled the sleeping bags, and the space inside the tent shrank.

Mason felt self-conscious. They'd been neighbors for as long as he could remember, and although they had run through sprinklers, built forts in the forest, and had late-overs, this would be the first time they were sleeping so close to one another. He wondered what Addie's dad would've said about the trip if he'd seen the tent before they left.

Addie maneuvered to position the sleeping bags, wiggling from side to side. Her black shorts crept up her thighs, and Mason forced himself to look away. How would he be able to sleep inches from her without touching her? He did the only thing he could think to do to distract himself: he grabbed his pillow and hit Addie in the back of the head.

"Oh you didn't!" She said as she swung her pillow to hit him.

He ducked out of the way and her pillow landed on Indy.

Indy barked, ready to play.

"Nice one!" Mason said with a laugh.

"Sorry, Indy!" Addie petted the dog to calm her down and looked at Mason. "Hey, I know I've said this before, but I really appreciate you doing all this for me."

"No problem." Mason scratched Indy behind the ears. "I'm doing it more for your dog than you, anyway."

Before he could duck, her pillow struck the side of his head, and Mason sprawled out on a sleeping bag. He tucked his pillow under his head and stretched out.

"I guess I'm sleeping here." He relaxed into the sleeping bag and once again let the tension of the drive ease from his shoulders. It was good not to be on the road. But the vision of the old man lifeless on the street still clung to his mind. Mason was continuously haunted by all the deaths he'd seen but not heard, seen but not talked about. This trip was far from over, and as much as he wanted every minute with Addie to last, he wanted the visions of the accidents to end.

Up ahead, on a road they weren't even close to traveling yet, were the only skid marks he wanted to see.

"I hope you don't snore," Addie said.

"Are you talking to me or the dog?"

"Funny."

"No one ever said I snore."

Addie tilted her head and raised an eyebrow. "And who has never told you that you snore?"

"Is that what girls talk about at sleepovers?" Mason flipped over onto his stomach and put his hands under his chin.

"You're such a dork sometimes."

Addie shoved his shoulder, and he pretended the force knocked him over.

"Did you find any food options when you were walking around?" Mason asked.

"They have pizza delivery," Addie said.

Mason propped himself up on an elbow. "Great!"

"But it's closed."

He slumped back on the sleeping bag. "It's your fault. You insisted on that stop at Reagan's home."

"Listen to you whine. I thought camping was about roughing it. Grilling hot dogs over an open flame. Not pizza delivery." Addie pulled out a plastic container of peanut butter and jelly sandwiches from the cooler. "Good thing your mom packed lots of food."

"Just wait," Mason said. "When it starts to rain, we'll see how comfy you think camping is."

"Not funny." Addie's phone buzzed and she looked at it. "I guess I better call home."

Mason followed her out of the tent. After he called his mom, he searched for information on Kenna Cook. He hoped to find a new article about her being found, but that still wasn't the case. He reopened and reread articles from the different news sites, all saying what he already knew. The article from Fallon, Nevada, about volunteers who spent days searching for her, walking in lines across the desert, but found nothing. The mechanic who was examining her abandoned car. The pleas for anyone with information to contact the authorities.

Mason muted a news clip of an interview with Kenna's mother that he'd watched a week ago. He glanced at Addie, who was still talking with her mother, and walked off a little. In the video, Mrs.

Cook choked back tears and pleaded for anyone with information to please come forward. The worry in her eyes alone was enough of a reminder to Mason that this trip was important on multiple levels.

He wondered if all the volunteers, police cars, and news vans that traveled over the road since Kenna's disappearance would've worn away the skid marks that were near her car.

*Will I even be able to find them if they are still there? And if they are, will they tell a story that could help Kenna?*

# CHAPTER 17

Mason grabbed the Frisbee from the back of the Jeep and called Indy. Addie still chatted on the phone with her mom, so Mason walked Indy to the nearby fenced dog run to let her burn off some energy. It was getting dark fast, but Mason sailed the Frisbee and Indy ran after it. She seemed to be tracking the Frisbee in the air, watching its arc as she chased it. As it curved down, Indy launched herself into the air, mouth open for the catch. She missed the Frisbee entirely. It landed several feet behind her, so she jogged back to it and scooped it up in her mouth.

"Looks like Indy needs some practice catching," Mason said when Addie sat on top of a nearby picnic table. "Don't you ever play catch with her? Your dog is deprived."

"Trust me. Indy is anything but deprived. My mom cooks chicken breasts and cuts them up to mix into her food."

Mason pried the Frisbee from Indy's mouth. "And you drive across the country to make sure she's comfortable."

"Safe, not comfortable," Addie said. "There's a difference."

The cornfields rustled in the slight breeze, and Addie looked around. The sky was dark blue with a band of deep orange hovering on the horizon.

"It's kind of pretty, you know," she said. "Like rolling hills of corn."

"Wow, you just said that."

"Pretty in an I-don't-mind-stopping-for-one-day kind of way," she corrected.

"Be glad your dad didn't get transferred to Nebraska," Mason said. "I'm sure they have a Harlan Hotel around here somewhere."

He threw the Frisbee, and it dove hard into the dirt.

Addie hopped off the table and walked toward Mason and Indy. "I think you're the problem," she said. "If you could throw a Frisbee, Indy might have a chance of catching it."

"Salt. Is that what you're throwing?"

Addie smirked and leaned on the fence. "How was your mom? Mine sounded stressed. The moving van comes in two days, and she said she's not ready. Should I feel guilty that I'm not there to help her?"

"No. My mom said she was over for most of the day helping her. She'll be fine."

"True. I bet she's way more ready than she thinks." Addie pulled her phone from her pocket. "Let's focus on something important. There must be food trucks in Denver that we can visit tomorrow."

"You think about food more than any person I know."

Indy dropped the Frisbee at Mason's feet and sat down.

According to the map on Mason's phone, Ely, Nevada, was eleven hours from Denver. They would reach the place where Kenna disappeared in two days.

"Let's not stop in Guthrie," Addie said. "Looks like the only thing there is a prison."

Addie leaned into her phone. Mason loved the way she tilted her head slightly to the right when she focused on something.

*Maybe I should tell her about the missing woman.*

But what could Mason say? Would he tell her about the Kenna he knew when he was a kid, the Kenna who used to live in her house? That wouldn't explain why he thought he could do something to help this Kenna. And he certainly couldn't explain the tire tracks. He brushed off the idea.

"Is this all you do?" he asked. "Plan your next meal?"

"No, I'm also adding some sightseeing stops. There's a livestock auction house in Brush, Colorado. I always wanted to see a livestock auction."

"That might be the oddest thing you've ever said." Mason opened the gate, and Indy rushed to Addie. "Don't add too much. There's a rodeo starting in Fallon that would be fun to check out. You can get your fill of livestock there."

"A rodeo? Cool! I'm down for that."

"If you want to see the little kids ride the pigs like bulls, we'll need to get there in two days. That'll give us a day to take in all that the rodeo has to offer." The rodeo was part of his plan to get to Valterra sooner rather than later.

"So Wild West of you! We can't miss kids on pigs!"

They walked back to the tent and climbed in for their makeshift picnic. Indy had convinced them that she should sleep inside the tent, and, after eating half of one of Mason's sandwiches, the dog curled up by the entrance.

Addie scratched Indy with her toes.

If Mason positioned his legs just so, he could stretch out completely without hitting Indy in the butt.

Mason's initial self-consciousness relaxed as they avoided talk of Tahoe and laughed about the day's random sightseeing stops. They were sunburnt and wind-blown from their day of travel, but they didn't care.

"Why did you decide to run at Illinois?" Addie asked. "A couple colleges offered you scholarships, didn't they?"

"Yeah, I don't know," Mason said. "I liked their program and their coach. Plus, they have a good engineering school." He wanted to add that it wasn't too far from home, from where he thought she was going to be.

"Do you know what type of engineering you want to study?"

"I'm not totally sure, but I'm leaning toward environmental."

"Is that like landscaping or something?"

"No, not quite."

"Farming? All this corn inspiring you?" Addie swung her leg in the air to take in their surroundings.

"Definitely not," Mason said, laughing. "It's more like developing sustainable systems for water and soil use. That sort of thing. Making sure resources are maintained."

"That's cool. Sounds a little like what you did for your Eagle Scout project."

Indy sat up and peered through a gap in the tent flap. She let out a low growl.

"What is it, girl?" Addie asked, propping up on her forearm and listening.

"Probably a monster coming out of the cornfields to feed on campers," Mason taunted.

"That is *so* not funny." Addie swatted at his chest.

"Relax. She probably heard someone at another campsite."

Addie scratched Indy behind the ears until she relaxed, and then Addie rested her head on the dog's belly. "She hates when I do this."

Mason propped himself up to get a better look. Addie, with her eyes closed, let her head gently rise and fall with Indy's breaths. In the faint campground light that seeped through the tent, Addie's hair looked blonder. He followed the contours of her mouth, her lips turned up slightly as if a smile was about to break free.

Mason lay back down and focused his attention on the ripples in the tent top. "I guess we better go to sleep."

"Yeah, I guess." Addie moved back to her sleeping bag. "So, did your Eagle Scout project make you interested in environmental engineering, or did you pick cleaning the river because you were interested in environmental engineering?"

"Is this a chicken-or-egg question?" he asked. "I think I picked the project because it interested me. I wondered how the forest preserve took care of something as natural as a river, and I often run near the dam they built to help the flooding."

He wanted to tell her that he'd always been drawn to water because it didn't leave traces behind like skid marks on the road. He had grown up along the DuPage River, and although it wasn't the most beautiful river in the world, watching it had been a mental escape. He saw beauty in running rivers, knowing that as the water flowed, it was always new, always moving. Even though it carried bits of the land with it, that land was reconfigured. The river kept no traces of what had happened on it.

He used to sit and watch the water run past him, mesmerized by the fact that the speed of the water was dictated by what was hidden underneath or along the banks. As a kid, he even pretended to take up fishing so he wouldn't look odd sitting by the river, staring into it.

"It's kind of strange to think that something natural needs to be taken care of by people, you know," Addie said. "But I get it. If we hadn't built so much next to the river, then I guess we wouldn't need to worry about it flooding."

They lay on top of their sleeping bags, and the blowing breeze rippled the tent slowly. It was dark and quiet, with only the rustling of the corn, the chirping of crickets in the fields, and the low thrumming of tractor-trailers in the distance.

Mason's pulse raced at how close Addie's body was to his, how easily he could reach out and touch her.

"Yeah," he said. "A lot of it is trying to control what the river does."

"Maybe we should control ourselves and not build so close to it," Addie said.

Mason focused on the phrase "control ourselves" to slow his breathing. He narrowed his eyes, following the pattern of the ripples and pulling his thoughts back to their discussion

"Think of it as controlling our effect on the river," he said. "The Riverwalk is nice *because* it's close to the river." He rolled to face Addie, then realized how bad of an idea that was.

Her hair was spread out on her pillow, and her eyes were closed. He used all his mental effort to stop his hand from reaching over and running his fingers through her hair.

"And that's why you organized the clean-up?" she asked, opening her eyes to look at him.

Heat rose in Mason's cheeks, as if he had been caught with his hand outstretched even though it was still at his side. "Well, that's kind of the reason. That and the river is kind of a mess because people are slobs. It was cool of you to help me get all those volunteers. You have quite a network."

Addie dropped her chin slightly and raised an eyebrow. "Don't you mean I *had* quite a network?"

"You still do," he said. "Only now it spans multiple states."

Even though it was the whole reason for their trip, it had been hours since he'd thought about the fact that she was leaving Illinois. In a couple of days, she would be permanently far away from him. He only wanted to focus on the present. And in the present, he wanted to kiss her.

"I guess I try to block out the fact that I am getting closer to my new home instead of farther away from my old one," she said. "I haven't gotten used to the idea that there won't be a return trip, at least, not for me."

The sides of the tent snapped in the wind as if to punctuate her thoughts. "Man, the breeze is pretty incredible here," she added.

"The plains," Mason said. "Not many trees or buildings to block the wind." He rolled over to the window. "Want me to drop the flaps? I think we'll feel the breeze no matter what."

"Sure," Addie said. "I'll get this one." When she moved, Indy got up and stretched. She licked Addie's face before lying down on Mason's pillow.

"Oh no you don't," he said, pulling the pillow out from under her. "I have to put my face on this. You're shedding all over it."

The tent darkened even more with the window covers tied down, but a soft glow from the camp lights still permeated through the fabric.

"Good dog," Addie said. "He hit me with that pillow earlier. Payback."

"Careful." Mason smiled. "Or I'll hit you with it again."

Indy returned to her post at the front of the tent, and they climbed into their sleeping bags.

"It's kind of cozy," she said.

"It should be. That sleeping bag has an EN rating of +10 to +35 degrees. Actually, it might be too cozy for the summer."

"I don't know what you're talking about," Addie said, rolling onto her side and leaning close to him. "I meant this whole thing was cozy, the sleeping bag, sure, but the tent, the talking, the night, the dog, everything."

He felt her breath on his cheek. "Yeah," was all he could say. Her brown eyes were inches from his, and he held her gaze, mesmerized by the specks of gold that sparkled in them in the dim light. He could lean a little closer and kiss her, but he didn't move. Her eyes drifted to his lips, and his heart raced.

Then she rolled away from him. "Don't snore. You'll scare the dog," she said over her shoulder.

The memory of her breath on his cheek and the way she had looked at him blocked all thoughts from his mind. He had a sudden urge to tell her how he felt, how he had always felt about her.

Instead, he reminded himself of her comment in Des Moines. She didn't want to worry about a long-distance relationship. He would only make the trip awkward if he spilled his guts.

He rolled over and went to sleep.

Thursday, May 30, 2019

*Ely Sun*
Ely, Nevada

## Ely Mechanic Consulted in Missing-Woman Case

A serpentine belt failure caused the breakdown of the car driven by a California woman who went missing near Ely last week.

Bud Freeman Jr. of Freeman Mechanics, a trusted establishment in Ely for 34 years, examined the abandoned vehicle belonging to Kenna Cook, 24, of Daly City, California, and reported to authorities that the serpentine belt on the 2005 Honda Accord failed, causing the breakdown.

"That belt drives the water pump, which means no coolant would have been circulating through the engine once the belt snapped," Freeman said.

Cook was last heard from on May 22 and reported missing the following day when she failed to arrive at her new residence. She is still missing.

Valterra County and Sterling County police departments have followed up on numerous leads, but none have provided information to Cook's whereabouts.

"A crash-reconstruction expert from Fallon examined skid marks found near the vehicle," Lieutenant Dean Wallace of the Valterra Police Department said. "He reported the presence of decelerating marks, most likely caused by a vehicle coming to a quick stop." No other debris was found near the tire marks and a connection to Cook's car was not confirmed.

Anyone with information about Cook is asked to please contact local authorities.

# Chapter 18

"Rise and shine, sleepy head!" Mason called from outside the tent.

Mason had been awake for two hours, taken Indy on a run, showered, eaten a breakfast pizza from the camp store—the kitchen had two options: breakfast pizza and dinner pizza—looked for new information about the missing woman, walked Indy again, and was contemplating going for a swim in the campground pool. Since he didn't pack a bathing suit, and swimming in boxers seemed like a bad idea, he finally decided to wake Addie. He was glad he didn't spill his heart to her last night; it would've made the morning even more awkward, but he still felt self-conscious in her presence.

"What are you, my dad?" Addie sat up, rubbed her eyes, and tried to smooth down her hair.

"Not sure there's much you can do with that bedhead," he joked. "You should've seen you last night. I thought Indy was drooling on me, but it was you."

"What are you talking about?" She rubbed the sides of her mouth.

"Well, when you rolled over and put your arm around me, I woke up to a close-up view of your open mouth," Mason said. "Very cute, by the way. A good look for you."

"Funny. Now I know you're joking." Addie climbed out of the tent and was smothered by Indy's licks. "Now that's drool."

"I already took her on a run *and* a long walk. She took two dumps. What did you feed her last night?"

"Can we not start the morning talking about my dog's pooping habits?" Addie stretched her arms in the air and leaned back. Straightening, she looked around. "Where'd you put my coffee?"

"Now you want coffee delivery? You are a demanding camper."

"I think my lips are sunburned. I need Chapstick. What time is it, anyway?" She grabbed her bag and found her flip-flops. "I'm going to the bathroom."

"Seven forty-two. I let you sleep in. We need to get on the road if we want to make it to Grand Junction, Colorado, before it gets dark, even with the time change."

"Yes, you definitely sound like my dad," Addie said and walked off toward the bathroom.

"Don't worry about the tent," he called after her. "I'll take care of it while you shower!"

---

AFTER TAKING DOWN THE TENT AND ROLLING IT BACK INTO the bag, a feat of magic, according to Addie, Mason checked the traffic reports.

There'd been a semi-versus-car crash, thankfully with no injuries, near Fleming, Colorado, but that was three weeks ago. He didn't think those skid marks would still exist on such a heavily traveled road. There also was an overturned semi, but that was eastbound. The motorcycle crash with injuries worried him. It was westbound and only a week ago.

*Please don't let me drive over those skid marks.*

Mason knew he wouldn't be comfortable driving near Keenesburg, Colorado.

Every site he went on had different reports of accidents, and most of them were in places he'd never heard of. He didn't know the counties, the roads, or the towns where the accidents took place, not to mention the unreported quick stops, near misses, and dead deer. He couldn't begin to know what remnants existed on the road from the past weeks.

Mason gave up trying to predict the road ahead and the past it held and put his phone in his backpack.

"How about letting me drive today?" he asked as they filled up at the gas station. Mason figured that if he drove, he could potentially avoid some of the skid marks.

"OK. But that means I navigate to a real meal."

Mason scrubbed at the multi-colored bug splatter on the windshield with the gas station squeegee. "Sounds like a plan."

"You missed a bug." Addie pointed to one of many spots still on the windshield.

"You should see all the bugs decorating your front grill," Mason said. "You'll need a serious power washer to get them all off."

He dropped the squeegee in the blue liquid and ran into the station for supplies.

"Grab me a snack," she called after him.

Mason returned with a Mountain Dew and a Rockstar, some Chex Mix, two apples, Flaming Hot Cheetos, Sour Patch Kids, and a bag of popcorn.

"Healthy choices," Addie teased as he climbed in the Jeep.

"I try," he said. "Here, I also got you this." He flipped a Chapstick with SPF at her. "From the look of those red lips, you need some help."

"Good call!" Addie tore the package open and liberally applied it.

"You might consider putting it on your nose, too," he said, chuckling. "You look like Rudolph."

He pulled onto the highway, and settled into the drive. Cornfields hugged the road, occasionally alternating with soybean fields.

"How much longer on this beautifully scenic road?" Addie yelled over the wind.

"About an hour or two. Then we dip down into Colorado. I guess we're a little behind schedule."

"There is no schedule," she said, throwing her hands into the air. "Looks like good weather, again."

Indy barked in agreement. Mason thought about Kenna. Addie might not be on a schedule, but he was.

"Don't forget about the rodeo," Mason said, repositioning his hat to keep it from blowing off.

"Hey, another shoe." Addie spun to look at it lying on the shoulder. "Looked like a work boot."

"Maybe it fell off someone's truck," Mason offered.

"There it is... I got you thinking about them, didn't I?" Addie said, patting Mason's shoulder.

Mason smiled. "True. I'd never thought about all the single shoes on the side of the road before." Mason had only focused on the skid marks he might encounter.

Addie returned her focus to her phone. "There's a go-cart place before we get on I-76."

That thought horrified Mason. He had gone go-karting only once when he was twelve. Being trapped on a track covered with hundreds of skid marks was overwhelming. He didn't have to pretend that he felt sick to stop early; he barely made it to the bathroom in time to throw up.

"Getting out of one car to sit in another doesn't sound like much of a break," he said.

"True. Hmm." Addie leaned closer to her phone to block the glare from the sun.

"How about we get to Vail and walk around there," Mason offered.

"You're ambitious. That's seven hours away."

Indy rested her head on the center console and closed her eyes.

Mason petted the top of Indy's head. "Fair enough. How about you find a place we can stop for lunch that has a patio for Indy?"

"I'm on it," Addie said and returned to her phone.

The view through Nebraska was consistently flat, and the wind whipping across I-80 and through the Jeep with its top down was loud enough to make the radio pointless. Mason focused on avoiding skid marks, exhausted by the regular flood of cars skidding to a stop when an animal crossed the road—there were more coyotes than he would've thought—or items flying off of pickups or sleepy drivers crossing the median.

Near Ogallala, Nebraska, Mason asked Addie, "Did you see that sign? Can you imagine how boring a Petrified Wood Museum would be?"

When Addie didn't respond, he glanced over. Underneath her sunglasses, her eyes were closed. Indy slept, too, stretched out on the floor behind their seats, in the only shade.

Addie had tucked her hair into a baseball cap to keep it from blowing, and Mason saw three little birthmarks, perfectly spaced in an even more perfect row, near the hairline on her neck. He'd never noticed them before, probably because her hair usually covered them. He wondered what else he didn't know about her after all these years.

He had a sudden desire to trace the line of birthmarks with his thumb, connecting the three together. Instead, he gripped the steering wheel with both hands and focused on the road.

# CHAPTER 19

Mason did a good job avoiding tire tracks, but after getting lunch and gas in Julesburg, Colorado, they encountered a stretch of highway with multiple skid marks and what looked like white paint splattered in the bushes and on the grass at the side of the road.

"Did you see all that?" Addie asked. "What a mess. What do you think happened?"

"Umm." He contemplated what he should say. Of course he'd seen what happened, but the truth seemed too bizarre. "I'm not sure you're going to believe this, but a semi, one of those flatbed ones carrying huge metal pipes, drove right through the middle of a tractor-trailer."

"You're right, I don't believe you," Addie said with a laugh. "Don't you have to stay in the realm of the believable when you make stuff up?"

"No, really. The flatbed was over there." Mason pointed to the road across the grass median. "The driver fell asleep and drove right across the grass and across these lanes."

He continued to gesture in front of him, trying to depict the scene as he saw it. He felt Addie's gaze on him as he narrated.

"The driver of the tractor-trailer saw the truck coming, and he tried to speed up, knowing the guy was about to hit him, but he couldn't speed up fast enough. The driver of the flatbed hit the broadside of the trailer and split it in two, drove right through it. It was like it was perfectly timed to happen."

"That's outrageous!" Addie said. "How did you come up with that?"

"It's what happened." He glanced at her. The comment sort of popped out of his mouth, but now that he said it, he realized he wanted her to know. "It's the truth. The semi that got hit was hauling paint supplies. You saw all that white paint splattered everywhere, right? Cans of paint and boxes of brushes and rollers, even tarps were all over the highway. It was a huge mess. They had to bring in extra workers to power spray sections of road that were covered in paint."

"That's ridiculous! *And* that's the best story yet."

Mason wished they had power sprayed all the skid marks off the road and not left any for him to drive over. "You saw the paint on the bushes. If we went back, we'd probably find a bunch of those little sample cards, you know, with all the paint names on them."

"I'm sure. Colors like Concrete Cream and Reflective White," Addie joked. "You're so creative. I love that about you."

"But what if I'm not being creative?" His serious tone was a stark contrast to her laughter.

"Oh! That's right," Addie continued. "You're being scientific."

Mason wanted her to believe that there was more than either imagination or science behind his stories, so he piled on more details. "A minivan was involved too. Everyone in it was okay, but the whole thing, the surprise of one semi driving right through the center of another, freaked them all out. The minivan went from dark gray to eggshell white as he drove through a spray of paint before skidding off the road."

"Eggshell white? Don't you mean Expressway White?" Tears were rolling down Addie's cheeks from laughing so hard.

He knew he should just give up. The entire story had become a huge joke. But he persisted. "I know it is hard to believe. And I've never told you about this, but—" Mason exhaled slowly and tried again. "I can see things other people can't."

His tone must have registered with Addie because she stopped laughing, and he felt her eyes searching his face like she was trying to figure him out.

"What are you saying?" she asked. "That you're psychic or something?"

He didn't know how to go on. He had thought about telling her before but, even in his thoughts, he could never put the right words together to convey anything close to believable. He felt her gaze on him still, and he didn't dare look at her. He knew if he did, he would cave and pretend he was joking.

He chewed on his bottom lip and nodded, a barely perceptible nod to confirm what she had said. "Something like that," he said.

"You can see things," Addie repeated.

He knew she was trying to puzzle out what he was telling her, that she was trying to hear the truth behind his words, and that gave him hope.

"Do you mean," she continued, "like you could see who Declan really was and that I should've broken up with him a lot sooner?"

Addie had given him an out. He could take it. If he pressed the issue, everything between them could change.

*Would that be good or bad?*

He waited for a beat as he weighed his options, and Addie went on. "You're perceptive. I've always known that. You usually have a good read on people."

*Except you.*

"That's one way of putting it," he said. He was about to say more, but the warmth of her hand on his arm silenced him.

"I totally should've listened to you about Declan," she said.

"Look," he said, not wanting the focus of the discussion to change. "I don't make up stories quite like you think."

Addie turned to pet Indy, and Mason longed for her hand to return to his arm.

"I know," she said. "You read about that accident online or something. That's okay. You still know how to tell a good story."

"But I..." He didn't know what to say, and as he paused, he realized there was nothing more he could say.

Addie pointed to the horizon. "Does that look like rain?"

Mason shook his head at his own cowardice and let the conversation drop. Dark gray clouds gathered in the west. "Looks like it. But I can't predict the weather. You'd better check the radar to see if we need to put the top up."

The truth was out there for a brief moment, but it hadn't landed where it was supposed to. Now he knew there was no way he could tell her about the missing woman and his hopes of finding the skid marks that had been by her car.

Addie looked at her phone. "I think we're going to miss it. We should be closer to Denver by the time it reaches this area. And it doesn't seem to be going in our direction."

"I'll trust your judgment," Mason said. The storm clouds loomed in the distance, and his heart pounded, his personal thundercloud.

# CHAPTER 20

"I guess you are psychic. I was wrong," Addie yelled over the patter of rain hitting the umbrella.

Traffic had been inching along the highway when the rain started falling in big drops. Addie had scrounged under the seats and found the umbrella—probably her mom's doing. Thanks to the umbrella, Mason and Addie had been spared, but rain pelted Indy and drenched the sleeping bags and luggage.

"So much for trusting you!" Mason said. "I need to pull over so we can put the top up."

"What do you mean? This is fun!" Addie took a selfie of her and Mason under the umbrella. "I'll add that to the commemorative video. One of our finer moments."

"Wave to that guy and see if he'll let us over before our sleeping bags are a soggy mess."

"You promised we could drive top-down the whole way," Addie said with a pout. "This is an adventure."

Mason merged into the middle lane and looked over his shoulder to continue into the right lane. "Not for your dog. Look at her."

Indy blinked away the drops and tried to hide her nose behind the seat.

"Ok, girl. We'll put the top up for you," Addie said.

Indy stuck her cold wet nose and very wet face under Mason's arm, which he'd rested on the center console.

"Hey!" he yelled, pulling his arm away. "It was my idea to put the top up. Put your wet face on her."

THE RAIN HAD STOPPED BY THE TIME THEY REACHED VAIL, so Mason parked in the sun. While Addie ran to the bathroom, he put the Jeep's top down and spread out their sleeping bags to dry them out.

Then he searched the internet for new information about Kenna. Nothing.

Out of curiosity, he looked up the accident with the two semis. Sure enough, there was an article from a week ago that explained what happened, and it was exactly like Mason had said. If he showed it to Addie, it would only confirm what she thought—that he read the article before they saw the skid marks. He tucked the phone in his pocket when Addie returned.

The ski resort village was beautiful, with wide brick walkways, flowers blooming in planters, mountain bikers weaving between people, and ground squirrels. Lots of ground squirrels that Indy was more than willing to chase, yanking Mason with her as she did.

"Check out that shirt." Addie pointed to a shop window.

With a glance he knew which shirt she was pointing at. It was royal blue with bold white lettering proclaiming *Everyone in this town is high elevation 8,150'*.

"I'll get it for you," Mason said. "But only if you promise to wear it when we pull into Incline Village."

Mason ducked into the shop, and Addie followed with Indy.

"You know I could buy it," she said. "I don't mind using my dad's credit card."

"Sure, but it's more for me," Mason said, putting the shirt on the counter. "I want to see your dad's face when he sees it."

"I'll tell him that I'm trying to acclimate to mountain living." Addie laughed.

"I don't know if your mom'll understand though," Mason teased.

"So true!" Addie said. "I can imagine my dad explaining it to her."

"And, when we walk up to your new house, I'll have my arm around you," Mason said. And he did just that. He put his arm around her shoulder and pulled her to him as they left the store. It felt perfect.

"Yeah, make them wonder what happened on this trip," Addie said, sliding her arm around his waist.

His skin tingled with her touch. "Maybe that would be pushing it too far," he said. "I don't want your dad to hurt me."

"Did you just meet my dad? He's all talk."

"Yeah, but I don't want to hear all that talk," Mason said, breaking into a laugh. "He'll know where I'm sleeping. What if he busts into my room to attack-lecture me in the middle of the night?"

"You're too funny," she said, but she didn't remove her arm from his waist.

Mason's steps felt light with her so close. He didn't want to think of tire marks, the missing woman, or Addie leaving. He held her a little tighter. "I don't see any food trucks. What happened to your planning?"

The restaurant patios were mostly full since it was close to five o'clock, though it felt later because of the time change.

"Vast nothingness happened in Colorado," Addie said. "I don't remember it being this empty."

"What do you mean empty?" Mason said. "Didn't we see the Statue of the Popcorn Man in Huntley?"

As he finished his sentence, Indy bolted after a chipmunk, yanking Mason from Addie into a row of shrubs.

"Great control!" Addie yelled after him.

"Getting a closer look at these flowers, that's all. Very pretty," Mason said, climbing free from the bushes. "Man, there are a lot of squirrels."

"And it's crowded," Addie said. "Imagine what this place is like in the winter."

"I bet Tahoe will be a lot like this."

"Maybe." The bag with her T-shirt swayed at her side, and they walked in silence, watching the people.

Mason knew Addie would love Tahoe, and that Tahoe would love her. Perhaps that was what he liked most about her. She didn't know the effect she had on others. Sure she had her close friends, but she always included people. When she volunteered at the river clean-up for Mason's Eagle Scout project, he had marveled at her ability to move among groups so easily, encouraging and laughing with people she'd never met. She could've simply clocked in some volunteer hours, grumbling about how disgusting pulling old cans and soggy cardboard ice cream cups from the river was, but she didn't. She made it a positive experience for so many. She could be happy anywhere, if she gave it a chance.

"I'll probably only be in Tahoe for a year, anyway. I figure I can tread water for at least that long. This time next year, I'll be driving to college, so it doesn't really matter."

"I hear University of Illinois is a good school," he said. "We could be neighbors again."

"Did you know that U of I is nowhere near Nevada?" Addie joked.

"Funny." Mason tickled Addie's side, and Indy barked at him.

"Hey, let's grab a bite here." She pointed to a small café. "I'll order if you hang out with Indy."

"Sounds good." He stood in the doorway and squinted at the chalkboard menu. Indy tugged on the leash in an effort to eat the crumbs around the few outside tables.

"Grab a Pop-Tart sandwich for me...with ham," Mason said.

"What?" Addie looked toward the menu. "Really?"

"Who's the dork, now?" He gave her a playful shove.

"Good one. Sadly, it's your only one."

Indy pulled Mason toward the sound of running water. "Wow. Squirrels *and* a stream? I don't think I like Vail after all."

Addie laughed as Indy caught sight of a duck and lunged toward it. Mason partially tripped, partially hurdled over the bench separating the sidewalk—and all its inhabitants—from the stream, which he quickly learned was ice-cold mountain water.

When Addie found them, Mason was wet, nursing a bruised ego, and sitting under a tree. Indy splashed through the stream, chasing ducks, water bugs, and the waves she created as her leash trailed purposelessly behind her.

"What the heck happened?" Addie squatted next to Mason to take in his drenched state. "I think you should really sit over there, in the sun. You need to dry off before I'll let you sit in my Jeep. I'm hoping it's dried out from the rain by now."

"Funny. I think we should let the dog run alongside the Jeep *Vacation*-style," Mason said.

"Don't be mean to my puppy." Addie ruffled Indy's ears. "Indy likes to explore, don't you, girl? But I'm still tying you up over there."

Addie looped Indy's leash around an Aspen tree far from them. Addie claimed it was to avoid the wet-dog shakes, but in Mason's mind, it was Indy's punishment.

"You're grumpy because you're hungry," Addie said, handing Mason a sandwich. "You'll dry off, but I don't know about all that mud on your shoes. Really, couldn't you have taken them off before going for a swim?"

Mason threw a piece of bread at her.

"See? Grungry." Addie punched his arm, but he caught her fist before she could pull it back.

"Grungry?" he said. "How'd you get to be popular when you're so dorky? It's 'hangry,' not 'grungry.' What does that even mean anyway?" He wasn't focused on his words, only the softness of her fingers as she relaxed her hand in his.

"Grumpy and hungry," she said. "Hangry isn't right. You are more grumpy than angry."

Mason instinctively laced his fingers with hers, and when he realized what he did, he let go of her hand, the heat rising in his cheeks.

Her mouth curved into a slight smile as she took a bite of her sandwich.

"You might want to get established in Tahoe as the cool new girl before you start making up words," he said. Mason looked at Addie as the sun bathed her flyaways in golden light, framing her face.

"I think that's the hardest thing about the move," she said. "I mean, besides leaving all my friends. It's having to start over. And, in another year, when I go to college, I'll have to start all over again."

"This could be like a trial run," Mason said, brushing one of the loose strands from Addie's eyes.

"That's one way to look at it." She tossed a few pieces of bread into the water, and ducks swarmed after them. Within minutes, in an attempt to get the ducks, Indy wrapped her leash around the tree so many times that she pinned her muzzle against the trunk. Her chocolate brown eyes pleaded with Addie for help, her ear twitching each time it brushed against the tree trunk. Indy stopped barking only long enough to whine.

"I'd love to see her get out of this," Mason said, laughing.

"If anything, I have packing for college down to an art," Addie said, returning to their conversation as she freed Indy from her self-created prison. "My parents said they would fly the girls out to visit, but I'm not sure when that will happen. I guess I'll pretty much be on my own for a while."

Mason understood Addie's anxiety. He was nervous about going to college. He'd been in school with the same kids, for better or worse, since he could remember. Elementary school, middle school, high school all in the same town. Sure, he was ready for a change—some of the kids in his class were totally nasty—Declan, for example—but Mason was unsure of who he was going to be or how he was going to fit in at college. Addie wasn't going to be one of thousands of new freshmen like he was; she was most likely going to be the only Midwestern, Chicago-accented, flatlander among all the mountain locals for her senior year of high school.

"Check out Indy." Mason pointed.

Addie turned toward Indy as she was about to sit down. "Dufus! Stop!"

Indy was chewing her leash, probably still trying to break free and get to the ducks.

"She's like an unruly child," Addie said.

Mason stood. "And I hate to be practical and parental, but we probably don't want to drive at night if we can help it." Even though he was getting used to driving, he didn't want to come across any surprise tracks in the dark. At least in the daylight, he had a chance of preparing for what he ran over.

"Where did we stay last night?" Addie asked. "Grand Island? And tonight's Grand Junction? Did you do that intentionally, Mason?"

He wasn't going to admit that when he was planning, he considered it a romantic connection. Their trip was a grand adventure, after all. "Just coincidence," he said.

Addie pulled her iPhone from her back pocket. "Let's see how far it is to our coincidentally *grand* second night." She handed Indy's leash to Mason.

"Oh no you don't." He put his hands up and backed away. "I do not want to go swimming again."

"She's tired," Addie said. "Look at her."

Indy stood, tail wagging, ears up, tongue out, looking all innocent.

"That isn't the look of a tired dog. That's the look of a wild beast," Mason said, but he took the leash anyway.

"We're only a few hours away," Addie said. "We should be fine."

Mason should have known better. Fine was the last thing he would be.

# CHAPTER 21

"You hardly ate any of your ice cream. What's up?" Addie asked as they walked the dirt path along the ridge above the Gunnison River in Grand Junction, Colorado.

"I don't know," Mason said, even though he knew all too well why he didn't have a stomach for food, not even ice cream. "Maybe I drank too much spring water, thanks to your dog."

Below, the river was a brown snake in the darkening valley. Mason wished the water would carry off the vision from the skid marks outside of Grand Junction. But it clung to him, permanent and immovable.

Thankfully, Addie had been driving. The sight had flooded Mason's mind as quickly as the accident seemed to happen. The driver of a box-truck looked down at his phone, and the semi in front of him braked hard to avoid a car that cut him off. When the box-truck driver hit his brakes, it was too late. He rear-ended the semi, flattening his already flat cab into the back of the semi.

The accident crushed the box-truck driver, leaving his arm to dangle from the shattered window. Mason tried to block the vision of the man's head, the skull crushed by the crumpled cab. He wanted to laugh with Addie as they hiked their way along the dirt path high above the river, but the memory of blood dripping down the man's lifeless arm and pooling on the asphalt challenged his every smile.

Accidents like that reminded Mason of how much he hated the visions. They made him feel helpless and angry. Even worse, the fact that he couldn't share those emotions with anyone left him feeling alone. Maybe that was why he wanted to find the marks left near Kenna's car. He couldn't change the fact that she disappeared, but maybe he could help find her. It gave him a small glimmer of hope that his visions weren't totally useless.

Indy sniffed along the path. The sun dipped below the horizon and the pink glow faded into a purple haze against the indigo blue of the night sky. The mountains were dark silhouettes in the distance. They fit Mason's mood perfectly, but he tried to shake it. He focused on the distant bubbling of the rushing water below and allowed it to soothe his nerves.

"I bet the sunrise will be pretty," he said.

"You can tell me about it," Addie said. "Or, better yet, take a picture. I plan to sleep in."

"This is a good trail for a morning run. I may come back here with Indy while you're sleeping." Mason scanned the area and looked up at the sky. "We should probably head back since it's getting dark."

"It's so much more like a desert out here than I expected," Addie said. "Except for the river. I would've thought that was the Colorado River, it's so big,"

"Yep." The word was all Mason could muster in the darkness that settled on his mind.

They turned back, and Indy led the way. Addie threaded her arm around Mason's waist. "Hey, are you sure you're okay? You're not yourself tonight."

Mason wrapped an arm around her and let her touch lift some of the burden from his thoughts.

"A lot on my mind, I guess." His answer was a cop-out, especially since she undoubtedly had a lot on her mind, too, and wouldn't push him.

"Fair enough," she said.

Mason let the retractable leash out as far as it would go and still

Indy tugged ahead. "I think there was an informational sign near the trailhead," he said. "Maybe it has some information about the river."

"No more informational anything, please," she pleaded. "I'm still scarred from Reagan's boyhood home."

"That was your idea," he reminded her.

Indy explored the bushes, chasing whatever ground squirrels hadn't disappeared for the night. When they reached the clearing at the trailhead, Mason pointed toward the sign. "There it is."

"It totally smells like skunk, don't you think?"

Mason's thoughts flashed to the night in his yard. He had forgotten to look up what to do if Indy got sprayed. He glanced around but didn't see a skunk. "Let's hope it's long gone."

Mason approached the sign and turned on his phone's flashlight to see it more clearly. He read, "'The town of Grand Junction, Colorado, was named for its location at the confluence of Gunnison and Grand rivers.'"

"Grand River?" Addie asked.

"That's what the Colorado River used to be called, I think." Mason continued reading. "'The river was named for U.S. Army Captain John—'"

"You're quite an exciting date, Mason."

His breath caught at the word "date," and he looked up from the sign innocently. "I thought you wanted to know about the river."

"No. Not actually. I think I need to teach you about small talk. Generally, it doesn't lead to research."

"Are you giving me dating advice?" Mason asked. "And did you say this is a *date*? What exactly do you mean by that?"

Mason nudged Addie's shoulder.

"A figure of speech. Do I need to teach you that too?" Addie smiled, but before Mason could return it, Indy yanked the leash, wrenching his arm, as she ran after something.

"Indy!" Mason stumbled and caught his footing as Indy came to an abrupt stop. She whined and rubbed her face in the grass.

"Oh yuck!" Addie turned from Indy and covered her face.

"Skunk! Really?" The stench of sulfur and rotten eggs permeated everything, and Mason backed away from Indy, covering his nose with his T-shirt. "Guess it wasn't long-gone."

Addie gagged. "I can taste it. It's terrible."

Indy alternated between rubbing her face in the dirt and sneezing over and over. A streak of shiny black fur cut across her face where the skunk had sprayed.

"Geez, dog, what were you thinking? Full in the face, huh?" Mason said.

"What do we do? Everyone at the campsite will kill us if we bring her back there."

"I'm sure they can already smell her."

Indy rubbed her nose with her paws and started another fit of sneezing.

"Do you think she's alright?" Addie asked, watching the spectacle of sneezing, scratching, blinking, and rubbing.

"Yeah. I'm sure it's only the shock of it," Mason said. "Maybe we should at least go to the camp manager and ask her what to do."

He checked his watch. It was just after eight-thirty P.M.. He hoped the office was still open.

"I guess," Addie said. "We'll probably have to give her a bath in tomato juice or something."

"I don't think that works."

"What's with us and skunks?"

"I told you that skunk was a sign," he said.

"You said it was a sign that you should control the music, not that Indy would get sprayed." Addie shoved him toward the dog. "Now you get to deal with her."

They walked across the street toward the campsite. In the darkness, various campfires and lanterns dotted the campground like fireflies. Thankfully the "Open" sign glowed in the camp manager's cabin.

Mason stopped by the entrance to the campground with Indy. "I'll stay with her here. Ask if they have a hose or something. Maybe we can at least rinse her off."

"Ok." Addie started toward the office.

Mason called after her. "Find out where the nearest store is that might be open too. We'll need some supplies, unless your mom thought to pack an emergency skunk-spray kit."

"You're the Eagle Scout. Isn't that your motto: Be Prepared." Addie held up three fingers as she jogged to the office.

*I might have deserved that.*

Mason kneeled next to Indy and examined her face. Her eyes were red, and snot dripped from her nose. She continued to lick her muzzle.

"That can't taste good."

Indy sat and looked up at him, whining. He scratched her back, away from the wet spray on her face.

Indy sneezed on Mason, then lay down on her belly and covered her face with her paws, rubbing them against her eyes.

"Don't worry, we'll get you some water soon," he said, trying to search Google for advice but nothing loaded.

Addie called out from the distance. "It's okay. Bring her to the office."

Mason stood. "Really?"

"Yeah. Pam, the manager, said she has all the stuff we need. Apparently, Indy isn't the first dog to sniff out a skunk around here."

"It's your lucky day, Indy," Mason said.

In response, Indy sneezed five times in a row.

"Nevermind," he said. "It's my lucky day. Come on, girl. Let's get you cleaned up."

TWO BOXES OF BAKING SODA, A JUG OF PEROXIDE, A BOTTLE of Dawn dish soap, a hose, and two hours later, Indy smelled only mildly of skunk—that, or they had become used to the smell. By the time they had cleaned up the mess, thanked Pam, and tied Indy to a tree, Mason and Addie could barely crawl into their tent.

"Thanks," Addie said as she dropped her head onto her pillow. "Who would've thought a skunk could do so much damage."

"Vail seems like years ago," Mason said. "I think I'm high on skunk fumes. The gummy bears would've been less stinky."

He lay on top of his sleeping bag. He was too warm to climb in, and he needed to be free from the smothering sensation. Phantom skunk smells drifted through his nostrils.

"You were great, though, Mason, really." Addie's hand reached for Mason's.

He let her find it. She intertwined her fingers into his and tugged his arm. He rolled onto his side to look at her.

"You know," she said, "some guys would've spent the last two hours cursing everybody and the dog. But you didn't. You found humor in it all."

By "some guys," she probably meant Declan. "Well, it was pretty funny to see Indy covered in baking soda," he said. "I didn't know it would foam so much when we poured the peroxide on her. How could you not laugh? She was a science experiment in action."

Mason smiled, but his nerves were on fire. Addie, the sporty, smart, funny, very attractive girl who no longer lived next door that he had crushed over for years, had pulled him closer to her. After all the times he had wanted to pull her close.

"Thanks. For everything." As she spoke, a piece of hair slid from her bun and fell over one eye.

He reached out and tucked it behind her ear, his eyes falling to her sunburnt lips before he looked into her eyes.

She held his gaze, and he imagined she felt the same. But she only squeezed his hand, before letting it go.

*Maybe tomorrow I'll work up the courage to tell her how I feel.*

And then he remembered that tomorrow was when he would hopefully find the tire marks by Kenna's car. Maybe tomorrow had enough challenges already.

In the silence, exhausted, Mason fell asleep.

# KENNA

*He's a monster. I still smell the stale beer on his breath as he smothered me with the weight of his body.*

*I threw myself out the wooden door when he opened it and tried to knock him off-balance. But he's so big. I managed to squirm past him though and slip into the fresh night air. Freedom, I thought, before a sharp pain shot through my scalp. He yanked me by the hair, and I flew back. But I kept fighting. What do I care if he rips all the hair from my head? I need to be free.*

*I screamed, and I almost didn't recognize my own voice. It was guttural and fierce, from deep within. I felt strong, like my voice alone could shatter him into pieces.*

*But I was wrong. He didn't shatter.*

*"Enough playing," he said. He grabbed me around the waist and tossed me over his shoulder, pinning both of my legs together with one of his arms. He carried me as I hit wildly with my fists and grabbed for the door to the cave.*

*I watched the dark sky recede and gasped for one last breath of fresh air before he closed the door.*

# CHAPTER 22

Mason woke to Indy whining and the lingering sulfur smell of skunk, probably from his balled-up T-shirt in the corner of the tent. Addie was curled on her side, facing him. He wondered if either of them had moved when they were asleep or if exhaustion had rooted them to where they were. He lay there for a moment, listening to her soft breaths and thinking about last night. How she had held his hand and pulled him close. He couldn't believe how close he had come to kissing her. The moment had seemed perfect, but he was too afraid of ruining what they had.

*Would it ruin everything?*

She looked peaceful, with her mouth slightly parted and her hair spilling around her face. They would be at her new home in two days. He couldn't bear the thought.

He grabbed a clean shirt and put on his running shoes. When he crawled out of the tent, he came face to face with Indy.

"You're getting to be an old lady, aren't you?" Mason rubbed her graying muzzle and then held her head to get a better look at her blood-shot eyes. She squirmed back from his grasp. "Well, I guess you aren't in too much pain if you can still fight me. That means you're joining me for a run."

He stretched as Indy rolled over and scratched her back in the grass.

"From the looks of it, you need to clear your head about as much as I do."

They headed out into the quiet morning.

WHEN THEY RETURNED TO THE TENT AN HOUR LATER WITH coffee and donuts, Mason peeked through the tent flap. Addie was still asleep. She might've moved, but it was hard to tell. He set her coffee inside the tent on top of the cooler, where she wouldn't kick it, pulled his stinky T-shirt from the corner, and zipped the flap closed. Maybe the scent of coffee would overpower any residual skunk smell and wake her. Until then, or at least until eight A.M., he would wait. She could probably sleep until noon, if he let her. He couldn't remember what time they had actually fallen asleep, but it was late.

He looked at Indy's eyes again now that she was worn out from her run and didn't have energy to fight him. They didn't look too bad, definitely red, but hopefully more from the dish soap than the skunk. Thankfully, she didn't smell all that bad. The Dawn-baking soda-peroxide cocktail worked magic. That or the night had destroyed Mason's sense of smell.

He sat at the picnic table, drank his coffee, and ate two donuts while he got on the camp Wi-Fi and searched the internet for new information about Kenna Cook. There wasn't any. He reread the latest news article, dated June 5.

*Why wasn't there any more recent information?*

He hoped it was because she'd been found, but Mason reasoned that if she had been, there would've been a follow-up article, even a small one. There weren't any more recent articles because there was no new information.

He opened Google Maps. It was seven hours and forty-eight minutes to Valterra, Nevada, the town closest to where Kenna's car was found. Her disappearance would've brought a lot more people to the town, creating a lot more traffic on the road. What if the skid marks were already worn away? Then what?

He looked at the map again. Almost eight hours to Valterra and, from there, just under two-and-a-half hours to Fallon, Nevada.

*Thank goodness for another time change.*

It gave him one more hour of daylight before his last night with Addie. Tomorrow, they would be with her parents, but he couldn't let that fact distract him from today, which he slowly realized he was not prepared for.

Mason had worked hard to plan the trip, finding the rodeo as a reason to get to Valterra as soon as they could. His focus had been on getting there with enough sunlight to see the skid marks on either side of the road, since he didn't know which side they were on. Mason hadn't thought about what he'd actually do when he got close to Valterra.

At eight-fifteen A.M., he sent Indy into the tent to wake Addie. A cowardly move, he knew, but he couldn't help it. When he peeked in the tent to wake her and saw her curled up, her legs intertwined with the sleeping bag, his sleeping bag, he couldn't do it. He only wanted to crawl into the tent and kiss her forehead, kiss her cheek, her shoulder. Instead, he opened and closed the Jeep door a few times, hoping the noise would wake her. When she didn't stir, he sent Indy into the tent to kiss her awake.

"Hey, sleepyhead," he called from outside the tent. "How'd you sleep?"

Indy, with her tail wagging, absorbed much of the space inside the tent, and Addie pushed her away.

Mason called Indy, and she ambled back outside. He poked his head in. "Your coffee's on the cooler. It might be cold. I should've woken you an hour ago."

"Thanks." Addie put her hair in a ponytail and grabbed the coffee. "What time is it?"

"Almost eight-thirty," Mason said. "If we're on the road by nine, we'll be fine, but we're pushing it. It's a long haul to Fallon. We're going to get there after dark as it is. But you can sleep in tomorrow."

"Sleeping in," Addie said. "Now you're speaking my language. Is that smell Indy?"

Addie sniffed her hair and T-shirt. "No, I think that's me."

Mason's thoughts drifted to the drive ahead. He hadn't figured out how he was going to handle the day. Even if he could drive over the tracks, what would he do if he learned something about Kenna's disappearance? His planning had been faulty. He'd only focused on getting to the skid marks. He hadn't thought about what he'd do when he actually found them.

"It's not too cold," she said.

"What? The weather?" he asked, lost in his own thoughts.

"The coffee. Not bad. Cool enough to chug. Did you get me a donut too?"

"Chocolate or glazed?" he asked.

"Chocolate. What, did you just meet me?"

He grabbed a donut from the bag on the picnic table, half expecting to turn around and see that she had climbed out of the tent. But she hadn't.

"Are you expecting breakfast in bed now?" He fumbled with the tent opening while balancing her donut.

"Yes, donut delivery, just like coffee and pizza delivery," she said, flopping back on her pillow. "Isn't that the way camping works? Like room service, but tent service."

"Nope, you aren't a Harlan Hotel snob at all," he teased. He put the donut on the cooler and stole one more look as she sprawled out on the sleeping bag in the morning light. He grabbed his backpack and climbed out of the tent. "I'm going to jump in the shower. I suggest you do too. You stink."

# CHAPTER 23

"Check this out." Mason tossed a little booklet to Addie as he climbed in the Jeep. "A passport to the Loneliest Road in America."

"What does that mean?" Addie flipped through it before she started the Jeep.

"Pam, the manager, gave it to us. When I was checking out, I told her we were headed that way. She said it was a cute way to get to know the area. She used that word, 'cute.' Anyway, we're supposed to stop at all the little towns and get a stamp, like a real passport." He didn't tell Addie the first two towns in the passport were Ely and Valterra, and that somewhere between them were a set of tire tracks he desperately wanted to find.

"That does sound 'cute.'" Addie pulled into the Flying J. "We better get some snacks for the road if we have a long drive on a lonely road. And some water. Man, it's hot out here."

WHEN MASON RETURNED, ADDIE STOOD ON THE SIDE-
board, leaning over the windshield trying to scrape off the numerous
multi-colored bug splatters. She strained to reach across the front of
the Jeep, standing on her tiptoes.

Mason grabbed Addie's waist and pretended to make her fall.

"Hey! Want me to smear bug water on you?" Addie swung the
squeegee, and blue water sprayed the ground.

Indy barked, either wanting to protect Addie or to play.

"It's okay, Indy. We're going."

They alternated between blasting the Jeep's heat in the shade of the
mountains and turning the air to cool when the sun beat down on
open stretches of road. By noon, walls of carnelian, lit by the sun, rose
up around them.

Mason's thoughts could almost get lost in the striations of the
mountains, the variations in color indicating eras of history and
revealing shifts in the continent, but his thoughts kept returning to
Addie and his own shifting world.

They saw very few cars on the road, and Mason saw fewer skid
marks. He almost wanted the distraction of the skid marks to keep him
from thinking about how close Addie's lips had been to his last night.
He wanted to tell her how he felt, but then he thought about the tire
marks he hoped to find. He still hadn't figured out what he would do if
they gave up their secrets, whatever those secrets might be. He couldn't
call the police. What would he say?

Mason sat in silence as Addie drove, thankful that the wind in the
open Jeep made it hard to talk.

Even Indy curled up on the back seat and closed her eyes against
the wind.

Mason didn't know what Addie was thinking, but her words about
not wanting a long-distance relationship echoed in his mind. Obsessing
over what one night meant, one where he didn't even have the courage
to kiss her, wasn't going to change the fact that she said she didn't want
a long-distance relationship. They were going to be thousands of miles
apart. He couldn't get more long distance than that.

Under her sunglasses, her eyes focused on the road. She licked her
lips several times, so Mason handed her the Chapstick.

She smiled when she took it. "You read my mind."

*I wish.*

The sound of loud mufflers interrupted his thoughts. Four motorcycles passed to their left, the gray beard of each rider flapping in the wind. The last rider had a passenger clinging to his back, a girl probably no older than ten, wearing flannel pajama bottoms and a T-shirt, no helmet. She smiled and waved as they passed.

Mason and Addie instinctively waved back.

"What do you make of that?" he asked.

"The girl was smiling, that's a good sign. Maybe that's her grandfather, and he was babysitting her? And now he's taking her home."

"Let's run with that."

Addie pointed to a sign. "There's a viewing area up ahead. Let's stop and let Indy run around."

"Sounds good."

"Maybe those motorcycle guys will stop there too," Addie said. "We can find out what their story is."

"I'm not sure I want to know," Mason said.

Addie veered the Jeep toward the exit ramp. "This place is called Ghost Rock. Do you think it's haunted?"

"I want you to remember that you asked that question," he said. "So, when I start reading signs, you won't think I'm a dork. I'm trying to find the answer to your question. But my guess is that it is named for some old gold miner's superstitious belief."

"There goes your imagination again." Addie pulled into one of six open parking spaces.

"I guess this is the reason it's called Ghost Rock—it's empty," he said. "No motorcycle-riding babysitters."

Indy jumped out of the Jeep and sniffed the dry desert weeds as Addie and Mason walked toward the lone sign by the viewing area.

"The mountains look cool, don't they?" she said. "I mean, we drive through what seems to be a mountain, with walls of rock on either side, and then we're in the wide open with mountains that look like ghost towns in the distance. Hey, maybe that's why this is called Ghost Rock."

"Back in Grand Junction, I read that from a distance, in the evening, the mountain ranges looked like a city," Mason said. "People would travel to them, only to find more mountains when they arrived. Wouldn't that suck?"

"When did you read that? Before or after you let Indy play with a skunk?" Addie teased.

"That's a trick question."

At the sign, they each read in silence. Well, Mason tried to read, but he was more focused on the way the sunlight played with the freckles on Addie's shoulders. He wanted to hold her at Ghost Rock and become as still as the rock cairns that travelers had constructed at the vista. He pushed back at the thought that he should be driving toward the skid marks, not standing at a viewing area, trying to memorize Addie's freckles.

"This says," Addie started to read, "'Fog covered the basin and obscured the base of the rock formation from view, making the upper part appear—'"

"And you tease me about reading signs?" Mason interrupted.

"This is not the same," she protested. "We stopped to learn this information. You read those other signs for fun. That's what makes you a nerd."

"Point taken."

"And, if you weren't reading that sign about the river last night, Indy wouldn't have been skunked."

At the sound of her name, Indy, who had found shade near an outcropping of rocks, raised her head and barked.

"See, she's still mad at you," Addie said with a laugh.

Indy ran to greet her.

"Where were your powers of observation? I don't recall you being engrossed in educating me on the river's history." Mason knelt to Indy and scratched behind her ears. "I think Addie was neglecting you. She should've saved you."

Addie looked back at the horizon and the mountains in the distance. "I guess we figured out the mystery of Ghost Rock."

"Yep. Guess that means we should keep moving," Mason said. "We have some towns to visit."

*And I have a mystery of my own to figure out.*

# CHAPTER 24

Addie and Mason drove through the intense heat of the desert and the cool relief of the mountains that blocked the sun. Small towns appeared and disappeared like apparitions, the highway's own version of ghost towns: mirages of civilization hidden by vapors of heat rising off the dry ground.

The Jeep's thermometer registered 104 degrees Fahrenheit. Indy kept her head low, most likely either hoping the air-conditioning might reach her or seeking shade.

"Check that out." Mason pointed to a lone house off the road. It was surrounded by posts, the fencing between long gone. On top of each post sat a birdhouse. "Totally *Heart of Darkness*. But in a rural-America way—birdhouses not skulls."

"Wow," Addie said. "Your AP Lit teacher would be proud."

"We should pull over so I can take a picture of it. I could email her. Maybe she'd rethink my B-minus."

"Not a chance. You were lucky to get the B-minus."

"True," Mason said. "Hey, I'm hungry. What about you?"

"Definitely. And I need water or, at least, water that isn't boiling hot. Can we please remember to buy ice for the cooler when we stop for gas?"

Mason looked on his phone to see what town was ahead. He hoped they were coming up on Ely, so his search could begin.

"What do you want to eat?" he asked.

"Sushi," Addie said.

"Good idea. Your dad's paying, right?" They'd spent the better part of the day munching on gas station snacks, and Mason was ready for a real meal. He scrolled through his phone. "It doesn't look too good in Gardner."

"What?" Addie said. "Bad reviews?"

"Gardner has sixty-four residents. We'll be lucky to find a restaurant."

"You mean a sushi restaurant?"

"We're in the middle of nowhere," Mason said.

He threw a pretzel at Addie, but the wind caught it and sent it into the backseat. Indy poked her head up, ate it, and retreated to the shade behind the seat.

"We'll be lucky to eat at a gas station," he said.

"No," Addie said with a groan. "I can't handle any more granola bars and Sour Patch Kids."

He looked at his phone again. "Ok, they have a pub and a diner. Which do you want? Pour Parking or Jumpstart Cafe? Pretty ironic names for a town of sixty-four people. Oh, there's a coffee cart too. Do you think that's like a food truck for small towns?"

"How can a town exist without a fast food chain?" Addie asked. "No Subway? Or McDonald's?"

"Says the girl who wanted to eat exclusively out of vehicles," Mason teased. "The reviews are good. One says that Pour Parking has 'the most amazing root beer float—and plenty of parking.'"

Mason opened the almost empty bag of Chex Mix.

"I don't think I've ever had a root beer float," Addie said, grabbing for the bag.

Mason pulled it out of her reach.

"Well then, it is about time you had one," he said.

"I don't even know if I like root beer. How about you get one and I'll try it." Addie, eyes on the road, groped for the bag. "Give me the Mix!"

Mason put the bag under her hand. "Are you hangry or grungry? I can't tell."

She glared at him, then giggled.

"Root beer floats are best when the vanilla ice cream gets a little melty and mixes with the root beer. You'll love it."

"I'm not really a fan of vanilla," she said. "Hey, did you see that one?"

The Jeep drove over a clearly delineated skid mark. Two straight, short lines that curved slightly to the right. Nothing but the freshness of it was worth noting.

"A gopher, I think," Mason said.

"Gopher?"

"I think," Mason said. "It was nighttime. The woman in the passenger seat wasn't too pleased when the driver slammed on the brakes when the animal ran in front of the car. She was asleep and inconveniently flew into the dash, hitting her cheek on the rearview mirror because she forgot to buckle up. The little creature bolted across the road and lived another night, unless a coyote ate it. As for the man driving, I don't know. She was really pissed."

"You know you drive me crazy, right?" Addie said.

"Crazy-good? Or crazy-bad?" he asked.

"I don't know, crazy-crazy."

"Wow, that's serious," Mason said. "But remember, you're the one with the bad habit of asking questions you don't actually want answers to."

Addie seemed to ignore his comment and asked, "What the heck is a gopher anyway?"

Indy sat up and stretched, putting her paws on the center console and sticking her head out the top of the Jeep.

"I think Indy knows," Mason said. "That, or she needs to go to the bathroom."

"The gopher?" Addie reminded him.

"You asked: it's a small rodent that burrows," Mason said. "Like a prairie dog. Mostly known for its role in *Caddyshack*. Have you ever seen that movie? It's a classic."

"Ugh!" Addie said. "You're so annoying sometimes! Just get me some food!"

"Definitely hangry. Don't you think, Indy?"

Indy licked Addie's cheek, and she laughed.

---

AFTER THEY ATE, THEY FOUND A PARK WHERE INDY COULD run around, though the swans in a nearby pond weren't thrilled by her presence.

"I'm still torturing you," Addie said, flipping through the visitor's guide. "There must be something around here to do."

"The Lehman Caves would've been fun—I'm down for someplace cool about now," Mason said. "But dogs aren't allowed."

Indy was a convenient excuse. Mason was intent on pushing forward toward Valterra.

"Look at all the trouble you cause, Indy." Indy ran up to Addie at the mention of her name.

"Bummer." Mason pointed to an ad. "We missed the Snake Festival."

"That isn't even funny. Who lives in a town that celebrates snakes? And people go hiking around here?"

"Look, this says there's a wildlife viewing area nearby," Mason said. "Maybe we can view the snakes."

"Absolutley no!" Addie grabbed the visitor's guide from Mason and searched. "I've got it. In the next town, there's a ghost train. Ghosts seem to be the theme for the day. Want to go there?"

"But it's still several hours to Fallon." He was hoping to stop after he found the skid marks, not before.

"It'll be quick," she promised. "And if we get to Fallon after dark, oh well."

Mason looked at his watch. They still had plenty of time to get to Valterra while the sun was still out. "Alright," he said. "Ghost train it is, but not for long."

"Yay!" Addie looked down at the guide. "We're headed to the Nevada Northern Railway Museum in Ely. And that's perfect! Ely is the first stop in the passport. We'd have to stop there anyway."

They were close to the start of the Loneliest Road in America and were about to head into the most desolate stretch of highway in the U.S.

Somewhere on the one-hundred-and-sixteen-mile stretch of road that separated Ely from Valterra, Mason was supposed to find a tire track that he hoped was still there. He had wanted so badly to find a purpose for his visions that he told himself he could help. Now, faced with the reality of the situation, that possibility seemed like a ridiculous fantasy. Even worse, if he did learn something about Kenna's disappearance, he'd have no way of sharing that information.

He'd spent all afternoon thinking about what he could say to the police, and all his ideas left him sounding mentally unstable or involved telling Addie the truth about his visions. The closer he got to Valterra, the more impossible it all seemed.

# CHAPTER 25

After stopping in Ely, Mason and Addie traveled miles of flat, straight road separated by winding mountain passes filled with tire marks. They didn't see another car all afternoon, yet Mason was exhausted from the layered images of past drivers realizing they were taking turns too fast. On the flat stretches, he scanned both sides of the road for the skid marks he needed to find, but they were elusive. Had they faded already, or were they still up ahead? And if he did find them, what would he do? Stop the Jeep?

After miles of fumbling for answers, an idea emerged.

When they reached the next straight stretch of road, he pulled the Jeep onto the dirt shoulder.

"What are you doing?" Addie looked behind them, probably thinking that a cop had pulled them over.

The dust cleared and the road ahead disappeared into a mirage that was punctuated by distant mountains.

"This is perfect. I want to take your picture," Mason said.

"Where?" She looked at the brown horizon stretching to the right. "It's vast but not really scenic."

"No. There." Mason pointed toward the road. "In the middle. There's no one around and miles of road behind you. What a cool shot."

"You're crazy. What if a car comes? I'd be run over."

"We haven't seen anyone on this road since we left Ely. And look, you'll see them coming for miles. Come on, you know it would be a perfect shot." It would also allow Mason to get a close-up view of the road.

A smile slowly crept onto Addie's face. "Indy has to be in the pictures too."

"You read my mind."

While they walked on the road, Mason saw some faded skid marks, but they had nothing to do with Kenna's car. They were so light, he knew he wouldn't have seen them while driving. But at least he now had a plan. If he did see skid marks, he could pull over for another photo shoot without raising suspicion.

Addie walked down the center of the road with Indy. The fact that a car could come down from the mountains, even if it was in the distance, added energy to the moment. Mason took pictures of them walking away, of Addie doing cartwheels down the dotted yellow lines, of her dancing while Indy jumped at her side.

Then Addie took pictures of Mason pretending to be a yellow dash in the road, of Mason running down the middle of the road toward the distant mountains, secretly scanning the road for skid marks. She took selfies of them, cheek to cheek, sitting in the middle of the road with Indy's tail hitting them in the face.

"That was perfect," Addie said as they walked back to the Jeep.

"No, this whole drive has been perfect. And it was all your stubborn idea."

Mason and Addie leaned against the Jeep as Indy explored the brush, sniffing around rocks and tumbleweed.

"You're making this move more bearable, you know," Addie said. "It sucks, but this trip has been a blast." She curled into his arms and gave him a hug.

Mason held her tightly. Making the move more bearable for her was making it nearly unbearable for him.

Indy barked and ran up to them, trying to squeeze between them. Mason released Addie and patted Indy on the head. "Okay, girl. Back in the Jeep."

THEY PASSED VERY FEW CARS AS THEY DROVE, AND MASON saw a few visions from recent skid marks, dark and pronounced. He'd planned to pull over if he saw skid marks on the other side of the road, but the "Valterra pop. 604" sign told him he'd missed the skid marks if they were there. Did he dare venture back to see if he could find them? Maybe they were so light on the opposite side of the road that he didn't see them. Maybe they were gone. Should he let it go? He thought about Kenna's mother in the video, muted but saying volumes with her swollen eyes and deep wrinkles. Could he give up that easily?

"There it is." Addie pointed to a red brick building with thin white pillars. "Slow down. Don't pass it."

Mason pulled over next to an old-fashioned black lamppost, a stark contrast to the newly poured concrete steps and ramp behind it. "How will anyone in this town learn to parallel park if there are no other cars?" he asked.

"Very funny." Addie got out and marveled at the balcony on the second floor. "This looks cool. You could totally have a party up there. I thought it was going to look like some old museum."

"Do you still have something against museums? Did Willy scar you that much?"

Addie grabbed Mason's arm and led him to the front door. "Come on. We have a stamp to get."

While Addie tied Indy's leash to a bench in the shade, Mason glanced down the road, wondering how he was going to come up with a reason to turn around. Then Addie pulled Mason inside the theater.

The gray-haired woman in the front office of the Grand Theater seemed mildly entertained by them as she searched through desk drawers for the stamp to mark their passport.

"Here it is," she said, pulling a smiley-face stamp from her drawer and holding it over the page about the theater in the passport. She paused and looked up at each of them, her white curls hugging her head like a halo in the sunlight from the window. "Now, I'll only stamp your book if you promise to tour the theater. There's no charge."

"We have a dog," Mason said. He wanted to focus on his plan, not look at an old building. "She's outside, and we shouldn't leave her."

"No one's going to bother her." The woman punched the stamp on the passport and handed it back to Addie. "Now, when you go down those stairs, I want you to look at all the photos on the walls. Go ahead now."

Addie and Mason looked at each other then at the narrow wooden stairs where she pointed.

"Go on, now. Have fun." The woman half-patted and half-pushed them toward the stairs.

"Um, thanks, Ms...." Mason stumbled.

"Ms. Barker, dear," the woman said. "But you can call me Sheryl. Now, on the way down, you'll see photos of all different celebrities. They've all performed here. And check out the wall of signatures. It's tradition for performers to sign the wall. Oh, and when you get to the stage, don't be frightened if you see Old Temple Joe."

"Temple Joe?" Addie asked as they obediently headed down the stairs. Sheryl's once short, grandmotherly frame now towered over them from the top of the stairs. "He's a friendly ghost and won't hurt you. Enjoy your tour, now!"

Sheryl turned and stomped off.

"You aren't coming with us?" Addie called after her.

"I'm going to bring your dog some water." Sheryl's voice echoed above them. "Enjoy!"

Addie looked at Mason. "Another ghost? That Sheryl is definitely crafty. Sending us on a self-guided tour after dropping a bomb like that."

Mason pointed to a black-and-white photo. "Check this out. Gerta Hackberry. What an unfortunate name."

"Yeah, but look at that purse." Addie pointed to a shadow box with a silver mesh handbag and read the placard below. "'Gerta Hackberry forgot this in 1884. She told the theater director she would get it when she returned.' I guess she didn't make it back to town."

In the large theater area, chairs were stacked along the walls, leaving an open wood floor in front of the stage. Again, the contrast between new and old was obvious—the newly finished wood floor gleamed against the heavy red curtain that hung on the stage.

Addie climbed up on the stage and peeked behind the curtain.

"What are you doing?" Mason asked.

"I want to see if Temple Joe is hiding back here." Addie turned back to Mason and shrugged.

"Maybe we have to come back at night," he said.

"I guess." Addie jumped down from the stage and twirled across the wood floor. "It's like a ballroom."

Mason wished he knew how to waltz, just so he could move as one with her. Instead, he said, "We should probably get back to Indy."

They returned to the front office and thanked Sheryl.

"You kids come back anytime." Sheryl had settled behind her large wooden desk and was sorting through one of many stacks of papers. Mason wondered how there could be so much paperwork for an empty theater in a small town.

When Mason and Addie got outside, Indy was sprawled under the bench next to a water dish with half of its contents pooling on the concrete patio.

"What's the next stop?" Addie asked.

When Indy heard Addie's voice, she jumped up, tail wagging.

Mason flipped through the passport. "Looks like the Sterling County Courthouse in Liberty."

*Or about 60 miles back toward Ely, Nevada.*

Indy barked and bowed, leaning on her front paws, butt in the air. Addie tried to scratch her head, but Indy jumped back and barked some more.

"I think she needs to play a little before we stick her back in the Jeep," Addie said.

Mason looked down the road. Maybe he could say he forgot something in Ely. He ran through his list of potentially lost items... his phone was in his hand, his sweatshirt was balled on the back seat. What else did he own that would warrant more than an hour's drive to get?

He could buy some time if they found a park or something. He looked at his phone.

"Signal's weak," Mason said. "I'll run back in and ask Sheryl if she knows somewhere we can take Indy to run around."

***

NOT ONLY DID VALTERRA HAVE A PARK, IT HAD A DOG PARK. Even in a small town, there were dog lovers. They unleashed Indy, and she ran, sniffing the bushes and chasing any lizard brave enough to scamper across the rocks. It didn't take long for the heat to get the better of her, though, and soon, panting heavily, she crawled under the picnic table Addie and Mason sat on. Mason looked out over the hillside, at the town sloping toward the valley.

Finding a park for Indy would only stall them for a little while. Mason needed a plan. He ran a finger over the scar on his knee and traced the jagged pattern he couldn't remember getting. How was he going to get Addie to drive back the way they'd come?

"What's that?" Addie asked.

Startled from his thoughts, Mason looked up, confused.

"Your scar?" Addie asked. "Was that from when you tried to teach me to fish?"

Mason looked down at the scar he was mindlessly touching, and the memory returned. Addie had followed him to the river one day when he was pretending to fish. She wanted to try it, she'd said, and Mason didn't have the nerve to tell her that he never baited his hook. Together they'd dug worms, and Addie pierced a hook through one and tossed it into the river. She jumped up and down when she reeled in the small bluegill, but she refused to unhook it. Mason pretended he knew what he was doing and knelt down next to the fish as it flopped in the dirt. He eventually wrenched the hook free from the fish, only to embed it in his knee. He almost passed out at the sight of the metal buried in his flesh, the hooked end curved through, the tip poking out the other side.

"Yeah, I think so," he said.

"Way to terrorize me. I've never fished again." Addie leaned back on her hands to look up at the blue sky. "You said we're staying in Fallon? How much longer is that?"

"Almost three hours."

"I'm going to check in with my folks," Addie said. "How far are we from Incline Village?"

"Actually? From here, only about five hours. They won't want to join us at the rodeo, will they?" Mason's back stiffened at the thought of her parents driving to meet them. "The tent won't fit us all."

"Ha! That would be hysterical. I can imagine my parents camping. I'm sure they'd want to leave their hotel suite to sleep in sleeping bags. But there might be a hotel nearby..."

Mason's face fell, and Addie shoved his leg.

"I'm joking," she said. "Don't look so terrified. But I should call them."

She hopped off the table, and Indy crawled out from the shade and followed her.

Mason was grateful that he had planned the extra night in Fallon, but his stomach twisted at the thought of the tire marks he hadn't found. He searched again for new information about Kenna Cook, and while Google loaded—service was definitely slow out here—he fantasized that there would be breaking news: woman found. When results populated his screen, they were the same articles he'd been reading and rereading—woman missing; no leads.

"I found water for Indy," Addie said, returning with a full water bowl.

Indy slurped her water, splashing Mason's leg and making a dark brown circle in the dirt.

"You are not a normal dog," he said. Mason brought his feet up on the picnic table to avoid a further onslaught.

"There was a plaque by the water spigot," Addie said. "I know how you like to read those, but I beat you to it. This dog park was donated in honor of Gunner, the best dog in the world."

"That's pretty cool," Mason said. "Someone donated this whole park in memory of their dog? That must've been an amazing dog."

"Best in the world. Just like Indy here." Addie scratched Indy's ears, not minding when water dripped on her foot. "Totally the best."

Mason looked at his watch. It was almost seven o'clock. If they left now, that would put them in Fallon a little before ten, well after dark. He'd known today would be long, so he scheduled a late arrival before leaving Illinois, but with a drive in the opposite direction, their arrival would exceed late.

"Did you tell your mom to call my folks?" Mason asked. "Then I won't have to deal with my mother."

"I've got you." Addie dialed her mom again. "I told her the signal was iffy, and then we got cut off. If I get her again, I'll tell her to call your mom."

She held her phone to her ear and looked at Mason. "You know you can send her a text. Here, take a pic of me and Indy. She'll think it's cute." She squatted next to Indy and smiled, phone still at her cheek, as Mason snapped the picture.

"Hey, Mom. Can you hear me?" Addie stood and wandered off.

Mason looked at the picture. Addie's smile was broad, creating a slight dimple under her right eye. Indy's ears were flipped forward and her pink tongue hung out the side of her mouth. Mason's mom wasn't the only person who'd think this picture was cute.

He typed "staying in Fallon tonight" and attached the picture. Mom would probably save the photo, along with all the others they had sent and put them in the family "year-in-review" photo album she loved to create. Mason would pretend to be embarrassed by her including the pictures and secretly love that he would have them forever.

While Addie walked in circles in the dog park talking with her mother, Mason pointlessly searched the internet again for Kenna. No matter how much Mason wanted to move forward, he would have to turn back.

He felt a stab of guilt.

*Am I really so worried about what Addie will think of me that I won't try to help this woman?*

Mason looked at Addie again, assessing how she was going to react to what he now knew he had to tell her. She chatted with her mom, and Mason caught snippets of the ghost train and the Grand Theater.

He even thought he heard "elk watching," as if they had seen so much as a deer.

"All good." Addie returned and plopped her phone on the table. "I convinced them that this has been a very educational trip."

"I sent my mom the picture."

"Perfect. And I'm sure my mom will call her to tell her all about our adventures, and how sweet you are for taking me on this trip."

"It's hard not to love me, isn't it?" Mason flashed a smile and hoped she'd say yes.

"Maybe." Addie winked. "You do have a cute smile."

He'd been in love with her for years, though he rarely admitted it to himself. And now she was flirting with him; he was sure what she just said constituted flirting. Add that to last night, and there might actually be something starting between them. And yet, Mason knew that telling Addie the truth about the visions would ruin it all. For as long as he could remember, he complained about the pointlessness of his visions, and now, when there might actually be a point to them ... *these visions will destroy my hope of a relationship with Addie.*

"Look, I need to..." Mason started and then faltered. "Something has..."

"Hold that thought." Addie grabbed her phone and headed for the Jeep. "Tell me over food. I'm starving."

# CHAPTER 26

Kenna's picture stared out from the Missing Person sign tacked to the weather-beaten siding by the front door of the diner. It was further confirmation that she had not been found, unless the manager forgot to take it down. From the looks of the front window, opaque from a film of grease, Mason thought it might be possible.

As soon as they sat at their table, Addie stared at the menu, deeply absorbed. Mason watched her and prayed that his stomach would stop churning.

"What do you think the Santa Fe chicken sandwich is like?" The menu muffled Addie's voice. "Or maybe I should have a burger. That's probably the safe bet."

"We have to go back." Mason spoke softly, almost hoping she wouldn't hear him.

"Go back where?" Addie turned her head and seemed to be checking out what food the other customers had ordered. "I think I might be tired of burgers. Do you know what you're getting?"

Mason shook his head. "I don't know how to tell you this."

Her left eye squinted slightly as she looked at him, which he was learning meant that she was confused. As her lips parted with a question, the waitress joined them.

"What'll it be for you two tonight?"

A silent pause hung in the air as Addie cocked her head a bit to the right. Then she turned to the waitress. "I'll have a burger. Medium. Cheddar cheese. And fries. Thanks."

"I'll have a burger," Mason said, still looking at Addie.

"You want cheese on that?'

"No, thank you."

"Fries, coleslaw, or chips?" The waitress's questions did not draw his gaze.

"Fries," Mason said, trying to read Addie's expression to determine if she was ready for what he had to make her understand.

"How did you want your burger cooked?"

"Medium."

"Either of you want anything to drink?"

"Just water, please," Addie said.

Mason shook his head, then a thought occurred to him. He called after the retreating waitress. "Excuse me, I saw the sign on the door, about the missing woman. Has she been found?"

"Nope."

It was a slim chance, and her answer only confirmed what he knew he had to do.

"What's wrong?" Addie stared into Mason's eyes, and he looked away. "What was that about a missing woman?"

"I don't know." Mason folded and unfolded his napkin. "I mean, I do know, but I don't know how to explain."

He focused on his breathing, hoping to calm his nerves. He couldn't drive back pretending that he forgot something. He would have to stop at the tire tracks if he found them in order to gather all the details he could. How could he explain that? No pretend photo shoot could cover up what he needed to do.

If he could find information that might help the police locate Kenna, no matter how much he wanted to ignore everything and be with Addie, he had to look for it.

"I have to tell you something," Mason blurted, steeling himself for the truth and looking into Addie's bright and compassionate eyes. He loved the way her dark lashes, free of makeup, framed her big, brown eyes. Mason was afraid Addie would never look at him the same once she knew the truth he had kept hidden for all these years.

Every skid mark that flooded Mason's vision was a reality he didn't want to know. And even though Mason had tried to tell Addie the truth about his visions the day before, she suspected nothing. This time, though, Mason needed Addie to believe him, no matter how ridiculous it sounded. If the skid marks by Kenna's car still existed, he needed to discover the reality behind them—Kenna's life might depend on it.

The lump in his stomach tightened. The smell of grease that had been appetizing when they walked in disgusted him now.

Mason twisted his napkin. "It's something, well, that I should've told you long ago. I tried to tell you the other day, but it's impossible to understand."

"What could you possibly have to tell me that I don't already know?" Addie reached over and stilled his hands. "You've lived next door to me since we were kids. I think I know everything about you."

"Not quite." He smiled weakly.

"Don't look so stressed," she said. "Whatever it is, it can't be that bad."

He chuckled at the thought of how wrong she was, but she must've thought he laughed in agreement.

She gave him a wry smile. "You know, you're not the only one who eavesdrops. What do you think your mom talks about when she has coffee with my mom?"

"What?" His stress momentarily dissolved under a new panic.

"Don't worry," Addie said, patting his hand. "I never repeat anything I overhear about you. I'm only saying that I know a lot more about you than you think."

Mason could imagine what his mom talked about. She was an over-sharer by nature, and he cringed knowing how much she'd share when he wasn't around.

"And I know that you once went on a date with Melanie and forgot your wallet at home. She told me all about it. Did you really make her pay?"

Addie broke into a giggle.

Mason loved her laughter, even if it was at his expense, but he couldn't join her. He shook his head. What he had to tell her was far beyond the scope of what she expected. He didn't even know how he would make her believe him. "It's nothing like that."

Looking at Addie, Mason understood that she never truly knew him. He could pretend that she did, and she could think that she did, but that didn't change the fact that she didn't. She did not live in his world. She did not see the things he saw. No one did. No one could. She would not be able to fathom the reality of his life, the reality behind a lifetime he still didn't understand. But despite her oblivion, he had to tell her the incomprehensible truth, whether or not she was capable of believing it.

"No," he said again. "I'm going to tell you something much more than all of that."

And since he didn't know where to begin, he went backward.

*The Daly City News*
  Daly City, California

## Gas Station Security Camera Captures Video of Missing Daly City Woman

Authorities in Nevada have released gas station security footage of a 24-year-old Daly City woman who has been missing since May 22.

The released video footage shows Kenna Cook pumping gas at Gas-N-Go in Fallon, Nevada, and then leaving minutes later while talking on her phone and holding a plastic bag. The footage was captured on the gas station's security cameras on May 22, the day before Cook's family reported her missing after she failed to arrive at her new residence.

The Gas-N-Go is located 195 miles west of where Cook's vehicle was recovered on May 24.

Police are following up on Cook's cell phone records and other leads but still have not been able to locate the missing woman. Natalie Cook, Kenna Cook's mother, told police she talked with her daughter while she was in Fallon.

"She planned ahead," the elder Cook said. "Kenna told me she had everything she needed before heading out on that empty stretch of road."

Benjamin Hunt, the gas station manager who provided the video, said, "According to the register receipts, she purchased water and snacks. What you'd expect heading onto The Loneliest Road."

Valterra County and Sterling County police have conducted a multi-day search with the use of drones and have not discovered any new information. Police said there were no signs of foul play but have not ruled it out.

# CHAPTER 27

Valterra was quieter when they drove back through town, the way they'd come. Only two street lamps illuminated the empty streets, and Mason briefly thought of Temple Joe as they passed the Grand Theater.

Even though he and Addie had sat at the diner for close to two hours, neither had eaten much. Mason couldn't have predicted the conversation, though he'd tried numerous times, because it was worse than he thought possible.

For a while, Addie was convinced he'd only imagined the visions after reading articles about accidents, coming up with all the AP Psych terms she could remember from class: maladaptive daydreaming, OCD, schizotypal personality disorder.

Mason had bent over his plate, shoving French fries around, as she expounded on how it was common for people with SPD to believe in the supernatural. She wanted him to go to counseling, to get on medication, to put off college for a semester until he was more stable. And he wanted to give up, to admit that he suffered from fantasies like she claimed. But he couldn't relent, even if she didn't believe him.

Now, as they drove back over the miles, he prayed he'd find the skid marks that'd been near Kenna's car. If anything, maybe he could still help Kenna. If he couldn't do that, then it was all for nothing. He'd already ruined his friendship with Addie, let alone any chance they might've had at a romantic relationship. In fact, the entire trip was ruined because any positive memory from it would be blanketed by his confession, by his bizarre ability to see stories in skid marks.

Addie sat silently in the passenger seat. Only Indy, smelling familiarity in the air, sat alert between them, sniffing upward toward the emerging stars. Mason gave Addie space in the silence that separated them. She needed to process what he told her. He hoped her questions would come, even if he wasn't ready for them. If she asked questions, that would be a sign she was willing to understand, that she might believe he wasn't certifiably insane. He hoped her silence meant she didn't know which questions to ask yet.

More than anyone, Mason needed Addie to understand him; he needed her to believe him. Yet he knew it was too much to ask. Heck, even his own mother didn't understand. Addie's eyes remained focused on the road ahead. Mason wished she would look at him, wished she would see the person she knew for most of her life. But her gaze remained fixed on the road ahead.

The sun set behind them as he drove into the growing gloom. Hours ago, the trip had connected them, and now it was a rift between them, just like the visions had always been: a wedge between him and others—even if they never knew it.

Mason tried to distract himself by preparing for what he might see if he found the tire marks near where Kenna's car had been. He'd seen people get injured and die in horrific ways. An image of the crushed man in the box truck outside of Vail flashed into his mind. He'd even seen people unintentionally kill one another, the way the elderly man cartwheeled into the air in Dixon, Illinois. But all those visions dealt with what had passed. The vision he wanted to find dealt with the present.

He unclenched his fingers from the steering wheel and stretched them to get the blood flowing. It was possible that the skid marks near Kenna's car had nothing to do with her disappearance. Kenna might've left her car and tried to take a shortcut to the nearest town through the desert. There was even a chance that he would drive all the way to Ely and not see a thing related to Kenna and her gold Honda. The skid marks, even if they were related, could be gone. Or this whole thing might be a misunderstanding.

Mason thought about the first rescue he'd been involved with when he started lifeguarding at Centennial Beach. An emergency had been called that cleared the pool and sand deck and sent all the lifeguards diving. Tom, one of the experienced lifeguards, had been tracking an elderly woman swimming across the fifteen-foot deep end. She'd caught his eye because she was dog-paddling, slowly, and the pool was sixty feet across. Tom didn't trust her ability to make it. But when a group of teens started screaming as they tried to sink one of the floating platforms, he diverted his focus. He thought he looked away for only a couple of seconds, but when he scanned the pool for the woman, he couldn't find her. In his mind, she never got to the other side. He radioed her description to the perimeter guards, but no one confirmed seeing her. He had to call the possible drowning.

They evacuated the pool, called the fire department, ran their drills, and sent divers into the deep end. The woman was never found. She had dried off and gone home, probably oblivious to the fact anyone was looking for her.

Mason hoped that was the case now. The missing Kenna had gotten in a friend's car and driven off, oblivious to the attempts to find her.

But his gut told him that wasn't the case. He drove into the darkness and hoped that everything was alright with the woman—and between him and Addie.

"Look, we're not going that far out of the way," Mason said. "Maybe all this is nothing. I just need to check."

The sun had completely set behind them. In the glow of the console lights, Addie's eyelids looked heavy, but Mason knew it wasn't exhaustion.

"Once I drive a little ways, I'll know for certain," he said. "I just can't leave here without being sure."

Addie didn't look at Mason, but her face softened slightly.

"If you're afraid of your dad tracking us, we can tell him that I forgot something and we had to circle back." Mason wanted to chuckle at the irony of his story. He'd originally created it to give Addie a reason for why he had to drive back, but he thought it so unconvincing he hadn't even tried it.

Addie still said nothing.

"Hey," he snapped, "are you okay?"

"Yes," she murmured and continued to stare straight ahead.

In the daylight, the open-range highway had been vacant and without interest—aside from the occasional cattle gate and wildlife viewing area—but Mason hadn't felt alone. He had felt connected to Addie, even when they didn't talk. But now, in the closing darkness, the fact that they were in the middle of nowhere was ever-present, and in her silence, he felt more alone than ever.

When he first told her at the restaurant, and she didn't believe him, he'd been prepared for that. But the more he explained, the more her forehead furrowed as if realizing all the conspiracy theories about aliens inhabiting human bodies weren't a myth but a tangible reality threatening human existence. And the more silent she went.

When she stopped questioning him and theorizing about the possible causes of his belief in imaginary events, when she sat frozen in her chair, staring at her uneaten burger, he knew she'd retreated into herself and he could say no more. He walked with her to the Jeep, opened the passenger door, and let her climb in.

At first, she didn't flinch when Indy licked the tears that had dried on her cheeks. But then she cupped a hand around her dog and held Indy's face to hers. Indy's tail thumped against the seats, and Mason drove back toward Ely.

The Jeep's lights barely dented the darkness, but what Mason needed to see, he could see without the headlights. The chance of a rogue cow on the road was slim. And no headlights flashed ahead in the distance. It was indeed the Loneliest Road in America.

"I'm sorry," he said again. "I wanted to tell you, but I didn't know how. It took me years to believe the stories were real. How could I expect someone else to believe them?"

He drove into the darkness.

"I never meant to ... I mean they've ... It's something that ..." He gave up.

Addie said nothing to help him.

# Chapter 28

Desperate to explain, Mason began again. "The visions ... seeing them ... I didn't believe they were real for a long time. Like I said, I tried to tell my mother once when I was little, but she didn't believe me. I haven't told anyone since, except you, just now, and the other day, when we were driving in Colorado."

Addie chuckled ruefully. "'I can see things other people can't.'"

Mason's words came back to him, chilled by her tension.

She nodded her head slowly. "You said that about the semi accident with all that paint."

It was Mason's turn to be silent. She needed to process the past.

"You were trying to tell me, weren't you?" She finally turned to look at him, but he wanted to shrink into the seat.

"I've wanted to tell you for forever." Mason stole a glance at her. "But it's not the believable kind of thing."

Addie didn't reply.

Mason drove on, letting the isolation of the road and the isolation of his life rush past him. The dark flat stretch of Route 50 numbed his thoughts. Road signs hovered toward him like UFOs illuminated in the headlights.

"I'm trying to understand," she murmured. "You're saying that you can see what happened that caused the skid marks? But...how? That's not possible. It already happened."

"I don't know. It's something I've been able to see since I was young." After all the years of visions, the only thing he understood was that events existed and events ended, but events didn't want to be forgotten. And now, for the first time, he felt a responsibility to remember—for this missing woman.

"And you think you'll be able to tell what happened to the woman if you go over the skid marks that were by her car?"

"I know it sounds crazy, but yes, maybe," Mason said. "I don't know, but I have to try. Maybe they have nothing to do with her disappearance. Maybe a coyote ran in front of a car a day earlier, an hour earlier. But I have to check. It could mean her life. I know that sounds dramatic, but she's missing. I've been looking up articles since we left Naperville. No one knows where she is."

"Who is she?" Addie asked.

"A woman who was driving from California to Colorado to move in with a friend," Mason said.

"And you found out about her when you were doing research for our trip?"

Mason told Addie how the woman's picture and her name made him think of his old neighbor. How he might not have paid much attention if it hadn't been for the name. As they drove into the darkness, he told Addie of the guilt he felt when Kenna Sadler died, and how he thought he caused her death by calling out to her, distracting her.

"Whether or not you waved to her didn't change the fact that the guy was drunk," Addie said.

"I can't explain the sound of the tire screech, how it paralyzed me," Mason said. "I was terrified, and then my mom came flying out of the house. And Kenna's mom rushed past me, and everything went silent."

"I heard about them, the Sadlers. They moved away a couple years after Kenna died, and then my family moved in. The other kids talked about the accident, but I never asked you about her. I should have."

Addie put her hand on Mason's shoulder and gave him a light squeeze.

Her touch of reassurance made Mason's eyes burn with tears. He blinked and focused on the road. Occasional visions flooded his mind, but none of them dealt with Kenna.

"When I read about Kenna Cook, all my memories of Kenna Sadler came back," he said. "I'm sure it's just a coincidence, but I haven't been able to shake the idea that finding this Kenna is the reason I have the visions, like if they started with my neighbor then they'll disappear with her."

"This is all too weird." Addie shook her head and let out a slight chuckle.

The weight on Mason's chest lifted slightly at the sound. It suggested that Addie was settling into what he'd told her. He drove slower as they got further out of town and kept his eyes on the circle of light made by the headlights as the blur of asphalt disappeared under the Jeep.

"You can see something for every skid mark?" she asked.

"Yes. Even though I don't want to." Mason loosened his grip on the steering wheel.

Addie kept her gaze forward, looking at the road for marks.

"I try to ignore them, the visions," he said. "If I didn't, I think they'd make me crazy."

It was surreal to talk openly about the marks, like it was all a dream that would dissolve in the light of day.

"The original article I read said that her car was found between Valterra and Ely, and there were skid marks nearby," he continued. "I've been looking up information about her since we've been on the road, but all the news I find is old. I hoped she'd been found. And then I saw that sign at the restaurant..."

"And asked the waitress."

"I have to try, you know," he said. "It's ridiculous, but I feel like I might actually be able to help someone. For all these years, everything was in the past. There wasn't anything I could do to change the outcome."

"I don't understand how you can see what causes the skid marks," Addie said. "Those events don't exist anymore."

"I don't understand either," he said. "I never have."

He felt her eyes on him, and he hoped it meant that she was beginning to understand.

*Or maybe she thinks I'm a freak.*

"I guess we'll find out whether or not you can do anything to help this woman soon enough."

Mason didn't know what this new knowledge would do for their relationship. Certainly a new town miles away would give her plenty of distance from the freak who used to be her neighbor if that's what she wanted.

Mason kept an eye out for headlights from behind. He was well under the speed limit and didn't want a car to come up fast behind them. In the dark, it was hard to see the skid marks, and he focused on spotting them so he didn't miss driving over them.

As they drove, Addie started to ask, "What about the one with the commuter on a bike..." then stopped.

Mason didn't complete her questions, though he knew them. He understood the struggle to understand. He had lived it every day—piecing the lives of his neighbors together in the marks they left on the pavement.

"And the dog on Martin Avenue?" Addie was quilting a past together, one she thought was pure imagination, and it would not take shape easily.

He tried not to worry about her confusion or about what she would think of him. He concentrated on searching for skid marks. After all these years of trying to avoid them, he now sought them out. The curves through the mountain passes, which didn't have guard rails, flooded his mind with visions of other drivers who did not slow down. And on the long stretches of straight road, Mason cursed to himself when there were no skid marks for miles.

*The skid marks near Kenna's car had to be here.*

"By the way, I didn't purposely forget my wallet when I went out with Melanie," Mason said. "I tried to pay her back, like, ten times."

Out of the corner of his eye, Mason saw Addie smile.

"She refused to take my money. I even stuffed an envelope of cash through the vent thing on her locker. Really."

"Mason," Addie grabbed his hand in both of hers and whispered, "I believe you."

Tears stung his eyes again as he understood the depth of what she meant.

"And I love that you want to help this woman enough to tell me something you've kept hidden for years. Now, just find the skid marks."

# CHAPTER 29

Indy lifted her head from under Mason's arm as he stopped the Jeep and put it in reverse.

"Did you find it?" Addie sat up straight.

"I think so." He backed up slowly to find the tracks again. When the vision flooded his mind, he stopped.

After all these years, he had never intentionally stopped on a tire track before.

Addie pounded on his arm, bringing him back to the present. "What do you see?"

"Hold on." Mason put the Jeep in gear and rolled off the tire mark, leaving the sunny day in the vision behind. When he pulled the Jeep off the road and killed the engine, he turned his phone flashlight on and climbed out of the Jeep. Addie unbuckled and followed.

Faint skid marks, pale against the gray asphalt, were barely visible in the light from his phone. No wonder he missed them when they first drove past. Mason walked onto the marks and stood still. The whole scene enveloped him.

It was daylight. A woman stood near her car, holding a phone in the air, probably trying to get a signal. A pickup passed, headed toward Ely, and then slammed on its brakes. Kenna was startled and seemed to retreat to her car. The pickup reversed slowly and stopped. Across the hood, "PROBLEM WITH AUTHORITY" was printed on the bug shield. The pickup sat high off the ground, and the undercarriage was protected by a sheet of metal that looked like it was welded on by the driver himself, who, Mason could see, was hopping down from the truck and walking toward Kenna. He was young, maybe a couple of years older than Mason.

"I see her," Mason said, stepping off the mark and returning to the present.

"Holy crap." Addie stood next to Mason, eyes wide. "Are you sure? The missing woman? You saw her, like, just now?"

Mason nodded. "And I saw someone stop."

"There was someone else? What happened?" The tension in Addie's voice prompted Indy to jump out of the Jeep and run to her side.

"A pickup stopped. It was huge. And a guy got out. I need to see it again though, to make sure I saw everything."

"Tell me. Tell me what you see as you see it," Addie said.

Indy nudged Addie's leg, clearly trying to herd her back to the Jeep.

Addie snapped at the whining dog. "Stop! Go lay down!"

Indy sat at Addie's feet, waiting for the cue to jump into action. Silence, only interrupted by Indy's occasional whimpers and the thrum of insects, swallowed them as Mason stepped back onto the skid mark and left the present.

"There are two guys," Mason began. "Both look to be in their late teens or early twenties. I'm not that good at guessing ages. They're big guys, though. She's talking with them. She's smiling and nodding. They're opening the hood of her car. The guys are shaking their heads, pointing to something in the engine. She's looking and nodding. The driver of the pickup closed the hood, and they're walking. No, not a good idea. She's getting in their truck." Mason couldn't believe what he saw. He had braced himself to see a fight, for someone to knock her out and stuff her in their trunk. Not this. It all seemed perfectly normal like they were helping her.

*If this is what happened, where did she go and why didn't the guys say anything?*

"Did they force her to get in?" Addie asked.

"No. She's smiling. I can't hear anything, but it looks like she's thanking them."

"Did the guys give each other looks, like they have a plan?"

"No. They look like they're helping her. They're pointing back toward where she came from." He stood on the faded mark that was barely visible in the pale light of the sliver of moon, a brief trace of Kenna that was days from disappearing.

"You're really sure it's her? Maybe this is a totally different situation?"

"No, it's her. It's her car, the gold Honda. No doubt in my mind."

Mason walked a bit, to make sure he didn't miss another tire mark, but he found no other traces of the scene.

"Can you see their license plates?" Addie asked. "Tell me and I'll write it down."

She ran to the Jeep and scrambled through the glove compartment for a pen.

That morning, he was eating donuts and contemplating how to wake up his former next-door-neighbor-carpool-driver-crush. Now, he was a witness to the last time a woman was seen before disappearing.

"They didn't have a front license plate," Mason said. "But the bug shield is pretty distinct. We need to tell the police."

"Yeah. This is huge." Addie returned and stood on the skid mark. "Every time you step on it, you see the same thing?"

"Like a movie—a silent movie. Did I tell you that? I don't hear anything. I just see it all unfold. The story of the skid mark plays in my mind."

"Do you think, like in the movies, if you hold my hands and I walk on it with you, that I would see it too?" Addie held out her hands to Mason.

"If that's true, I will be so mad that I didn't think of it twelve years ago," he said.

He held her hands and they stepped onto the tracks. He saw the woman, again in the daylight, holding her phone up. Then the pickup with "Problem with Authority" in black block letters skidding to a stop just past her.

"Do you see it?" he asked.

Addie shook her head. "No."

Mason walked off the skid mark, and Addie dropped his hand. The brief warmth of her hand had given him hope, but now that hope faded.

"If anything," he said. "There can't be many pickups like that. The police can talk to those guys. Maybe it's all a misunderstanding or something."

"Maybe," she said.

Addie didn't need to articulate the big question that hung in the air. How would he tell the police what he knew? How could he give a detailed description of the pickup and the guys driving it without raising questions?

# KENNA

*I don't know how long I have been trapped here. I can't keep track of the days. I know he's still drugging me, but I have no choice. The bottles of water and bits of food he brings are all I have.*

*Everything is foggy.*

*I tried to count the days by looking at the light from the wooden door, but sometimes I fall asleep and don't know if I slept for hours or for minutes. Is it the next day or the same one?*

*I know my family is looking for me. I can't imagine what my parents are going through. Why did I go on this trip alone? Grant said he'd go with me, but I laughed at him. Why did I laugh? Why didn't I want my cousin to go with me? What was I trying to prove?*

*"Oh God, please help me."*

*I talk out loud, just to cut into the silence. I bargain.*

*"I'll go to church every week. I'll be nice to everyone. I'll call my mom regularly. Take care of the poor. Teach Sunday school. Do whatever you want. Just please get me out of here."*

*I want to live. Someone has to find me. I can't disappear.*

# CHAPTER 30

Addie and Mason sat in the Jeep, and Indy, with her paws on the center console, poked him with her wet nose, probably trying to make sure everything was okay.

"It wouldn't be hard to believe that we drove past Kenna however long ago it was when she went missing, would it?" Mason asked.

"No, I don't think so," Addie said. But what will we say is the reason we waited so long to tell the police? That we didn't hear that she was missing until now?"

"What day was it that she drove on this road? Was it the twenty-second of May or the twenty-third?" He swiped his phone to search for the article. "There's no service. Probably the same problem she had."

Addie rummaged in her bag for a sweatshirt and checked the time. "It's almost midnight. We need to go to the police, but we need a story they'll believe."

"This is all absurd," Mason said. "I've never seen anything like this. It didn't even look like she was in trouble, I mean, other than her car breaking down. It looked like they were helping her."

"Let's go back toward Valterra," Addie said. "That way, we'll be headed in the direction the guys pointed. Right? And we'll be headed in the direction we need to go. On the way, we'll come up with a plan."

Mason started the engine. "Thank you. For all of this. I can't believe I've gotten you in the middle of this. And I can't believe I told you the truth about the visions, and you didn't run away."

"I don't have many places I can run to yet." She gestured to the darkness around them. "Plus, I'm the one who got you into this mess since I wanted to drive to Tahoe. Remember?"

"True point. This is all your fault."

"Don't push it. You volunteered."

The night sky was speckled with stars, and the temperature had dropped. Mason cranked the heat in the Jeep. "I think we might be below your sixty-degree threshold."

"It was so hot earlier. I didn't know the desert got so cold." Addie held her fingers over the vent to warm them.

"You can undo one of the sleeping bags and use it as a blanket," Mason offered.

"I'm fine. So, you think that Kenna looked okay? Like she wasn't in trouble?"

"Nothing bad happened in the vision. But that doesn't explain what happened to her or why she hasn't been found yet."

Addie shifted in her seat and tucked her knees under her sweatshirt. "I can't get over these visions you get. There has to be an explanation for them." She stared out the window into the darkness.

Mason didn't say anything. He'd researched possible reasons for his visions, but he never found anything that could explain them, except that he had some psychic ability, and that wasn't an explanation at all.

"For Halloween, you should've been Super Skid Mark Man instead of Super Marathon Man," Addie said with a chuckle. "I know the perfect design for your cape."

With mock seriousness, Mason said, "I'm glad you can find humor in my disability."

"Disability? Are you kidding? It's more like a hyper-ability. And yes, I am trying to find humor in it 'cause it freaks me out."

"Fair enough. Any bars yet?"

She looked at her phone. "No. What are we going to tell the police?"

"I don't know. I guess we say that we saw a pickup stop and the guys were talking to Kenna," he said.

They drove toward Valterra, creating distance between them and Mason's memory of "PROBLEM WITH AUTHORITY" written across the bug shield. He didn't know what had happened to Kenna, but what he saw didn't suggest that she was in danger. Could this all be a miscommunication like the situation at the beach?

"Where are we going to sleep? We are clearly not going to Fallon," Addie said.

"We'll find a place. Remember the Grand Theater? Maybe Temple Joe wants a late-night visitor. Or we could find a spot to camp and go into town in the morning. That might be better than showing up at the police station at one A.M.

"Camp? Out here?"

"Our options are pretty limited at this time of night. And it's wide open out here."

"What? We just camp anywhere? Can we do that?"

"Do you see anyone who would stop us?" They hadn't seen a car in close to an hour. "We'll find a pull-off area, like one of those wildlife viewing areas we saw earlier, and camp there. We have a tent."

"That's not sketch or anything," she said.

Mason slowed the Jeep as they passed a sign for a wildlife viewing area. He could make out the outline of an RV in the dim solar light by the picnic table.

"Want to find the next one?" he asked.

"Please," she said. "I'll have enough trouble sleeping out here already. I don't want strangers nearby. And I don't feel up to small talk if they're still awake."

"I don't remember seeing that trailer when we drove by earlier, do you?" Mason asked.

"Are you trying to make me lose it?"

"Sorry." He continued driving and focused on the imminent problem. "So, we just tell the police what we saw and let them do the rest?"

"Yes," Addie said. "We can say that the pickup stuck out in our memory because of how unusual it was. We need to be sure about the dates, though, to make sure they take us seriously. And we should figure out the time of day. We can go to the station once we get our facts straightened out. We need them to believe us."

Addie looked at her phone again before dropping it back in her lap.

"You're really good at this," he said. "Thanks for not totally freaking out."

"The night's not over, Mason. I haven't processed it all yet. Trust me, I'll freak out when I do."

"Fair enough," he said with a smile. The sign for another viewing area floated toward them out of the darkness. "Ready for some real camping?"

Addie nodded. "There better be a bathroom out here."

Mason slowed the Jeep and turned in.

# CHAPTER 31

"It's kind of spooky out here," Addie whispered as she walked around the Jeep. Indy followed and sniffed the ground.

Moths thwacked into the single, solar-powered light, which illuminated a small circle of ground and the corner of a picnic table.

"Should we set up the tent?" Mason asked, scouting the area with the flashlight on his phone. "Or do you want to sleep in the Jeep?"

"No offense to the tent, but I think the Jeep is a good idea. I don't want to find out what wildlife lives out here. Or people, for that matter."

"Good idea," he said.

Mason busied himself with the Jeep top, and Addie cleaned out the day's worth of travel. They put down the back seat and moved as much as they could into the front to make room for the sleeping bags. Mason finished zipping the rear side window panels and walked to Indy, who sniffed around the picnic table.

"Come look at this," Mason called to Addie. He sat on top of the table and leaned back to take in the spray of stars across the black sky. A sliver of moon, nestled in the stars, barely sliced the dark. He lay back on the table to take it all in.

Addie joined him, pulling her oversized sweatshirt over her knees as she tucked her feet up. "Do you know any of the constellations?"

"Well," he said, pointing, "that's the Big Dipper."

She hit him on the chest. "Duh. You know what I'm talking about. Any others?"

"Wait, let me find it. Yes." He pointed again. "There's the Little Dipper."

"I'll take that as a 'no.'"

"I could never quite understand how the stars form all the pictures they're supposed to form. All I can see are the Dippers."

"And yet, you can see the pictures left by the skid marks?"

"Yeah, well, that's a whole different thing." Mason was glad he had the stars to look at because he didn't trust himself to look at Addie.

"And you don't know why you can see those?"

"I don't understand it any more than I do the constellations," he said. "And I've lived with it all my life."

"Or at least since your neighbor Kenna died."

He let the hum of insects fill the silence, and he drifted into his thoughts.

Kenna's death had been traumatic: the ear-ringing squeal of tires, the crunch of metal, the contorted face of her mother's anguish. But there was no logic to suggest that the accident made him see things that had happened in the past. He wondered if he had seen the visions all along, but in the funny way memory works for kids, he couldn't retrieve those memories.

"Did you ever go to a doctor?" Addie asked.

Mason cupped his hands behind his head and closed his eyes. "My parents never believed me when I told them about the visions, so they didn't take me to a doctor, not that I think a doctor could do anything except lock me up."

"What about Google? Did you look it up?"

He gave Addie a side glance to see if she was being serious, but no trace of a smile crossed her lips. Instead, her tongue moistened her top lip before she rubbed her lips together. A warm tingle surged through his body.

"Sure, I tried looking it up," he said.

Addie turned to him. "Yeah? What'd you find?"

"I don't recommend Googling 'visions' and 'skid marks.' You will be grossed out by the results."

Addie broke into a laugh. "Yeah. I guess you have a point."

"I gave up after finding too many websites about hygiene. And the pictures that people post—gross. Sure, there was information about tire skid marks, but nothing about seeing the stories surrounding them. I figured there was no answer. You know, like in those movies where the mom and daughter switch places or the guy suddenly hears everything women think. It's just the result of magic or something."

"Maybe you're wired differently."

"Wired differently," Mason repeated. He hadn't thought about it that way, that it was some hardwiring issue in his brain. "I guess I'm waiting for the perfect electrical storm to heal me of this affliction."

"So," Addie said, leaning back and resting her head in the crook of his arm, "you get these visions, and yet you offered to drive all this way with me?"

Addie's head was heavy as she relaxed against Mason, and he didn't dare move.

"As I'm sure you can imagine, I typically try to avoid long drives," he said.

"And then you said you'd take the longest drive ever so I could annoy my parents?" she said.

"Don't you mean take care of Indy? I really do love that dog."

"The dog?" Addie challenged.

The heat rose in Mason's cheeks.

"You drove because you love my dog?"

Their feet dangled over the edge of the picnic table as they lay across the top looking at the stars. Addie's leg rested against his, and he held his breath as he took in her warmth.

*Did I just confess that I love her?*

He forced a laugh if only to release the tension growing in his chest. "Please. A road trip without parents? You were a bonus."

"A bonus? Like a free gift?" Addie hit his stomach.

*Did her hand linger?*

Mason brushed off the idea as wishful thinking. "That came off wrong," he said. "I didn't mean *that*."

Mason rotated to face Addie, and her head slipped from his arm and hit the table with a thud. Indy barked.

"Oh! Sorry!" he said, his cheeks flushing again with his stupidity.

Addie sat up, rubbing the back of her head. "I see where I stand in all this. Come here, Indy. You love me, don't you?"

"I didn't mean to bang your head," Mason stammered. "I hope you know, I would travel anywhere with you."

She stopped petting Indy and looked at him. "Yeah?"

His face burned at his honesty. "Well, your parents *are* paying me to keep an eye on you."

Mason wanted to sound offhand, but he could hear his nerves vibrate through his voice. He smiled and hoped she could see the blue of his eyes, what he thought of as his best feature, in the dim solar-powered light.

Addie raised an eyebrow. "And you're keeping an eye on me by making me spend the night on the side of a road after taking me to the place where a woman disappeared?"

Mason bit his lower lip and bowed his head. "When you put it like that, I guess I'm not doing a very good job."

"I forgive you," Addie said as she leaned into him.

Just as Mason was about to wrap an arm around her, Indy nudged between them and barked.

"I'm hungry too," Addie said to Indy. "I'll never be able to sleep if I don't eat something."

*That dog's timing is terrible.*

Addie hopped off the table and went to the Jeep in search of food.

# CHAPTER 32

"Help me understand," Addie said, returning with a bag of pretzels and a couple bottles of water. "You're a runner. Don't you run on tire marks?"

They sat cross-legged on top of the picnic table.

"Have you seen my stride?" Mason replied. "I've learned to land where I want to land."

"Please. You must've run across skid marks at some point. I mean, you're always running."

"Sure, but it's instinct to avoid them," he said. "Sometimes, though, if I'm zoned out, I'll go over one, like the day after you told me you were moving. I blame you for my lack of attention to my run."

The vision returned to him, and he sat in quiet contemplation before he continued. "A little boy, like four or five, with dark brown hair, chased his soccer ball into the street and almost got hit by an SUV."

"Geez! Was he okay?"

"Yes, thankfully, but it scared the crap out of me. That's why I prefer to run on the paths."

Not a single car passed on the highway, and it was easy to forget they were near a road.

Addie pointed a pretzel at Mason. "You know, I thought I knew everything about you, but clearly I don't," she said. "There's a lot I don't know about you."

He mimicked her move, pointing his pretzel at her. "I was thinking the same thing about you."

"Remember that trip to the dunes? The one a group of us went on when Neha was dating that friend of yours?"

"Mickey?"

"Yeah. Last minute you bailed 'cause you had to cover someone's shift at the beach? You didn't really have to work, did you?"

"How do you remember that?"

Addie ignored his question. "Tell me, how has the trip been so far? As bad as you thought it would be?"

"More fun than I thought possible." Mason's smile faded. "Except the missing woman part. I still don't understand what I saw. It all looked so regular. I don't know why she's missing."

The evening had been a challenge, from telling Addie the truth to finding the skid marks. Tomorrow—actually today, since it was almost one-thirty in the morning—would bring a whole new challenge: convincing the police they were giving them a real lead.

"Before we started this trip," Mason said, "I was more afraid than anything else. I've avoided going places, seeing people, doing things all because I was afraid of seeing something tragic. It took this whole trip —missing woman included—to learn that I don't need to be afraid. You're helping me understand that."

"I can't imagine how hard it's been to keep everything to yourself all this time."

Addie said exactly what Mason needed her to say, and what he didn't know he waited a lifetime to hear.

"Thanks." He looked up at the sky to control the emotion that welled in him. He finally felt understood for who he was, completely. "Do you see those three stars, right in a row?"

"I think." Addie pointed. "Those three, in a line?"

"Do they look familiar?"

"Umm. Should they?" She raised an eyebrow and looked at him.

Mason lifted the hair along the left side of Addie's neck. "You have them right here," he said. He traced her freckles with his thumb, connecting each dark spot to the other.

Addie noticeably shivered. She said nothing, just looked into Mason's eyes.

"I think they're called Orion's Belt," Mason said, holding her gaze.

"I thought you didn't know any constellations."

"This one has been right in front of me, and I didn't realize it."

It was her turn to blush. "I have so many freckles. How could you spot those?"

"I saw them when you were sleeping yesterday when I was driving."

*How was that only yesterday?*

"Checking me out while I'm asleep, huh? Should I be worried?"

"With me, never."

"Wow, that was Declan-smooth," she said.

"Way to ruin a moment," Mason said.

*Had Declan been on her mind?*

Mason's doubts rushed back. He didn't have as much courage as he thought. He couldn't handle rejection, not after everything that had happened. Plus, she didn't want a long-distance relationship. She made that clear. He needed to let it go, let her go. He climbed off the table.

"You know that I'm the same person I've always been, right?" he said.

"If you mean the same dorky, uber-skinny, runner-boy who can't do backflips? Yes, I know."

"I'll take it." He held out his hand and helped Addie down. "Tomorrow's going to be a long day. We need to get our stories straight."

Mason grabbed the bag of pretzels and empty water bottles from the table.

"You'll describe the pickup. We'll say that I was driving and didn't see much."

"True. I'll just tell them what I know."

"And why didn't we say anything earlier?" Addie drilled. "What if they ask us that?"

Indy joined them by the Jeep, and Mason leaned down to pet her.

"We can say that we didn't realize anything about a missing person until we saw the news."

"And when did we see the news? On what news station? I doubt there've been any recent news reports on TV if there haven't been any new articles."

"We can say we saw an old article on the internet," he offered.

"And how did we stumble across it?"

"Geez, what are you, a district attorney?" Mason massaged the back of his neck.

"I don't want them to ignore us because they think we're full of crap," Addie said. "It looks like nothing happened, but we don't know. What if those guys weren't all nice after all?" She leaned against the side of the Jeep and rested her head against the door.

Mason felt the seriousness of the situation return. "You're right," he said. "We need to get our story straight. I expected to see something terrible, and when I didn't, I figured everything was okay. But she's still missing, so everything isn't okay."

Addie bolted upright and pointed at the sky. "Hey, did you see that?"

"Was that a shooting star?"

"We should make a wish."

They were both silent for a moment.

"Well, what did you wish for?" she asked.

"How many wishes can you make on one shooting star? Because I made a lot." And he had. So much had happened that day, and there were too many unknowns.

"Me, too." Addie yawned. "I'm exhausted. I think everything is catching up with me."

"Let's figure out how we're going to sleep in the back of the Jeep." Mason opened the tailgate and spread out the sleeping bags. Indy jumped in as he finished and settled in the middle.

"Oh, no you don't, bed hog," Addie said, maneuvering around the space. "You have to share space. This is even smaller than the tent."

"We'll figure it out. Right, old girl?" Mason scratched Indy's head, and her tail thumped. "Just like the tent, we can unzip the windows to get some air."

"And we can lock the doors." Addie leaned into the front and hit the lock. "Even better than a tent."

It took a minute for the three of them to get settled. Mason lay at an angle since Indy curled up by his legs. He didn't complain, though, since his head was close to Addie's.

"Remember that accident that Tammy got in?" Addie asked. "She swore she had the green light when she hit that car. Did she?"

He laughed. "No, but we all knew that anyway."

"How many skid marks did Declan make?"

"Lots. But do we really have to talk about him, again?" Mason tried to maneuver to see Addie more clearly, and Indy yelped. "Sorry, dog."

"You said that you tried to tell your mom, but she didn't believe you."

"Yeah. But how could she have believed me? I mean, I was a kid. Who believes wild stories from a six-year-old? I never really tried to tell her when I was older. They did send me to therapy after Kenna's death. My mom said that aside from nightmares, I had a fear of cars and driving because of the accident. I don't remember too much from then, but after a while, I got better."

"Or better at hiding your fear," Addie said.

Mason closed his eyes and listened to the hum of the insects. He was suddenly exhausted by it all.

Addie rested a hand on his chest. "When did you know it was real? That you weren't hallucinating or something?"

Her hand felt so natural on his chest, rising and falling with his breaths. He stared out the back window into the darkness and told her about the hot pink sunglass case. And because it felt natural to talk with Addie, Mason told her about the truck accident outside of Vail—the reason he couldn't eat ice cream. About the man in Dixon that he pretended was a bee sting. The teenage girl and her father in Schaumburg. He knew he shouldn't tell her any of it, that it would only upset her, but he couldn't help it. Each story he told released him from its burden.

Hot tears dropped from Addie's cheek and rolled down Mason's neck as she squeezed his arm.

"I've spent a lifetime questioning these images. There must be a reason. A reason other than to totally upset me, and now you. Sorry."

Mason brushed the tears from her cheek.

"Maybe this is the reason, to find this missing woman," Addie said.

Mason had felt that since the moment he saw the article about Kenna Cook. But the vision he saw didn't match the fear he typically had when he crossed a skid mark. Now he doubted the certainty he once felt.

"Maybe," he said. "As selfish as it sounds, I think I was happier when I only saw the past, a past that's over, not a past that might be a clue to something in the present. What if I don't really know anything that can help this woman?"

He felt responsible for Kenna Cook. He knew he would have to get his story straight like Addie said. If Kenna really did need his help, he couldn't mess it up.

Addie sighed and melted into him. He was tired, too, but now his mind wouldn't stop.

"If you've done everything you can, you've done something," she said.

"Inspirational poster?" he teased.

"I know you, and you suck at lying." Her words came slowly as she fought sleep. "You have to be telling the truth about these visions. Strange as it is."

"You never told me how you remembered that I bowed out of the trip to the dunes."

The heavy rhythm of her breathing told him she was already asleep.

He gently kissed the top of her head and tried to match the rhythm of his breathing to hers as he thought through all the events. Their stops, the accidents, the deaths, the fact that he told Addie the truth—and, the more surprising fact, that she understood. The Kenna from his childhood and the missing Kenna. The two guys that seemed helpful despite their intimidating truck.

*She's probably fine.*

He ran through different versions of what he could tell the police, but nothing seemed believable. Mason felt like he was lying because he *was* lying.

*Didn't Addie just tell me I suck at lying? How are the police ever going to believe me, when everything points to the unbelievable?*

Addie's breath tickled his neck, and he tried again to sync his breathing with hers. He focused on her, on how close her body was to his.

*Tomorrow*, he swore to himself. *I will tell her how I feel tomorrow.*

SATURDAY, JUNE 1, 2019

*Sierra Nevada Star*
Fallon, Nevada

## Ex-boyfriend of Missing Calif. Woman Questioned; Aunt Pleads for Her Return

The ex-boyfriend of a missing Daly City, Calif., woman has been questioned in connection with her disappearance. Police have declined to comment, outside of stating that Eric Prosser, 27, of Oakland, Calif., has been questioned and is cooperating with police in regard to the disappearance of Kenna Cook, 24, who drove through Fallon on May 22 and has been reported missing since May 23.

Marley Mirtz of Oakland, Calif., friend of Prosser and Cook, said, "He would never hurt Kenna. They broke up on good terms and were still friends." Another friend of Prosser, Amelie Hudson of Pacifica, Calif., stated, "Kenna and Eric haven't been together for over a month. He never threatened her or wished her harm. We all hope Kenna is found and that she's safe."

Emily Higgins of San Francisco, Calif., aunt of Cook, questions the focus by police on Prosser. "Someone knows what happened to her, and I'm sure that person is in Nevada. Kenna needs you to speak up, whoever you are."

The Sterling County Sheriff's Office asks anyone who traveled Route 50 on May 22 to come forward if they have any information.

# CHAPTER 33

Mason woke but didn't move. Lines of yellow pierced the indigo sky, and as beautiful as it was, he wished the day hadn't begun. Addie's head rested on his arm, which was numb, and he was increasingly aware that her leg was out of her sleeping bag and intertwined with his. He resisted the urge to run his hand along her thigh and feel her smooth skin.

Indy sat up and looked at him.

*What? You can read my mind too?*

Mason shifted to a less-tempting position.

"No coffee this morning," he said when Addie lifted her head.

She moaned and dropped her head back onto his arm.

"We have some water in the cooler. Want me to get you one?"

He felt her head nod, so he slid his arm out and leaned into the front seat. In the growing light, he could see that he missed the parking pad by about fifteen feet. Thankfully, he also missed the fence that kept the wildlife separate from the wildlife viewing area. He reached into the cooler and pulled out a couple of waters. He handed one to Addie, then opened his door and climbed out. Indy jumped out after him.

"Yeah, water for you too," he said.

After he filled Indy's bowl, he took a long drink and looked around. They were certainly in the middle of nowhere. Or, depending on how one looked at it, exactly in the middle of somewhere. Across the plain, in the distance, a cloud of dust trailed a pack of fast-moving animals.

"Come here," he called to Addie. "You've got to see this."

She moaned but opened the door and leaned out. "What?"

Mason pointed at the trail of dust, and Addie crawled out of the Jeep with the sleeping bag wrapped around her. She stood next to Mason in time to see a herd of horses run past. They weren't close, but close enough that they could make them out. Five or six brown horses running full-speed, no one to ride them, manes and tails flying.

"Wild?" she asked.

"They must be," he said, his eyes following the trail of dust as it faded into the distance. "Welcome to the wildlife viewing area."

"They're beautiful. I can handle that type of wildlife. I can't handle the type that slithers. Protect us from that, Indy."

"Your dog doesn't have a good history with wildlife. She can't even protect herself."

"True." Addie wrapped the blanket tighter. "It's cold out here. What time is it?"

He checked his phone. "Five forty-one. Still no bars."

"Guess we better go find some," Addie said.

---

As HE DROVE, MASON NARRATED EVERY SKID MARK THEY passed at Addie's request. Most were similar: sudden braking because an animal darted across the road, taking a turn too quickly, or a quick stop to retrieve a shoe that slipped off a foot hanging out an open window.

He pointed out marks made by anti-lock brakes, their signature intermittent light and dark patterns, and marks where the tires locked up, creating solid dark lines. He explained that marks made when decelerating start light and get dark while the opposite is true for marks made when accelerating. By the time they got close to

Valterra, Addie could correctly identify marks created by cars drag racing.

"How about those?" She pointed to the line of intermittent skid marks, evenly spaced, that stretched out on the road.

"Skip skids. They annoy me because the visions come and go with them. With this one, a semi braked hard because there was an oncoming car and a group of bicyclists on his shoulder. Sometimes, when a semi brakes like that, the cargo shifts and causes the trailer to bounce, which makes those marks. That's why they're called skip skids."

"Bizarre."

"Those," Mason pointed to the marks coming from an unmarked side street. "Those are called 'yaw marks' because the tire is still rotating as it slides. Whoever lives down that road takes his turns fast."

"Kind of like the marks we saw going to school. What was it you said? Something like, 'What if I told you Declan made those?' Well? Tell me. Were they actually made by Declan?"

"Remember the bashed mailboxes in the neighborhood?"

She whipped her head to look at him. "That was Declan?"

"And a few of his close friends."

"Why didn't you say anything? The victims could've made him and whoever he was with—"

"Peter, Andy, and Zayd."

Addie raised her eyebrows. "Well, Declan, Peter, Andy, and Zayd could've paid for whatever damage they caused. You should've said something. At least to me."

"What was I going to say? I wasn't there," Mason said, as a sign for Valterra appeared, as if on cue. "Guess that's not stopping me this time."

They parked outside of the diner where he had told Addie about his visions and got on the free Wi-Fi. It seemed a fitting place to figure out the details of their story before going to the police.

When they were confident they knew dates and times, Mason pulled into the parking lot of the police station. The white block lettering on the side of the red brick building proudly proclaimed "Valterra County Justice Department."

All they needed to do was go in, report what they saw, and leave. At least, that was the plan.

"I guess I understand why you didn't say anything," Addie said, standing in front of the large front door with the town crest painted on it. "This is intimidating, and I haven't done anything wrong."

"I hope I get this right," Mason said, drawing in a deep breath. "I can't mess it up. A woman's life could be on the line."

From the Jeep, Indy barked after them as they opened the glass door and entered. When Mason told the young cop at the front desk that they might have information about the missing woman, he made a call and then led them down a hall, past a large mural of the town with the mountains in the distance, to an office.

Mason felt guilty, simply being in a police station.

*Just breathe.*

"Tell me what you saw," the cop who introduced himself as Deputy Burke said when they sat down. His voice was deep and gruff like he'd smoked unfiltered Camels since he was ten.

"Well," Mason started and looked to Addie, who gave his hand a quick squeeze for reassurance, "we were driving on Route 50 when we passed a car on the side of the road."

Deputy Burke wrote notes on a yellow legal pad as Mason gave him the information.

Mason looked at Addie for reassurance, then continued. "We're sure it was the same car that we read about in the *Sierra Nevada Star*, the one that belonged to Kenna Cook."

Deputy Burke looked up at Mason. "Where'd you see the car? What was the make and model?"

"It was a gold Honda," Addie added.

"And a pickup truck was pulled over near it," Mason continued.

Deputy Burke hovered his pen over the pad and looked between Mason and Addie. His eyes were watery and looked burdened by eyelids that threatened his vision. "Tell me about the truck."

"It was big, not just the truck, but the wheels. They were huge. Tall, you know? It was silver. I remember the truck because the words 'Problem with Authority' were on the bug shield."

"Travis Ray and Bobby's truck, no doubt." The deputy chuckled more to himself than to them.

"Yeah, there were two guys there."

"The Norris boys," Deputy Burke said, tossing down his pen. "Hard to mistake that truck."

Mason and Addie looked at each other, eyebrows raised in surprise.

"I think I saw her get in the truck with them," Mason added quickly.

"You see all this driving past?" The deputy clasped his hands behind his head and leaned his full weight back in the chair, keeping his eyes fixed on Mason.

The creaking of the springs filled the silent space as Mason marveled at the way Deputy Burke's neck disappeared, making his head appear as if it protruded out the middle of his chest. It was an optical illusion, but the visual was so disturbing, Mason could only sit, open-mouthed.

Addie answered for Mason. "I was driving, so he had a better look."

"They have a recognizable truck," Deputy Burke said. "You're sure you saw it there, and not somewhere else? Sometimes memory's like a woman—she doesn't look the same in the full light of morning."

"I'm positive," Mason spat. "That was the truck by the missing woman's car."

"Alright." Deputy Burke leaned forward and put his elbows on the desk. "I'll talk to them. But if they stopped to help her and didn't tell me, well, that isn't like them."

"Just because you know them—"

Deputy Burke raised his hand to silence Addie. "I'll call them and find out what's going on."

The deputy stood, and Mason and Addie stood with him.

"Thank you for coming in," he said. "We've been chasing down a lot of leads. Most of them are unrelated, and they distract more than help."

"Well, this one should help, if you look into it," Addie said. "Will you tell us what you find out? We'd like to know."

"Trust me, we all want to know what happened." Deputy Burke laid his fat hand on Addie's shoulder and she reflexively took a step back. "There hasn't been a missing person in these parts for almost a decade. I'll talk to Travis Ray and Bobby to see if they were there. If they gave this woman a ride somewhere, they'll tell me."

"But how will we know," Mason said.

"Dave, get the Norris boys on the line, will you?" Deputy Burke yelled down the hall, then turned back to Mason. "Come to think of it, I haven't seen their truck around here in a while. Maybe they aren't even in town."

"Look, I know what I saw, and—"

"They're out at the Maxxim Race," yelled Dave. "You know, Vegas to Reno. They haven't been home in weeks."

"Does everyone know everyone?" Addie accused.

Deputy Burke turned toward Addie and sighed. "We're a town of 600, in a good year. Yes, we know everyone."

"I hope that fact helps you do your job—and not the opposite," Addie said.

Deputy Burke shook his head slightly and gave a half-grin. "I have a teenage daughter myself, so I'm not new to the sass. Rest assured, we're doing all we can to find this woman."

"Kenna," Mason stated.

The deputy turned to him. "'Scuse me?"

"Kenna Cook, the missing woman. She has a name."

Deputy Burke looked between Mason and Addie and sighed. "Her family's still in town."

"They are? We'd love to talk to them." Addie looked at Mason, hopeful.

"If you did, they'd tell you everything we're doing to find their daughter."

"Where can we find them?" Mason asked.

Deputy Burke let out a chuckle. "It's a town of 600. I'm sure you can figure it out."

# CHAPTER 34

"He was pleasant," Addie said as they stood in the parking lot of the police station. "Let's get breakfast, and then we can stalk the streets of Valterra looking for people who don't belong."

"Why didn't he tell us where the family is staying?" Mason asked. "Would he be breaking some kind of law if he told? Like HIPAA, or something?"

"Those are for doctors, not police," Addie said, getting in the driver's seat and scratching Indy on the head. "He's just being difficult."

When Mason got in, Indy licked his cheek, leaving a trail of drool. "Thanks, I think." He wiped his face.

"Deputy Burke could've been more helpful," Addie continued. "He was a jerk, after we handed him a major clue."

"A major clue that makes them look foolish," Mason said. "If the Norris boys are locals, and no one knows a thing about them helping the woman, it looks suspicious."

"Definitely. We need to find Kenna's family and tell them what we know. Who knows, maybe Deputy Burke has no intention of telling them what we saw."

Addie turned left onto Highway 50, the main road through town.

"The family might not be in any condition for two random

teenagers to get in their business," Mason said. "I don't want to give them false hope. What if what I saw doesn't help?"

Mason ran his fingers through his hair. After talking with Deputy Burke, he doubted how useful his information was. He'd expected the deputy to send out an APB for the pickup truck, and he and Addie would be on their way to Fallon while police across the state searched for the pickup. He hadn't expected the police to know the guys driving it. Maybe they weren't the reason she disappeared.

"What if the Norris brothers started driving her to town," Mason said, "but she decided she should stay by her car? And then someone else saw her walking and pulled up alongside her. No skid marks or anything. And hit her over the head and stuffed her in their car?"

"Your imagination again," Addie said. "You have to go with the most economical interpretation; isn't that what we learned in English class?"

Addie pulled the Jeep into the diner parking lot. "Breakfast, first. It will help me think."

The diner was lighter inside than it had been the night before, but the dark wood-paneled walls still shrunk the interior space. The smell of fried bacon hung in the air, and Mason's stomach rumbled. He was thankful when they took a seat at a different table than the one they sat at the night before.

"No more major revelations," Addie said, pointing a finger at Mason as they sat.

He thought about his desire to share how madly in love with her he was. That would have to wait. He couldn't drop that bomb in the same place he told her about the visions.

After they ordered, Addie flipped through her phone. "I need to find something to do in the area, so I can tell my parents why we returned to Valterra. They don't have to know we didn't actually go to Fallon."

Mason watched her long lashes flutter as her eyes darted across the screens she flipped through. She hadn't worn make-up the whole trip, and she looked simultaneously younger and older, like she was comfortable enough to be in her own skin. He envied that assurance and then wondered if he was projecting his own hopes onto her.

Addie glanced at him. "We'll find something to do and then send my mom a picture. Otherwise, she's going to think I've decided to run away. We don't need the cops looking for us too."

"Take a picture of Indy." Mason pointed out the window at Indy, who was sitting in the back of the Jeep, staring at the diner, tongue hanging out.

"She'll need more than that." Addie returned to scrolling through her phone. "How about riding some ATVs? We can take some video of us on an ATV, and then we can find Kenna's family. I'll tell her we're on a half-day guided tour or something."

"Is she going to ask about the rodeo we told her about?"

"I'll come up with something."

"There's a news report with Kenna's mom. It was heartbreaking, but you'll be able to see what she looks like. That'll help us find her." Mason searched Google, then held his phone out to Addie. "I wish we could've gotten here sooner. How will we explain not calling the police earlier? I don't know if I can talk to her."

"We could've gotten here sooner if you told me about it sooner," Addie said, taking his phone and hitting play.

"I wasn't going to tell you at all," Mason said.

Addie watched the video with the volume on low. When she finished she looked at Mason.

"You're right. This is going to be hard." Addie handed the phone back to him. "But we have to talk with them. How else will we know if Deputy Burke told her about the pickup truck? Heck, I don't even think he believes us. If the Norris guys say they were never there, how do we prove it?"

"What's talking to her mom going to do, though?" Mason was having second thoughts about this whole thing. "It's not like she has reason to believe us, either."

"Unless..." A sly smile slid across Addie's face.

"Here we are." The waitress set their plates down. "Bacon'll be right out. Need anything else?"

"All good. Thanks," Addie said.

When the waitress left, Mason dropped his voice. "You better not be thinking I should tell her about ... you know what. It took a lifetime to tell you. If I start proclaiming it to the world, I'd be locked up so fast."

"It might make her push Deputy Burke to investigate if he isn't," Addie said.

"Addie, she wouldn't believe anything we said if we told her something that outrageous. I've kept it a secret for a reason." Again, Mason's eyes darted around to see if anyone was listening to them. "Remember how hard it was for you to believe me? And you know me."

She reached across the table and squeezed his arm. "You're right. Sorry."

"This isn't a party trick, Addie. It's plagued my life, tortured me with horrible accidents. Remember? I told you because I trusted that you'd believe me *and* that you wouldn't say anything."

Addie took both Mason's hands in hers. "We'll stick to our story. It will all work out."

Mason took a deep breath to calm his racing heart. He squeezed her hands. "Thank you."

"Maybe by the time we find her family, Deputy Burke will have news about the Norris guys," Addie said.

"This is way messier than I thought it would be," Mason said. "We told the police. Why don't we leave it to them now?"

"We'll just double-check with the family, to make sure Deputy Burke, despite being rude, is doing his job," Addie said. "Then we can go to the rodeo. But first, we need to get a video of us riding some ATVs."

"Where do we go for the video?"

"Down the street." Addie's eyes twinkled with mischief. "I'm thinking it wouldn't hurt if we asked about the Norris boys when we're there. After all, everyone in town knows everyone, right?"

# CHAPTER 35

"Who made those skid marks?" Addie asked as she turned into the parking lot of Smith's ATV Rental, Repair & Sales.

"Navy blue pickup, with a gun rack."

"Don't they all have gun racks around here?"

"True. The driver looked like a teenager. He was peeling out. Seems like that's the only way to turn onto the main road."

"Well, I guess that's one way to make some excitement. The other is this." Addie parked at what looked to be a converted gas station, with the metal roof canopy covering several rows of ATVs facing the road.

"Are you sure about this? I could just take your picture sitting on one of those, then we can walk around town to look for the family."

"I need to show my mom some videos of us doing things. She thinks I'm sulking and refusing to get any closer to 'our new home.'" Addie put air quotes around the phrase and affected her mother's overly sweet tone. "Come on, we'll go for a quick ride. That'll give Deputy Burke a little time to talk to the Cook family and hopefully find out what's going on with the Norris brothers. By the time we find the family, maybe we'll all know what happened to Kenna."

"What about Indy?"

Addie opened the door, and Indy jumped out. "We'll see if there's someplace she can hang out."

THE FRONT DOOR CHIMED AS THEY WALKED IN. THE PLACE was empty, except for a few vinyl chairs and an end table covered with magazines. Mason scanned the titles: *Sand Wheels, UTV Nation, ATV Off-Road Dirt*. Indy sniffed the ground. A dark-haired boy about their age came in, wiping his hands on a dirty towel. "Hi. What d'ya need?"

"We were driving through and saw your place," Addie said in her perkiest voice. She glanced around the place, probably trying to gauge if the kid was alone. "We'd love to take a couple ATVs out on the trails."

"Sure thing." The boy went to the counter and fished for some papers. "Have you ridden before?"

"Um..."

Mason could tell that Addie was contemplating saying yes, so he quickly interjected, "No, we haven't. Is that a problem?"

Addie shot Mason a look. Apparently, he hadn't masked his hopeful tone.

"Nope," the boy said, setting a couple sheets of papers on the counter and starting to fill one out. "Just need to know how much to tell you. What's your name?"

"Addie, what's yours?"

Mason couldn't hide his eye roll.

The kid looked up and squinted his dark eyes at her. He pointed his pen at the name embroidered on his shirt.

"Nice to meet you, Danny. This is Mason." Addie waved a hand in Mason's direction and then circled it around the room. "Is this your place? It's pretty cool."

Danny snorted. "I wish. Guy owns it. I work for him. Maybe someday I'll have my own place. You need to sign this. Says we're not responsible if you get hurt. And I need to see your license." He slid the waiver in front of them.

Mason grabbed the pen and wrote his info and signed. He held the pen to Addie, hoping he could move her along.

"So," she pointed the pen out the front window at the variety of vehicles lined up. "Why are those ATVs bigger than those?"

"Those are dune buggies. They have a 1600cc engine; most of our ATVs only have a 450cc engine. And see the roll bars? ATVs don't have those."

"Great," Mason said, pulling his license from his wallet. "Maybe we should rent dune buggies instead."

"You don't wanna take those out around here." Danny repositioned his baseball cap and cracked a smile. "They're great for Sand Mountain out by Fallon though. Sign here."

Mason tapped the paper in front of Addie. He knew where this conversation was headed. "We should get going."

Addie signed and pushed the paper back to Danny. "Sand Mountain? Sounds like fun."

"Sure is, if you have the right equipment. Nothing beats hanging with the boys out there." His face softened, and Mason realized he was probably younger than they were.

"I can imagine," Addie continued. "Let me guess, you hang with the Norris brothers?"

Danny's head snapped up, and his jaw tightened. He glared at Addie.

"I guess not," Addie said. "That's probably good. I hear they aren't very nice."

Danny held out their licenses. "You both're from Illinois." He pronounced the "s" at the end of Illinois. "Why you asking about the Norris boys?"

Addie took the licenses. "We've been in town long enough to hear about them."

Danny pulled a laminated sheet from a drawer and set it in front of them. "These are the trail rules. You'll see other riders. People go out on the trails all the time. No matter what they do, though, you got to stay on the trails. It's when you go off them that you run into trouble."

"What kind of trouble?" Mason asked.

"Ravines, barbed wire, boulders. That kind of thing. If you're going fast, you don't want to run into anything unexpected."

"We'll stay on the trails. Got it. How about Indy?" Mason looked at Indy splayed out on the linoleum. "Can we tie her up somewhere in the shade?"

"Out back's fine. How long did you say you wanted? It's $125 for an hour or $400 for four."

"One hour," Mason said.

Addie handed Danny a credit card as she gave Mason a wink. "Dad owes me much more than that."

Danny ran the card and set a pen on the counter by the receipt. "Sign there, and then we'll go around back."

Instead of signing, Addie rested her elbows on the counter and cupped her face in her hands. "You don't want to talk about the Norris brothers. Why not?"

Danny stiffened. "I don't hang with them or their pa. And I don't know what you mean by asking. If you wanna ride, sign this and let's go." He pointed at the receipt.

"Enough," Mason whispered.

As soon as Addie signed for the charge, Danny turned and walked out the side door, the dirty towel swinging from the back pocket of his worn jeans.

Mason and Addie followed as Indy ran ahead of them.

"Sorry about that," Addie said when she was alongside Danny. "I didn't mean anything by it. Just trying to learn more about them is all."

"I suggest you don't." Danny handed them helmets. "Make sure you wear your helmet at all times."

"How long has Guy owned this garage?" Addie asked, surveying the row of ATVs.

Danny let out a sigh, clearly annoyed by all the questions. "He opened it shortly after he came to town. That was about ten years ago."

"Did you hear about the woman that went missing last month?" Addie persisted.

Mason choked down an audible moan.

Danny crossed his arms over his chest, eyebrows furrowed, staring at Addie. "Yes."

"Do you know what happened?" she pushed.

"No."

"But it's a small town. There must be rumors."

Danny pulled the rag from his back pocket and fiddled with it. He looked at Mason, his eyes seeming to plead with him to make Addie stop asking questions. Mason could only shrug his shoulders in silent apology.

"Not as many as you'd think," Danny said. "Least not that I hear."

Addie leaned closer to Danny, waiting for something more.

Danny sighed, and then offered, "I heard that her family is in town."

"Do you know where they're staying?" Mason asked.

"No." Danny wiped down the ATV with the rag he pulled from his back pocket.

"We heard there hasn't been a missing person for years, until now." Addie was definitely probing. It would've been easier to simply Google the missing person from the past than ask this kid, and Mason didn't know why it even mattered.

"Ten years ago or so, the whole town spent weeks looking for Kat Wallace when she disappeared, but she probably ran off with some guy and wasted all our time. Look, do you want to ride these or not?" Danny shoved the towel back into his pocket and crossed his arms over his chest.

"We do," Mason said quickly. "What do we need to know?"

"These are nerf bars. They stop your feet from getting caught in the back wheel. Keep your feet on them when you ride." Danny tugged on them to make sure they were stable. "Ok, sit here."

Addie climbed onto the ATV, but the faraway look in her eyes let Mason know that she was trying to piece something together and not listening to Danny's instructions.

"They're pretty easy to work. But if you hit the gas too hard, it'll be like you're in the rodeo. Got it?"

"Got it, Addie?" Mason repeated.

"What ever happened to the girl who went missing?" Addie asked instead.

"Kat? Who knows. No one ever heard from her again. Like I said, she probably run off."

Addie opened her mouth, and Mason knew it was to ask more

questions. He sped off before she had the chance, forcing Addie to follow.

ONCE THEY DROVE A DISTANCE FROM THE GARAGE, MASON stopped and turned to Addie. "What the heck? I thought that guy was going to lose it on you. You wouldn't stop pummeling him with questions."

"He does not like the Norris brothers. Or their 'pa.' I didn't even mention him. I need to Google them." Addie pulled out her phone. "The reception here sucks."

"That's why the woman went missing in the first place," Mason said. "She couldn't call anyone. Really though, you couldn't have been more obvious."

"Are we supposed to be undercover? Who cares if I annoyed him? He'll get over it."

Addie waved her phone in the air in an obvious attempt to get a signal. She reminded Mason of Kenna standing at the side of the road trying to get a signal.

"I'll have to look up Pa Norris later," she said. "Can you believe the story about Kat Wallace? Ran off with some guy. Ha!"

"She might've," Mason said. "What do we know? It was ten years ago. Don't you remember all those lessons on internet safety we suffered through in school?"

In the distance, a dust trail followed what must've been another ATV. The sun beat down on them and sweat dripped from under Mason's helmet.

"I don't know," Addie said. "Danny certainly didn't like the Norris brothers."

"And Deputy Burke said they were harmless."

"What does he know?" The glint in Addie's eye returned. "Or maybe Deputy Burke does know something, and he's covering it up."

"Who has the imagination now?" Mason said. "Come on, let's get some video for your mom so she doesn't think you've run off. Then we'll find the family and see if they learned anything new from Deputy Burke. This was your idea, remember?" He held up his phone. "Smile."

"I'm sure Danny knows where her family is staying," Addie said. "I should've pushed for more information."

"You don't stop. We can go back to Sheryl at the Grand Theater. She seemed like the type of person who would know if new people came to town."

Addie smiled. "You're right."

"I'm sorry, I didn't hear you." He hit record on his phone. "What was that you said?"

"You wish! Just try to keep up!" With that, Addie sped off.

# CHAPTER 36

"He was charged with attempted murder? And arson?" Addie's eyes were wide as she read the article Sheryl gave them on Jed Norris. "Oh man! No wonder Danny didn't want to be connected to them."

Addie handed the article to Mason, who scanned it. "This says he was accused but the case was dropped," he said.

"Keep reading," Addie said, pointing. "It says something about evidence that was mishandled by the police. The case was thrown out. He might've had a friend who happened to be a police officer. That'd come in handy."

Sheryl interjected. "It may sound worse than it is. They're small-town boys, but there's a line that doesn't get crossed."

Indy sniffed around Sheryl's office. Addie and Mason had gone right to the Grand Theater after their ATV excursion. Mason found riding the ATVs surprisingly fun, driving over miles of dirt paths without any skid marks to worry about.

"She won't eat my furniture, will she?" Sheryl nodded toward Indy.

"Not unless you rub bacon on it," Mason said, looking up from the article.

"It sounds like Jed Norris has some serious anger issues," Addie said. "I can't imagine what you'd turn into growing up with a dad like that."

"T-Ray and Billy are good boys," Sheryl said. "I've known them all their lives. They learned to stay clear of their Pa's goings-on."

Mason handed the newspaper back to Sheryl. "Then what do you make of us seeing their truck by Kenna? Why wouldn't they have said anything about picking her up?"

"I said they're good kids, not smart ones." Sheryl put the article back in a filing drawer. "I don't know why they didn't say anything."

"Thanks for showing us that," Addie said. "I'm glad you had it."

Sheryl sat in her desk chair and scratched Indy behind the ears. "I feel like the town historian of sorts, so I like to hold onto things."

Mason looked at Addie and then back to Sheryl. "You don't happen to know where Kenna's family is, do you? Deputy Burke said they were in town."

Sheryl chuckled as she pushed herself out of her chair. "I do, honey. They're downstairs."

"What?" Addie looked towards the stairs they had climbed down only a day ago. "Like right now?"

"They've been staying at a friend of mine's since they came to town," Sheryl said. "He's been out of town, and we couldn't see the poor family having to pay for a place, going through what they are."

Sheryl left the office and stood at the top of the stairs, almost like she was guarding the family. "They came over when they heard about T-Ray and Billy. They wanted to know what I knew about them."

"I'm glad Deputy Burke told them," Mason said, turning to Addie. "Maybe he's not a bad guy."

Addie shrugged, like she wasn't sold on that fact quite yet, then she drew in a sharp breath. "You didn't tell Kenna's family how evil Jed is, did you?" she asked Sheryl.

"My dear, the more information they know, the better," Sheryl said.

"Yeah, but..." Addie rubbed her forehead.

Sheryl looked down the stairs and then back at Mason and Addie. Her voice dropped. "Look, they're trying not to get their hopes up.

There've been so many false leads, leads that sound as promising as yours."

The intensity of her stare wasn't lost on Mason. She didn't fully trust them or their story about the pickup truck. The hallway suddenly felt smaller than Mason remembered with the three of them huddled together at the top of the stairs and Indy nudging their legs.

"We'd never do anything to intentionally hurt them," Addie assured Sheryl. "We're trying to help."

"Let me tell you, there are some seriously deranged people who've tormented this poor family," Sheryl said. "Some even blame Kenna's mother. Said a mother who allowed her daughter to get a nose piercing had to know that no good would come to her. Can you believe that?"

Mason remembered seeing the glint of a nose piercing in one of the pictures he had looked up. "How can people be so cruel?" he said.

"Do you think they'd want to talk to us?" Addie looked past Sheryl and down the stairs.

"I'll ask them, but you have to promise to stay up here until I return. Don't come down unless I tell you."

"We promise," Mason said.

"Not sure Indy can make that promise, though." Addie pointed at Indy who had already climbed down a few stairs.

"She might be a pleasant diversion for them," Sheryl said with a chuckle.

Indy raced ahead as Sheryl descended the stairs.

Addie turned to Mason. "What are we going to say to them?"

"I don't know. Maybe tell them what we told Deputy Burke?" Mason said. "They'd at least have the chance to ask us questions about what we saw."

Addie paced the hallway but turned when she heard the jingle of Indy's collar on the stairs. "I thought you'd come back when you realized I wasn't there," she said as the dog raced toward her.

Indy circled her legs and then lay at Addie's feet.

"I think she feels bad for leaving you," Mason joked.

"I forgive you." Addie knelt down and Indy rolled over to expose her belly. As Addie scratched Indy, she asked Mason, "Do you think they'll be mad that we didn't say anything earlier?"

Before Mason could answer, Sheryl returned.

"You can come on down. They want to talk with you. I gave my word that you two aren't crazies." Sheryl stared at each of them in turn. "Don't make me look like a fool."

"No, ma'am," Mason said.

"We won't," Addie added.

"All right, follow me." Sheryl headed down the stairs and led them behind the stage.

Circle light bulbs surrounded a mirror in what must've been a dressing room. Mason saw two women sitting close together on a large brown sofa in the mirror's reflection. He turned to greet them and noticed a gray-haired man standing in the corner next to a younger man.

"Mr. and Mrs. Cook," Sheryl said, holding out a hand to indicate Addie and Mason, "these are the youngsters I told you about."

The older man stepped forward and the two women rose from the sofa.

"I'm very sorry for what you're going through," Addie said.

"So am I," Mason added. "We shared what we know with Deputy Burke, but we wish we'd known sooner."

The young man in the corner snorted.

Mason glanced at him, and he glared back. He looked about Mason's age, but Mason didn't remember reading about Kenna having a younger brother.

One of the women stepped forward, first taking Addie's hand, and then Mason's. "Thank you," she said. "I'm Natalie, Kenna's mother."

Mason remembered the video and her pleas for the return of her daughter. Now, standing in front of Mrs. Cook, Mason saw the worry etched into her face. Her shoulder-length, dark brown hair, which resembled her daughter's, was streaked with gray.

Mr. Cook's voice was deep and controlled. "You saw Kenna get in a pickup with two men?"

Mason nodded. He wanted to say something reassuring, but what could he say? There was nothing reassuring about the fact that Kenna willingly went with two tall, very muscular young men in a pickup that had "Problem with Authority" written across the front.

Addie filled the silence. "We gave Deputy Burke a description of the truck, and he knows who it belongs to. Hopefully he's already talked to them."

"They tell us they are doing everything they can," Mrs. Cook said. "But we still don't have her back."

The other woman came to her side and rubbed her back. "Thanks for telling Deputy Burke what you saw. I'm Emily, Kenna is my niece."

Mason nodded a hello and glanced at the young man who still refused to join them.

"We thought that maybe Deputy Burke would've learned something by now. Hasn't he?" Addie asked.

"Everyone here is slow to get things done. Even you two." The words traveled from the corner of the room and landed on Mason's heart. "She disappeared weeks ago. What took you so long to tell anyone what you saw?"

"Grant, that's enough," Emily hissed. She turned to Mason and Addie. "I apologize for my son. We're all having a difficult time with this."

Indy returned from checking out the room and stood by Addie. The dog seemed to have sensed the hostility in Grant's voice and wanted to protect Addie.

"No, we get it. We didn't pay attention to the news," Mason lied. He'd been hyper-focused on news about Kenna. "When we realized she was missing, and that she might be the woman we saw on the side of the road, we came here in person to make sure they'd listen to us."

Grant paced the back of the room, raking his fingers through his dark hair. He was shorter than Mason, with broad shoulders, like a swimmer's. Pacing as he was, he looked like a caged pitbull ready to fight.

"Tell me," Mrs. Cook asked, leaning forward. "How did she look when you saw her?"

"Honestly, she looked fine," Mason said.

"She did? Really?" Mrs. Cook's eyes seemed to light up with hope.

Up close, the dark circles and bags under her eyes were even more pronounced. She was clinging to Mason's words. The fact that Mason may have been the last person to see Kenna alive, even if it was only in a vision, slammed into his chest. Mason had been the last person to see his neighbor Kenna alive before she died too. Kenna Cook had to be okay. History could not repeat itself in such a horrible manner.

"She did," Mason managed to say. "Addie was driving, and she slowed a little as we passed. Kenna was talking with two guys. They were all smiling. I thought they knew each other, you know, like they were driving together or something."

Mason wanted to believe that he was narrating a scene that had played out live in front of him; it felt like it had. And now, hearing the desperation in Mrs. Cook's voice, Mason realized he'd been fooling himself by thinking he could do something to help.

"Look, we appreciate that you made the effort to talk to the police in person," Mr. Cook said. He put an arm around his wife and pulled her close. "We're still hopeful that Kenna will be found and be okay."

"If I'd known they weren't traveling together..." Mason trailed off. What could he say that wasn't pure fantasy. Even if Mason wished he'd been there to help, he'd been 2,000 miles away when Kenna disappeared.

He couldn't help the present. Mason could only witness the past, and like all the other visions he ever had, he could do nothing to change what had happened.

Mason dropped his eyes and stared at the floor.

# KENNA

*I know the sounds that warn me when he's coming. First, there's the rumble of a loud motor, like a truck or something without a muffler. Then, keys jangle and I know he's unlocking the bolt on the door. And when he pulls the door open; if it's dark outside, the headlights are pointing right at me, blinding me to what is out there. Now that I know what to listen for, I always lunge at the door to push past him. I can't tell if anyone else is there, but I scream as loud as I can. I just need one person to know that I'm here, and I know I'll be saved.*

*Every time I try to run though, he catches me and laughs. He says I can scream as loud as I want cause the coyotes don't mind.*

*I've kicked and hit and scratched him, but it does nothing.*

*My fingers are raw from digging around the door. I don't use the precious flashlight battery to look at my fingers, but I can tell they're in bad shape. I've asked him to give me a fork or spoon to eat with instead of my fingers, but he's not as dumb as I hoped. He knows I'll use it to dig.*

*I have to get out of here. I will not die like this.*

# CHAPTER 37

Indy nudged Addie's leg and let out a single bark. When Addie looked at her, she trotted to the stairs.

"I think she has to go to the bathroom," Addie said. "I guess we'll leave you."

"There's a grass yard out back," Sheryl said. "Come this way; I'll show you."

Mason and Addie followed Sheryl down a hallway at the back of the Grand Theater and up a few stairs to a door under a glowing red EXIT light.

"I'll just prop this open and you can come back in when she's done." Sheryl ignored the "Alarm will sound if opened" sign and pushed the door open, exposing a fenced yard with party lights strung from tree to tree.

"Wow! Addie said. "It's like an oasis back here. I never expected this."

Sheryl looked across the yard and smiled as Indy rolled onto her back and scratched herself in the grass. "We have receptions and whatnot out here. Need to keep it looking special. So make sure you clean up after her if she leaves any gifts."

"Certainly," Mason said.

The fenced-in yard was beautiful—the contrast of all the green against the brown of the mountains. He could envision how magical it would look at night with the lights on.

"You have wedding receptions back here?" Addie asked.

"I'm sure you're not surprised to know that there aren't many venues for big events in these parts. We rent it for wedding receptions, quinceaneras, birthday parties, funerals, you name it. The Grand Theater serves many purposes."

Grant stood in the doorway for a moment before walking into the yard. "My mom told me I had to apologize for my attitude," he said.

"On that note," Sheryl said, "I'll be right inside."

"You don't need to apologize," Addie said.

Indy jumped up and followed Addie as she walked over to Grant.

Indy sniffed Grant's legs, checking him out.

Grant knelt down and scratched behind Indy's ears. "You're beautiful. Aren't you?"

"And she's a pain in the butt," Addie said with a laugh. "She's the reason we're driving in the first place."

Mason shot her a look, suddenly realizing that their story wouldn't add up if they were driving from the Chicago suburbs to Nevada. There would be no way that they were here to drive past Kenna three weeks ago.

"Grant, are you still in high school or are you in college?" Mason said to change the subject.

"High school senior."

"Me too!" Addie said.

Mason could already tell that this line of discussion could only lead to Addie explaining that she was starting a new high school in the fall. Which would turn into her explaining about our road trip. They hadn't discussed their story much beyond what to tell the police about where and when they saw Kenna.

"Where are you from?" Addie asked.

"The Bay Area." Grant picked up a stick and held it out to Indy before tossing it across the yard. Indy dutifully ran to retrieve it, then returned to drop it at Grant's feet.

"The Bay Area? That sounds too much like Green Bay. We're from Chicago." Addie motioned to Mason.

"San Francisco Bay Area," Grant said.

"Do you get to any 49ers games?" Mason asked. Again trying to keep the conversation away from anything too personal.

Grant threw the stick again. "No."

"Mason here is going to college in the fall. He's going to run cross country for the University of Illinois." Addie patted Mason's arm like his mom did when she said the same thing to relatives.

Grant nodded and continued playing with Indy, clearly uninterested in anything about Mason.

"So," Addie started. She looked at Mason and shrugged. "What are you most excited about for senior year?"

"Graduating," Grant said.

Mason returned her shrug.

"How are your aunt and your mom holding up?" Addie went in for the direct question.

"They're barely holding each other up. It sucks. There's nothing we can do now but wait. We walked for miles along that road, for weeks. It's empty."

Mason understood Grant's one-word answers. He was focused on the one thing he needed to be focused on: finding Kenna.

"I can't imagine how hard it is," Addie said.

"She didn't just vanish. And she wouldn't go somewhere without telling us. Our family has always been close. She's my cousin, if you didn't figure that out."

Mason kept his eyes on Indy as the dog again retrieved the stick.

"I know she's in trouble," Grant continued. "And I can't do a single thing to help her."

Indy dropped the stick at Grant's feet, and Mason noticed how dusty and dirty his sneakers were, a testament to the searching they'd done.

"Maybe the info about the truck will help," Addie said. "Maybe they'll find her soon."

"Maybes. That's all we've had." Grant looked between Addie and Mason as if seeing them for the first time. "What are you doing out here if you're from Chicago?"

The question ushered back all of Mason's fears about their incomplete planning. What could they tell him that would maintain the integrity of their story?

"Well, I'm soon to be from out here, sort of," Addie began. "My family is moving to Incline Village. Have you heard of it?"

Mason looked at Addie, wishing she could read his mind.

*Careful.*

Grant snorted. "Yeah. It's where the Bay Area-rich vacation. You're moving there?"

"What? Is that bad?"

"No. Just bougie. Good for you."

"Have you been to Tahoe?" Mason asked.

"Yeah," Grant said. "It's nice. If it weren't so expensive, it'd be a great place to live."

Indy dropped the stick at Addie's feet and lay down, panting heavily.

"I told Kenna she should go there instead of Copper Mountain. I didn't want her to move to Colorado. It's so far away."

Mason understood that feeling. He looked at Addie, who sat in the grass next to Indy.

"She's such a fun cousin; more like a sister," Grant continued. "Our families used to go to Tahoe sometimes in the summer when we were kids."

"Did she have friends in Copper Mountain?" Mason asked, although he already knew that she did.

Grant stiffened as he glared at Mason. "*Does,* not did. Don't talk about her like she's dead."

"I didn't mean anything by that, bro," Mason said. "Just trying to make conversation."

Addie jumped up. "He's not trying to upset you. We're trying to help."

"Yeah. Well, maybe we should go back in," Grant said.

Addie rested a hand on his arm as he turned to go in. "Sure, but, do you have any pointers for me? About Tahoe?"

Mason figured she wanted to get Grant in a better mood before they went in. It wouldn't look good if we returned and Grant was as hostile as when he first came out.

Grant's shoulders seemed to relax under her touch. "The water's cold. Like really cold. All the time."

"What did you do with Kenna when you went there as kids?" Addie asked.

Grant leaned against the fence and talked with Addie about hiking and swimming, about boat rides and bears. This was Addie's talent, making people feel comfortable. She listened and smiled. Mason wanted to be jealous of all the attention she was giving Grant, but he couldn't be, not really. It was who she was. Open and caring. And Mason had been on the receiving end of that for much of his life.

Sheryl stuck her head through the door. "There's news from Burke."

Grant walked away from Addie and squeezed past Sheryl before she had a chance to move out of the way.

"It's good, but not great," Sheryl said to Mason and Addie, as she watched Grant race back to his family. "I hope I didn't give that boy false hope."

"What is it?" Addie asked.

Sheryl joined them outside. "Burke talked to the Norris boys, and they said they helped her."

"Helped her do what? Disappear?" Addie scoffed.

"They said they brought her to a mechanic. They aren't sure who, but they're going to take Burke there."

Mason's heart fell. That wasn't news. That was buying time.

"When?" Addie insisted. "When are they taking Deputy Burke to this mysterious mechanic? I thought everyone in town knew everybody. How could they drop her off at a mechanic they don't know?"

"It does sound strange," Sheryl agreed.

"Are they taking Deputy Burke there right now?" Mason asked.

"Burke's going to meet the boys at seven o'clock, when they get back in town. They've been out of town since the day they helped her, they said. So they didn't know she was missing."

"What's Deputy Burke thinking, waiting like this?" Mason wondered.

They heard Grant yell, "Are you kidding me?" Apparently, he had learned what Mason and Addie did.

"I think we should let them be," Addie said. "Will you give them our best? We've intruded on them enough today."

Sheryl nodded. "There's still hope. Burke'll go to the mechanic and find out what happened. I know it."

"I hope so," Mason said. "Will you let us know?"

"Of course, dear."

Addie left her phone number, and Sheryl showed them out through the side gate.

When they were back in the Jeep, Mason dropped his head into his hands. He thought his vision would lead to answers, but it only led to more disappointment.

"I give up," he mumbled.

"No, you don't," Addie said, putting the Jeep in reverse. "We're finding Deputy Burke."

*Golden Valley News*
Fallon, Nevada

## Family Increases Reward as Hope of Finding Missing Calif. Woman Alive Dwindles

The family of Kenna Cook, 24, the Daly City, Calif., woman who was last heard from on May 22, has increased the reward to $50,000 for any information that leads to her safe return.

Authorities believe that Cook's gold Honda Accord broke down after driving through Fallon on her way to Colorado, and she may have left the vehicle to find assistance. Cell phone and credit card records show no new activity since her disappearance.

Anna Herneda, long-time resident of Valterra and member of the search party, speculates Cook may have left the road and encountered a venomous snake or mountain lion. Nevada is home to five different species of rattlesnake and some 3,000 mountain lions.

Cook was reported missing by her family on May 23. The stretch of desert along Route 50 is vast, and without water, chances of survival are minimal.

Contact the Sterling County Sheriff if you have any information.

# CHAPTER 38

The sun was still high on the horizon, but Mason knew nightfall wouldn't be long. He checked his phone. Five-thirty P.M. The day seemed to have melted away. Addie gripped the Jeep's steering wheel with both hands and sat erect in her seat, no foot perched casually on the seat.

"What's your plan?" Mason asked.

"I told you. Find Burke."

The town passed by, and Mason realized she wasn't headed toward the police station.

"Where do you plan to find him?" he asked.

"Duh. Where do you think?"

"Then you might want to turn around." He pointed at the "Thanks for Visiting Valterra" sign they were about to pass. "That's a literal sign that you are headed out of town."

Addie slammed on the brakes and skidded to a stop.

"Watch it!" Mason said. "Now I have to relive this moment when we drive over it."

Addie glared at Mason. They locked eyes for a second, then burst into laughter. The sheer absurdity of the idea that Mason would have to relive that moment, a moment of shared annoyance, gave them a much-needed emotional release.

"Sorry." Addie made a U-turn and headed back through town. "I think I'm directionally challenged."

"And hostility-driven."

"Can I add that to my college application?" Addie asked. "And will you write a letter of recommendation for me?"

"The college process. I would gladly never live through that part of senior year again."

"Careful. You're treading in sensitive waters." As if to punctuate that sentence, Addie slammed on the brakes again.

"Again?" Mason hissed, putting out a hand to brace himself on the dash.

Addie hushed him with her upraised hand and pulled into a parking lot.

"Who is going to hear us?"

Addie slid down in her seat to hide and motioned for Mason to do the same.

"You pulled into a parking lot for an abandoned building," Mason whispered, though he wasn't sure why. "We're the only vehicle around. Not a good cover."

"Crap. I suck at this." She sat up and drove out of the lot. She found a street that looked down on the main road, and parked before hopping out.

"Hey," Mason called after her. "What are you doing? Indy'll lose it if you run off. And so will I."

Addie stopped and looked back at him. "Sorry. There's a police car down there. At the ATV place we were at. I want to check it out."

"Stop," Mason said, catching up to Addie and grabbing her arm. "First, you said you wanted to talk to Deputy Burke. Now you want to eavesdrop on a police officer where we rented ATVs? Do I need to worry about you?"

"We need to hurry. I want to hear what they're talking about."

"But why?"

Addie pulled free from Mason and pointed. "It's a garage. Danny's a mechanic, remember."

"You think he did something to Kenna?" Mason found it hard to believe that the wiry kid who squirmed under Addie's questioning was capable of something so sinister.

"It's quite a coincidence that the police show up at the garage after we learn that Kenna was dropped off at a mechanic. And you saw how uncomfortable he was when I asked about the Norris brothers. If we don't overhear anything about Kenna, we'll find Deputy Burke." Addie turned to go down the hill to the garage.

"Stop. I don't want to call your folks for bail money when you get arrested for obstructing the police."

"You wouldn't bail me out?" Addie batted her eyes at him.

"Let's not find out," Mason said. "You stay here and keep Indy quiet. And I'll go down there and see what's going on."

"But—"

"I'll be back in a flash."

Mason sprang down the hill before Addie could protest. He climbed over the chain-link fence at the back of the property and ducked behind an ATV. He waited, listening to see if anyone heard or saw him. No one came out or yelled at him, so he crept closer to the building. He wished it were dark so he'd be hidden but, at least in the light, he could avoid tripping on the abandoned ATV parts strewn around the yard. He moved from one object to another, trying to hide himself, like a kid pretending to be James Bond. When he got close to the building, he heard voices. He squatted under the open window and focused on breathing slowly so he could hear what was being said.

"It sounds bad. Just tell me what you know. I can help."

It sounded like Deputy Burke's voice, but Mason couldn't be sure. The other voice didn't sound like Danny.

Mason waited, squatting down further, afraid his head was visible.

"I don't know anything, Stan. And I don't appreciate what you're implying."

Stan? Mason tried to remember Burke's first name. Was it Stan?

"I'm not implying anything, Guy. But Travis Ray said..."

"Was his dad holding a gun to his head? You don't know, do you? Of course not. What were you thinking questioning them over the phone? Of course Jed would make his boys feed you information so you didn't look at him. And here you are, questioning me instead of him."

It was definitely Deputy Burke, and did he say Guy? Danny said Guy owned the place. Mason fought his urge to stand up and peek through the window. He wanted to get a look at the man Deputy Burke was talking to. Was Guy the mechanic that the Norris brothers brought Kenna to?

"You know Jed's in jail in Ely, right?" Deputy Burke challenged.

"Bail was posted this afternoon," Guy said. "Don't you listen to your radio? How incompetent do you have to be to miss that? I should run for sheriff next term just so I can fire you."

"Jed was questioned early on," Deputy Burke retorted. "He wasn't in town when the woman disappeared."

"But his boys sure were," Guy said. "Bet they didn't tell you that, did they? Some random witness did. Now Jed's boys suddenly decide to tell you that they brought the missing woman to me? And you believe them?"

Mason heard a loud clatter. He could only imagine Guy's hand slamming down on the desk.

"I'm just saying I have to follow up on their claim. If it's false..."

"If?" Guy bellowed. "Get out!"

"You know I can get a warrant."

"Then get one. You need to talk to Jed, not me!"

Mason heard the bells on the front door chime, but he didn't move, even after he heard Deputy Burke drive off. He didn't know what Guy would do, and with the sun still bright, Mason couldn't risk being seen. He heard a door slam nearby and held his breath.

"What an idiot!" The yell was punctuated by something getting kicked across the yard and a string of swear words. "I'm going to make him pay. How dare he, after all this time."

Mason peeked out from behind the ATV as a man, built like a linebacker with dirty blond hair, stomped through the yard and threw something into the bed of his silver pickup truck.

Mason flinched at the clamor of metal hitting metal.

The truck left a spray of dirt and dust in its wake as the man drove off.

Mason climbed back over the fence and scampered up the hill to the Jeep.

Addie and Indy were gone.

"Addie," he called. No response. "Indy?"

He walked around the Jeep in disbelief, but they were nowhere.

Then Indy came panting up the hill from where Mason had come. Addie's voice followed behind her.

"Service is so slow..." Addie looked at her phone as she finished climbing the hill, her arm raised in the air as if the additional two feet might improve her internet service. She looked at her phone. "Got it! Let's go."

"What are you talking about? Where were you?" Mason asked.

"Guy. I Googled where he lives. Let's check out his place. I heard everything."

"You were down there? I didn't see you." Mason looked down the hill toward the garage.

"I was near the front. What?" Addie smiled at him. "Why do you look surprised? Did you really think I wasn't going to go down there?"

Mason shook his head in disbelief. "I guess I should've known better. Well, if you heard all that, then you know that it's the Norris family that needs to be checked. Not Guy. It sounds like the dad is trying to frame him."

"Maybe. But Guy was super pissed. Like maybe he was really angry at Travis Ray but taking it out on Deputy Burke." Addie opened the back door of the Jeep, and Indy jumped in. "Good girl!"

"Didn't you hear Guy when he was leaving?" Mason asked. "It was an impressive, albeit highly offensive, string of insults directed at Deputy Burke."

"How do you know he wasn't cursing out Travis Ray for talking?" Addie stared at Mason and shrugged. "Just saying."

Mason ran the rant through his mind. He couldn't tell. There wasn't anything specifically referencing Deputy Burke. But then, there wasn't anything referencing Travis Ray, either.

"What do you hope to accomplish by going to his place?" Mason said. "If he's responsible for whatever might have happened to Kenna, what are we going to do?"

Addie sat in the driver's seat, engine running. "I don't know," she said. "But Deputy Burke isn't going to check him out. I heard him on his radio. He's stopping at the station before going to talk with Jed."

Mason stood by the Jeep, knowing that the moment he got in, she would drive to Guy's house. "What if Guy's headed home? He's in no mood to talk to strangers."

"My guess is that he's going to pay Travis Ray a visit." Addie banged her hand on the steering wheel. "Can we go now?"

"You know, I miss the girl who was afraid of corn in Nebraska," Mason said, climbing in the passenger seat.

# CHAPTER 39

They stopped for gas, and drove back toward Ely, watching for Byrne Mountain Road.

"Are you sure this is the right address?" Mason asked. "We don't even know his last name."

"Guy Smith. I looked that up, too. He owns the garage." Addie glanced at Mason. "Don't look at me like that. It's public information. And Danny told us too. As the owner of a garage, he's probably a mechanic. Coincidence?"

"Danny's a mechanic," Mason said. "I think there are a lot of mechanics around here."

"Deputy Burke must have lied to the Cooks," Addie said. "He said the Norris brothers couldn't remember who the mechanic was. If that's true, then why did he talk to Guy?"

"I figured the Norris brothers were trying to buy extra time with that comment," Mason said. "Instead, it was Deputy Burke who was trying to buy time? Something is definitely going on. We should go to the Cooks, instead of Guy's house. Or Sheryl. Maybe she'd know what's up."

Mason didn't have bars on his phone.

"I thought about that," Addie said. "But what if Guy is going to try to hide evidence now that he's a suspect? I think we need to keep an eye on him."

"I think you watch too many crime shows. Did you have a chance to send the ATV video to your mom?" Mason asked. "I'm sure she's wondering what you're up to."

"Yeah, and some pics," Addie said. "She texted back that she was glad to see we were wearing helmets. What a mom-thing to say. I told her to share the pics with your mom too. I told her we'd be in Incline tomorrow afternoon."

"Tomorrow? She's fine with a whole extra night?" Mason was surprised and thrilled with the idea.

"I told her we were having fun getting to know Nevada." Addie smiled. "So now we have plenty of time to check out Guy."

"Great. That's exactly what I want to do with our extra time." Mason looked at his phone again. "As soon as we have service, we should call Sheryl."

"Let's see what we find first," Addie said. "I don't want to get them more upset than they already are."

"This has been quite a day," Mason said. "It feels like years ago when we woke up and saw the wild horses."

Addie smiled. "That was an amazing way to wake up."

He loved her smile and the messy bun on her head, the strands of loose hair whipping in the wind. Even covered in dust and windblown, Addie made his heart race.

Mason forced himself to focus on the picture of the map on his phone. "It should be up here a little ways, on the right."

"What's with all these signs?" Addie pointed at a road sign.

Mason squinted at the approaching sign, a picture of an elk or a deer with antlers. Light shined through the image. "Bullet holes."

"What?" Addie twisted to see it as they passed. "A lot of the signs are like that, with holes in them."

"Target practice," Mason said.

"They shoot the signs? When they're driving?"

"I'm guessing, but probably," he said.

"Where the heck are we?" Addie said with a sigh. "Is that supposed to be fun?"

"I'm guessing it's about as much fun as knocking mailboxes off their posts," Mason said. "Target practice, batting practice—what's the difference?"

"I guess you had a lot of reasons not to like him, huh?"

"You figured out some of them on your own," Mason said. "Not that I'm happy about that."

"Well, good riddance," Addie said.

Several dust tornadoes danced along the ground in the distance, and Mason pointed. "At least you won't have to worry about those in Tahoe. I looked it up. The place is beautiful."

"No Tahoe-nadoes?" she joked.

"Please," Mason said, breaking into a smile.

"I love that you Googled Tahoe. That's so cute."

"I needed to see where my neighbor was going. I wanted to know if I should visit you."

"And?"

"Are you kidding? I would visit you, even if you lived in Valterra. But Tahoe is much better."

"Don't you mean Tahoe-geddon?" Addie said.

"No, please don't," Mason pleaded.

"Hey, that sign ... Byrne Mountain Road is up ahead." Addie slowed the Jeep and pointed to the right. "There's our mountain."

She slowed even more as they approached the gravel road, which seemed to lead to nothing.

Yaw marks layered the turn, and Mason focused as they drove over them. Multiple visions flooded his mind. "We've got the right place. I know that pickup."

"So freaky," Addie said. "I don't think I'll ever get used to that."

"You wouldn't," he assured her.

The Jeep bounced along the road, hitting holes and ruts where the gravel wore thin. Indy braced herself to stop from falling into the front seat.

"It's kind of creepy, being way out here," Addie said. "But this road must lead to somewhere."

"That's totally an inspirational poster, by the way," Mason said.

"I always wanted to take the Jeep off-roading. Do you think this counts?"

"Technically, you're still on a road, I think." Mason reached over to pet a whining Indy. "You're okay."

They climbed in elevation, and the air cooled slightly.

"It should be up there." Mason pointed toward a turnoff, and Addie stopped the Jeep. Mason's eyes traced the two ruts as they curved left around the back of the mountain.

Addie turned. "Here we go."

Half-buried tires painted white read "KEEP OUT" along the drive. "Yeah, he'll be happy to see us," Mason said. "Especially with how pissed he was when he left. This is not one of your better ideas."

Addie drove slowly along the road, and Mason prayed that Guy's truck wasn't there. Around the last turn, they came upon what looked like an extra-wide trailer across from an even larger, light-gray metal garage. No pickup truck.

Mason let out the breath he was holding. "Thank God."

"His truck could be in that garage." Addie pointed.

Mason was annoyed at how easily he had let his guard down. "Look, we could be in way over our heads."

Addie parked between the two buildings. "I'll go up and knock, just to make sure no one is home. If someone is, I'll pretend like I have the wrong house or something."

"You're not going up there alone." Mason followed her to the door. "Who will we say we're looking for if someone does answer?"

"A cousin or something who moved out this way." Addie knocked.

Indy whined from the Jeep as they waited silently at the door. No one answered.

"I'll try." Mason banged on the door.

Addie stood on her tiptoes and peered in the small diamond-shaped window in the door. "I don't see anyone." She walked to the side of the trailer and looked in the other windows.

"What are you? A professional snoop?"

A single window sat high on the backside of the trailer, too high for Addie. "You're tall," she said. "Come look. Tell me what you see."

Mason stood on his tiptoes and cupped his hands over his eyes. "I can only see the ceiling, maybe the top of a headboard."

Addie moved an upturned crate toward him. "Stand on this."

"I think the sun has gotten to you," Mason said, looking down at the crate. "This has to be illegal, even in Nevada. We should go back to the Grand Theater and tell Sheryl what we know."

"Just look!" Addie said.

Mason huffed but climbed on the crate, hoping it would support his weight. "It's a bedroom," he said. "I was right. That's the headboard."

"What else do you see?"

"Nothing. Whoever lives here's a slob. The bed's unmade, and clothes are everywhere." Mason turned to step off the crate but Addie pushed him back on.

"Men's clothes? Women's? Look."

"I don't know what that'll tell us." But Mason looked through the window again. "It looks like all men's clothes. Dude really needs to do some laundry."

"Just hope your college roommate doesn't live like that," Addie said. "I didn't know you were such a neat freak."

They walked to the garage and checked the doors since there were no windows.

"These look like ATV tracks." Mason pointed to the ground at the back of the garage. "Looks like they head out into the mountains."

"I wish we could see inside." Addie tried the doors again, but they were all locked.

They walked back to the Jeep.

"Look, it's almost eight o'clock," Mason said. "Who knows when he'll be back, and the sun is setting. We need to go back to town."

Addie looked at the sky, as if noticing the pink cotton candy clouds that brightened the darkening sky for the first time. "Wow. How about we go a little higher up on the mountain and watch the sunset, and then we can go back. Maybe we'll even be able to get some cell service further up."

Mason didn't think they'd get service but figured it wouldn't hurt to try. Plus, he liked the idea of watching the sunset with Addie on their last evening together.

"That sounds like the best idea you've had all day," he said.

Mason thought about Deputy Burke, hopefully going to see the Norris boys. Maybe everything will work out. He got in the Jeep, and Addie followed Byrne Mountain Road higher.

"There is seriously nothing up here," she said. "I thought pine trees grew in the mountains."

"They do in Tahoe," Mason said. "This is the desert."

They found a flat area near some boulders and pulled over. Route 50 in the distance was true to its name. The Loneliest Road was empty.

"If he came home, do you think he'd see us up here?" Addie asked.

"We probably blend in."

"My Jeep is white. What part of 'blend in' do you think that is?"

"It was white in Chicago," Mason said. "Now, it's beige. Relax. Plus, he wouldn't know to look for us, and it's getting dark."

Mason walked to the edge and looked down toward Guy's house. He couldn't see much except part of the garage. He held up his phone. Still no service.

"Help me with this, will you?" Addie was spreading a sleeping bag out on the ground.

"That better be yours," he joked. "What's your plan for this?"

"Sit and watch the sunset. Duh. Hurry, before we miss it."

They spread out the sleeping bag, and Addie grabbed a few waters from the cooler. "Here," she said, tossing one to Mason. She poured another into Indy's bowl.

Addie sat next to Mason and kicked her legs out, resting back on her hands. "Now this is beautiful." The sky stretched out in front of them. Orange burned behind the pink clouds and rested on a layer of deep blue.

"You know, I never imagined my visions would lead to any of this."

"It's all been totally surreal and unexpected," Addie agreed.

"In a good way? Or a bad way?" Mason looked at Addie, wondering if the shock of everything was wearing off and making her rethink her opinion of him and his visions.

"Please. The drive, hanging out with you, that's been the best part.

But the rest is almost too much to take in." Addie leaned back on the sleeping bag. "Who would've thought that you would have information about a missing woman because of some psychic power of yours?"

"When you put it like that," Mason said, laying his head back and gazing at the sky, "it definitely sounds surreal."

The pinks and yellows and oranges melded together and slowly faded into the indigo sky.

Addie turned to him, her face close to his. "You're going to miss it if you keep waiting."

Mason looked at her. "What do you mean? Miss what?"

"Miss the chance to kiss me during the sunset."

Mason tried to speak, but couldn't form words.

Addie smiled. "About four different times on this trip, I thought you were going to kiss me. But you never did. Why?"

Mason could only smile back. "Was I that obvious?"

"Worse than you think," Addie said, laughing. "Well? The sun's almost gone."

# CHAPTER 40

Mason tucked the loose strands of hair behind Addie's ear and trailed his fingers down her cheek to her chin. He leaned in and kissed her.

He started tentatively, and then pulled back, gazing into her eyes. "Are you sure?"

In answer, Addie kissed him. Her lips, slightly rough from being chapped, were warm against his, and when her lips parted, goosebumps raced down his arms.

Addie ran her fingers through Mason's hair and trailed her hand down his back, pulling him to her. Her lips tasted like salt and spearmint lip balm, and he drank them in. He ran his hand along her back, and she kissed his ear.

Mason leaned back to look at her. "I've wanted to kiss you for as long as I can remember." He brushed the hair from Addie's eyes.

She smiled. "Did you know that one of your eyes has green in it?"

"And yours are definitely hazel."

"That's what I like to hear." She kissed him, but Indy stuck her nose between their faces and nudged Addie.

"It's okay, girl." Addie tried to push Indy away, but she wiggled her way in between them.

"What? Are you a chaperone?" Mason teased. Indy sat with her tongue out, breathing heavily into Mason's face.

"Go on, Indy," Addie said.

Mason lightly brushed Addie's cheeks with his fingertips and ran his thumb over her collar bone. "I had no clue you liked me."

"Neither did I, not really, until this trip." She traced circles on his back. "Being with you made me realize that I've liked you for a while. I just didn't admit it to myself. Plus, I thought you liked Sophie."

Mason grazed his lips over her ear and whispered, "I've only liked you."

"I was prepared to make the first move before we got to my parents if you didn't," Addie said. "Looks like I had to after all." She ran her fingers through his hair and kissed him.

Their tongues met briefly before Indy sneezed on Mason.

"What was that for?" Mason asked, wiping his neck.

"That's her defiant-sneeze." Addie sat up to pet Indy. "She's mad at you. She thinks you're attacking me. Don't you, girl?"

"Come here, Indy." Mason scratched both her ears and kissed the top of her head. "You love me, remember? I take you on runs."

"It's getting pretty dark." Addie looked around. "We should go."

Mason pointed up at the sky. "First star. Make a wish."

"Star light, star bright, first star I see tonight. I wish I may, I wish I might..."

"...have this wish I wish tonight," Mason finished. "Don't tell me what you wished for. It might not come true."

Addie rested her head on Mason's shoulder, and he held her. So much of what he wished for was already in his arms.

Headlights pulled off the highway. Addie pulled away and pointed. In the dim light, they saw a dust trail behind a pickup.

"Is it him?" she asked.

Mason looked down to where the house was. Headlights reflected off the garage. "Looks like it."

"Maybe we should creep down there a little closer and see if he does anything."

"I think we should drive back, like we planned. We can touch base with Sheryl to see what Deputy Burke found out."

Addie nodded and wrapped her arms around Mason. "That would be sensible."

"Why does that sound like you're about to drop a big 'but'?"

The temperature had dropped with the sun, and Addie shivered in his arms.

"I'll grab you a sweatshirt, if you promise not to run down there," Mason said.

"We should put the top on the Jeep," she suggested.

"Good idea." Mason pulled his "U of I XC" sweatshirt from his backpack and handed it to Addie.

"Does this mean we're going steady?" she asked as she pulled it on.

Mason liked the idea. "It looks good on you." He kissed her again before latching the top on the Jeep.

Addie piled the sleeping bag and water bottles into the Jeep and then made Indy jump in. She closed the back door and turned to Mason. "Ok. We'll climb down a bit, enough so we can at least see his trailer. Maybe we'll hear him cursing out someone again, and that'll give us a clue about what's going on."

Mason looked toward Guy's place. "There's nothing we can do here."

"But we can't leave now. He'll hear us drive past. We have to wait a little, at least until he's too engrossed in something to notice us or care."

Mason couldn't argue with her logic, even if he didn't like the thought of spying on a potentially dangerous man in the middle of nowhere without cell service. "If he's involved in Kenna's disappearance, I don't want you to get anywhere near him."

"I won't," Addie said. "Just going to get a little closer."

Addie headed down the mountain.

Mason could only follow her toward the yellow glow that came from inside the trailer where the shades were open.

Addie sat on a rock. "We'll wait here."

"Umm. Couldn't you at least find two rocks together?" He pretended to look for another rock.

"Shhh. Come here." Addie scooted over on her rock.

"I have a better idea," he whispered. He helped her up, sat down, and pulled her onto his lap. "We can keep each other warm."

She scooched back and leaned into him. "How's that?"

"Don't wiggle so much. You're killing me." He buried his head in her neck and kissed her hair.

"I'm trying to get comfortable." Addie wiggled a little more to tease him and settled on his lap, looking down toward the house. "What do you think he's doing?"

"Who knows. Making dinner. Drinking beer. Farting."

"Gross." She shifted to look at Mason. "Thanks for telling me about Kenna and your visions. You could've done nothing and kept it all to yourself."

"Trust me. I contemplated that." He wondered what would've happened between him and Addie if he didn't tell her. And if something did start between them, could it ever be an honest relationship if she didn't know about his visions? "I trusted that you'd understand somehow. Kenna's disappearance was too real to ignore."

"You're one of the good ones, Mason." She leaned her head on his shoulder. "What would I do without you?"

He lifted her chin. "You don't have to worry about that. I'm here for you no matter where you are." Mason traced his thumb along her lower lip, and she kissed it. Tingles electrified the hairs on his neck.

He drew her into a tight embrace and whispered, "I wish we were back on the sleeping bag. This rock is killing my butt."

She giggled into his neck.

Then a door slammed.

# KENNA

*I've taken apart the little flashlight and unwound the coil for the battery. Positive or negative side, I don't know. I just know that the edge of the wire is sharp. I'm using it to pick at the mattress seam. If I can rip open the mattress, I can get at one of the metal springs. I know I can hurt him with one of those. He'd never expect it.*

*I fantasize about stabbing him in the eye or in the neck.*

*The thought of causing him pain erases the pain in my fingers. If I can rip open this mattress enough to get a spring. I don't even care that I've ruined the flashlight. The batteries were going to die anyway, and I definitely don't want to see this cave he keeps me in like an animal.*

*I'm going to make him pay for what he's done to me.*

*I just need to rip open this seam. I've propped the mattress against the wall to pick at the underside with the wire. If he comes, I can easily drop the mattress down and hide my progress.*

*I wish my fingers weren't so swollen. The wire is so small, and I keep dropping it. Then I have to feel around in the dirt until I find it. I only need a little opening though, then I can tear the mattress open.*

*I sit and pick at the seam and listen for the sound of a motor.*

# CHAPTER 41

Mason and Addie looked toward Guy's trailer.

"He's leaving." Addie tied her hair back and squinted down the mountain. A man's silhouette pulled open the door to the garage and disappeared.

They stood, waiting, as crickets thrummed around them.

Light flooded the ground behind the garage as one of the doors rolled up. Then the roar of an engine broke the silence. Guy, on an ATV, headed out toward the mountain.

"Oh no." Mason tracked the headlights that seemed to head in their direction. Then they curved right and headed away, into the darkness.

"Remember the trail we saw behind the garage? He must be on that." As he drove out of sight, Addie ran after him, and Mason ran after her.

"What are you doing?" he yelled, no longer afraid of Guy hearing them. "We need to go back. This is a perfect time for us to drive off without being seen."

"We have to find out where he's going. This doesn't seem like a good time for a joy ride." She stumbled over rocks in the darkness but continued chasing the sound of the ATV.

Mason cursed the fact that the sliver of moon had disappeared.

Where was it when they needed it? The sky was a deep navy, and the shadow of the mountain covered them. The roar of the ATV echoed over the mountain and, in the distance, the glimmer of Guy's headlights raced away. Mason turned his phone's flashlight on, hoping to avoid some of the rocks and brambles.

"This is nuts," he said after again stubbing a toe on a rock. "Why did I switch out of my running shoes? Slides are not made for this."

"Who knew he'd go for an ATV ride at night?" Addie said, still racing ahead.

"And who knew we'd chase him? How do you think this will end?"

Addie slowed. Mason thought his question might have landed as he intended. That, or she was running out of breath.

"I have no clue," she said, walking with her hands on her hips, breathing hard. "I hope you know how to get back."

"He's probably out for a late-night ride after having a few after-work beers," Mason said. He feared that at any moment, Guy would head back home and Addie and Mason would be caught in his headlights like deer, frozen.

"You're the Eagle Scout. Can't you follow the stars or something?"

"You know how good I am with stars. And there's only one I'm following right now—you."

"Aren't you sweet?" Addie reached out and took his hand, just in time for him to catch her when she stumbled over a rock. As they rounded a large boulder, they saw the ATV stopped in the distance, with its headlights still on.

Mason killed his flashlight, and they tucked back behind the boulder.

"Is he peeing?" Addie whispered.

Guy stood in the light of the ATV headlights, facing what looked to be the sheared wall of the mountain.

"That's gross," Addie said.

"Why would he come all the way out here to pee?" Mason whispered. "I'm sure he has running water."

Addie inched a little closer.

"Addie," Mason said in the loudest whisper he dared, but she didn't acknowledge him. He had no choice but to follow her.

The ATV motor still growled loudly and, as they got closer, Mason caught the glint of metal in Guy's hands. Keys. What does he need keys for on the side of a mountain? Mason looked at Addie and motioned that he was unlocking something, but Addie wasn't looking at Mason. She had her phone up, recording.

Mason prayed that Guy couldn't see beyond the glare of the headlights to notice them hiding in the darkness. Whatever Guy was unlocking gave way.

Screams filled the air.

Addie gasped and dropped the phone. Guy turned to face them, his face lit by the ATV headlights. Mason didn't know if Guy could've heard them over the sound of the woman screaming or the idling ATV, but they froze. Guy stood still, searching the darkness, and behind him, in the oversized shadow he created, a woman's arms reached for the air, fighting to get past Guy. Her screaming was continuous; her voice so hoarse that Mason could tell she'd been screaming forever.

Mason slowly reached down and picked up Addie's phone which had tumbled by his feet. It was still recording. He pointed it at Guy and prayed again that Guy couldn't see them. Addie was on her knees, hands covering her face. Guy stayed still, intently watching the darkness.

Abruptly he turned, pushed the woman back, ducked his head, and closed the door, muffling the woman's screams. The ATV continued to idle with its headlights shining on the small door in the mountainside.

"We need to go!" Mason whispered, grabbing Addie by the arm and pulling her. "Now!"

"We can't." Addie's voice trembled, matching the shaking of her body. "Oh my god. He's going to hurt her."

"He already has." Mason didn't know what had happened, but he knew he needed to get Addie out of there. Right now. "We need to go! We'll go right to the police. They can save her."

Mason pulled Addie to her feet, held onto her arm and ran, dragging her with him.

Addie stumbled to her knees. "We can't leave her. We can't," she whimpered.

"We have to. Hurry! He left that ATV running. He doesn't plan on being in there long." Mason put his arms under Addie's shoulders and hoisted her up. One of his slides slipped off his foot as he tugged her forward, but he didn't bother to search for it. He could run in his sock. "Come on. We have to get to the police."

"What if he kills her?" Addie said. They stumbled over rocks, and Addie fell again. "Oh my God! Did you see her trying to get out?"

Mason pulled Addie up and grasped her by the shoulders. No reminiscence of times past flooded his mind now. He was solely focused on getting Addie out of there and to safety.

"Addie, I need you to get to the Jeep," he said. "That woman trapped in there needs you to get to the Jeep. We need to get to the police, and they need to save her. Come on!"

Mason kept his arm around Addie's waist as he tried to remember the way they had come. It had gotten even darker, but he didn't dare turn on his phone's flashlight. They stumbled forward, putting space between themselves and the lights of the ATV.

In the distance, Mason heard Indy bark.

*Thank God for Indy.*

They scrambled toward the sound.

# Chapter 42

Mason drove fast, ignoring the now-familiar skid marks they passed. Addie sat silently next to him, tears streaming down her face.

"Where's my phone?" she asked abruptly.

He had forgotten about her phone and rummaged in his pockets. "Here."

She found the video, and the woman's screams filled the Jeep.

"Turn it off," Mason snapped.

Addie muted the sound and replayed the video, pausing and zooming in.

"Don't," he said. "Do you have any bars? We need to call the police. They'll help her."

"There's no service." She typed at her phone and then pounded on it. "Message failure. I can't even text."

"We'll get service when we're closer to town," Mason said. "Keep trying."

"I can't believe we left her," Addie said. "Look, the light from the ATV shines right on her." She zoomed in on the woman's face.

Mason hated to ask, but he couldn't help it. "Can you tell if it's Kenna?"

"It's too pixelated. Oh my god, I can't believe we left her," she repeated.

"We had to. It's the only way to help her. Check your bars."

"I am! Drive faster!" Addie zoomed on a stilled frame of the video and held the phone close to her face.

"Stop looking at it, please," Mason said, his tone almost a plea. "Just focus on contacting someone."

Addie closed the video, and her phone returned to the home screen, to her smiling selfie with Becca, Grace, and Sophie. "This can't be real."

Mason reached over and squeezed Addie's leg. "It's going to be okay." He wanted to believe that, too, but even he wasn't convinced.

"I've got bars!" Addie yelled.

"Call the police. Dial 911."

Addie dialed and put the phone on speaker. As it rang, she said, "What are they going to do? Wait until tomorrow to talk to Guy?"

"911, what's your emergency?"

"A woman is in danger on Byrne Mountain. Guy Smith has her—"

"Hello? 911, what's your emergency?"

"Can you hear me?" Addie yelled. "Hello?"

A dial tone filled the air.

"Are you kidding? 911 hung up on me."

"Try again." Mason sped toward town, hoping it wouldn't be too late.

When he swerved into the station, he didn't bother finding a parking spot. He stopped in front of the main doors, and they both jumped out, leaving Indy to bark after them. The front desk officer yelled after them as they burst into Deputy Burke's office. Addie thrust her phone at him as he stood.

"Guy's trapped a woman. You have to save her," Addie said, out of breath.

"Hold up. What's going on?" Deputy Burke waved off the other cop, who had followed them, and took Addie's phone, which had gone black. "I thought you kids had left town by now."

"There's a video." Mason pointed to the phone. "A woman..."

"She's trapped. Guy has her…" Addie grabbed the phone back and unlocked it.

Deputy Burke put on his reading glasses and took the phone as Addie pressed play.

The woman's screams filled the air. Addie collapsed in a chair, and Mason fought the urge to vomit. They had been right there, with Guy staring into the darkness trying to see them.

"Lieutenant Wallace?" Deputy Burke yelled. "Come here!" He didn't wait for the lieutenant but headed down the hall. He must've hit play again because the woman's screams trailed after him.

Deputy Burke turned the phone to a gray-haired police officer as he came out of his office. The man hunched over the phone.

*Wallace. Kat Wallace's dad?*

"That son of a b—" Lieutenant Wallace looked up at Deputy Burke then back down at the video. Guy Smith was clearly visible in the lights of his own ATV. "It can't be."

Lieutenant Wallace slumped into a chair and replayed the video.

"You've got to do something," Addie yelled, immediately at his side. "Now!"

"Where'd you get this?" Lieutenant Wallace asked her.

"We were there, behind his house. We took the video tonight," Mason said.

"If this is some kind of joke…" Lieutenant Wallace's eyes, laden with bags, seemed to implore Addie to tell him that what he just saw was not true.

"Joke? What is wrong with you?" Addie spun from one police officer to the other. "Go save her!"

"To think," Deputy Burke said to Lieutenant Wallace. "We've known him for years."

"Can you reminisce some other day?" Addie demanded.

Mason understood what had happened in those years. The words of Danny came back to him:

*"No one ever heard from her."*

Maybe Kat Wallace hadn't run off after all. Was the woman they discovered Lieutenant Wallace's daughter, trapped for ten years in that mountain? Or Kenna Cook?

Lieutenant Wallace and Deputy Burke exchanged a long look, and Deputy Burke nodded slightly.

Lieutenant Wallace got up and ran out. His heavy movements from moments ago were fueled with a fire only anger could produce.

Deputy Burke reached for his keys and said to Addie and Mason. "Stay here."

He ran after Lieutenant Wallace, who was probably already speeding toward Byrne Mountain.

# CHAPTER 43

Addie called Sheryl as soon as Deputy Burke and Lieutenant Wallace left, and without pausing to see the video, the Cook family and Sheryl followed Mason and Addie to Byrne Mountain.

Mason looked at Addie, who sat frozen in the passenger seat with her knees tucked up to her chest.

"Are you okay?" he asked.

"No. You?"

"No." Mason turned off Route 50 and followed the now-disturbingly-familiar road. "Do me a favor. Grab my running shoes from my bag."

Addie raised an eyebrow. "Planning a jog?"

Mason reached for his remaining slide and held it up. "I lost the other one when we were trying to find the Jeep."

"That couldn't have felt good," Addie said, rummaging in the back seat for his shoes.

"Didn't feel a thing." It was true. He had been so determined to get Addie to safety and make it to the police, that his adrenaline blocked all sensation of pain.

By the time they got to Byrne Mountain, flashing red-and-blue lights had transformed the mountainside, and the fear Mason had felt only an hour earlier welled up in his gut. Visions of the woman rushing the small wooden door as Guy pried it open, the sound of her cries, her voice hoarse from screaming, it all filled his mind in place of the silent visions he had seen over the years.

They parked just beyond the painted tires, which looked less threatening in the glow of emergency lights from the vehicles that crowded the drive.

Kenna Cook's family bolted toward the officers standing around Guy's house. Addie, Mason, Sheryl, and Indy followed.

An ambulance stood behind the garage, its back doors open, waiting. Mr. Cook ran past the few police officers standing around it, breaking free of their attempts to stop him.

"That's my daughter out there!" he yelled, and he disappeared down the police-lit path Guy had taken earlier on his ATV.

Emily and Grant struggled to help Mrs. Cook, whose small frame was racked by tears. She stopped in her steps often, bent over sobbing violently, before they too disappeared up the mountain.

Mason didn't know for certain who the trapped woman was. The video was grainy, and the woman was shadowed by Guy's huge frame. He wanted Kenna found, but the reality of what most likely happened to the woman who was trapped there was terrible. He didn't wish that on anyone.

A radio nearby crackled and then they heard, "We are bringing her out. She is conscious but severely dehydrated."

Addie collapsed into Mason's arms, sobbing in relief. Whoever it was, she was saved.

Sheryl came alongside Addie and Mason, and encircled them in her arms. "Whoever she is, she's going to be alright. Thanks to you two."

Two EMTs, carrying a stretcher, emerged from the path. Mr. Cook held the woman's hand and bent over her, whispering in her ear. Mrs. Cook held her daughter's other hand and leaned in, tears streaming down her cheeks. They all climbed into the ambulance, and the doors closed behind them.

"Where is he?" Grant demanded, looking past Deputy Burke, and back down the path they had come.

"Soon to be on the way to the county morgue. He's dead."

The tightness in all of Grant's features melted. He no longer needed to prepare for a fight. "Good. He can rot."

"Where are they headed?" Emily motioned after the ambulance. "We need to meet them there."

"Sterling County Hospital. It's in Ely." Deputy Burke rubbed his hand on his forehead.

Emily turned to Mason and Addie. "We'll never be able to repay you for finding my niece." Tears slid down her cheeks.

Addie gave her a hug. "I'll pray she recovers quickly."

Emily wiped away her tears and turned toward her car.

"Thank you," Grant said, choking up as he stepped toward Mason and Addie. "I'll text you and let you know how she is."

Grant pulled Addie into a hug and gave Mason a fist bump.

"Didn't Deputy Burke go to see the Norris brothers tonight?" Addie asked as Grant headed to his mom's car. "What happened with that?"

Grant looked back at Mason and Addie as his mom honked the horn. "Nothing," he said.

"What!" Addie exclaimed.

"They weren't there." Grant ran the rest of the way to his mom's car and raised his hand in a wave. "Thank you!"

Their car disappeared around the turn, and Mason wrapped his arms around Addie, pulling her close.

Deputy Burke walked up to them. "You never told me, what were you kids doing out here in the first place?" He ushered them to a makeshift command tent that had been set up.

Mason hadn't expected this question—or any question, for that matter. He told a partial truth. "We went up on the mountain to watch the sunset."

"And it was so pretty, we stayed to look at the stars," Addie added.

Deputy Burke stared at one, then the other. "The sunset and the stars? Really? Not sure that explains how you got that video though."

Mason and Addie remained silent as Deputy Burke stared at them, waiting for an answer. When they said nothing, he let out a long sigh.

"Well, I'm mighty glad for the coincidence," he said. "You saved that woman's life with your appreciation for nature."

"'Mighty glad' should only be the start of how you feel, Stan." Sheryl came up alongside Addie and Mason. She squeezed Addie's shoulders. "I'm mighty glad too. And I'm thankful that neither of you were hurt."

Addie gave her a hug and turned to Deputy Burke. "What happened with the Norris boys? Grant said they weren't there when you went to meet them."

"Found them at Sterling County Hospital," Deputy Burke said. "They were both beaten pretty badly with a tire iron."

Addie gasped, and Mason asked the question they already knew the answer to. "Who did it?"

"They said they didn't know who he was. Gave a vague description that could be half the men in Nevada." Deputy Burke looked toward the EMTs loading a stretcher into the back of a second ambulance, this one with a white sheet draped over the body. "I imagine they'll remember who did it now."

"They told you that Guy was the mechanic, didn't they?" Addie challenged.

Deputy Burke didn't know that they'd overheard his conversation with Guy, but it would've been a good guess.

He stared at the stars peppering the sky, then looked at Addie. "Yes. One of the boys did, but the other said it was someone else. There's a long history there, and it seemed plausible that Travis Ray threw Guy's name out as some sort of revenge."

"I don't get it," Mason said. "They didn't get along, but the Norris boys still brought Kenna to Guy? And then they didn't say anything? Why?"

"Like I said, they have a complicated relationship. But my guess is, Guy was the closest mechanic. Her car needed fixing, and T-Ray and Billy took her to the nearest garage. Then they went to the race in Vegas. As simple as that. In their minds, it'd little to do with liking someone."

The ambulance with Guy pulled out, and another ambulance backed in.

Mason motioned toward it. "Is someone else hurt?"

"Look, we didn't just find Kenna Cook out there."

Lieutenant Wallace helped load a stretcher into the ambulance, the occupant shrouded in a white sheet.

# CHAPTER 44

As he drove, Mason's mind raced through images of the mountainside and Guy standing by the crude wooden door. He didn't remember seeing another door, but then he was too shocked to notice anything else.

Mason and Addie had declined both Deputy Burke's and Sheryl's offers to stay the night in Valterra. They wanted to get away from there, from the dust, the ATV trails, the thought of Guy Smith. Deputy Burke had a copy of the video, though he figured there was enough evidence at the scene to make the video irrelevant, and Addie erased it from her phone.

But even with it deleted, the sound of Kenna's screams etched themselves into Mason's memories.

"Do you think the other woman was Lieutenant Wallace's daughter?" Addie asked.

"Maybe." Deputy Burke's words echoed in Mason's mind: "We found the remains of a body, mostly buried and pretty decomposed, in another cave near Kenna. And there's a good indication that we'll find more." Mason shivered at the thought.

"Can you imagine how many times Lieutenant Wallace talked to Guy?" Addie said. "Joked with him. He said he rode ATVs with him on his property. And all the while, Guy..." She couldn't say it out loud.

"Don't," Mason said. "Heaven knows Lieutenant Wallace will never stop thinking about it."

Indy, sensing her owner's sadness, rested her head on Addie's arm. If Addie moved, Indy was up, sticking her nose in Addie's face, ready to lick her tears.

"I'm sorry about all of this," Mason said as they drove through Liberty, Nevada. He briefly thought about the Loneliest Road stamp they had planned to get at the courthouse. That had only been the day before, but it felt like the universe had rippled time since then.

"Don't be sorry," Addie said. "Because of you, we saved Kenna." Light from the town's two street lamps reflected in the Jeep's windows. "If you didn't say anything, heck, if you didn't have that vision in the first place, that woman would still be a prisoner."

Mason thought about Kenna from his childhood, riding her bike and waving to him. He wished he could've done something to help her too.

"Your stubborn desire to check out Guy's house—that's what saved her," Mason said. "It's like you knew."

Addie rubbed her eyes. "I watch too many Netflix shows, like you said. I don't know. He was so angry when Deputy Burke suggested he knew something. But I didn't think he was such a monster."

Mason nodded, replaying the vision of Guy's huge shadow over the small wooden door. "Let's talk about something else and try not to think about him anymore tonight." Mason knew that was impossible, but he wanted Addie to rest.

A faint smile came to her lips, and she squeezed his hand. "We haven't driven this road before. Why don't you tell me stories about the skid marks? Like you used to. Except this time, I'll know they're real."

The night hid the marks on the road, and the small beam of the headlights didn't do much to illuminate them. "There must not be any," he said.

Mason thought about their drive. Had he seen any skid marks since they left Byrne Mountain? He must have seen the one Addie had made when she thought she was driving to the police station. Maybe his mind had been too absorbed with what they'd seen tonight to notice them.

"Ok, let me know when you see one," Addie said, leaning back into her seat and staring at the darkness out her window.

They passed through Fallon. He didn't know where they would stop for the night, but he was certain he wasn't ready to stop yet. He knew the events of the day, of the last couple of days, would catch up with him at some point, but for now, he wanted to get Addie as far away as he could.

When he saw a dark skid mark outside of Fallon, he braced himself for the vision he knew would come, but he saw nothing.

*Did I miss it?*

He'd trained himself to avoid skid marks whenever he could, so it was possible he'd avoided it. He sat alert, watching for other marks, intent on driving over them.

When he knew without a doubt that he hadn't missed a skid mark, and when the vision never came, he was baffled. He didn't know what to think. Mason glanced at Addie, about to say something, but her eyes were closed and her head was propped on the window.

*Good.*

Mason hoped she wouldn't have nightmares. She needed rest. As for him, he was wide awake with the possibility that he could no longer see visions left in the road.

Random visions had plagued his mind for most of his life, and now, without them, he felt ... free. A smile grew as the feeling took root.

He purposely ran over skid marks he could've avoided, testing this new sensation. He relished the lack of knowledge he gained. Anything or nothing could've happened, and he was unaware.

After his euphoria wore off, Mason thought about the timing of his loss of the visions. If this torment, or gift as Addie called it, disappeared days earlier, he wouldn't have been able to help Kenna Cook. Kenna. He thought of his neighbor, how her mother's face was twisted in anguish over her daughter's body, but he never heard her screams. Mason didn't think he'd ever stop hearing Kenna Cook's screams.

He glanced at Addie. Indy lifted her eyes to look at Mason, leaving her head resting on Addie's arm.

"Good dog," Mason whispered and scratched Indy's head. She thumped her tail against the back seat.

*What now?*

That question seemed to encompass everything. What would help Kenna Cook heal from such a trauma? What would a whole town who trusted Guy do with this knowledge? What will help Lieutenant Wallace forgive himself? What would they tell their parents about Valterra? And what would happen between him and Addie? He was thankful that his thoughts remained uninterrupted, even as they got closer to Reno, and the skid marks on the road increased.

When he couldn't avoid it, he pulled into a gas station.

"Just getting gas," he said as Addie stirred.

"Where are we?"

"Near Reno."

"Wow." Addie sat up. "How long did I sleep?"

"About two and a half hours."

"I need to pee." She slid into her shoes and climbed out of the Jeep. "I'll be back in a minute."

Under the lights from the Chevron station, Mason could see how dirty both he and Addie were, covered in dust and tear-stained.

"How about you, girl?" Mason said to Indy. "Do you need to pee?"

Mason walked Indy to the small patch of grass and checked his phone for a nearby campground. He knew they couldn't show up at the Harlan Hotel now, not looking the way they did. It was a little after two thirty A.M.

"What's the plan?" Addie asked when she returned. He could see that she'd washed her face, probably the best she could in a gas station bathroom sink.

"Mt. Rose Campground," he said. "It's only about thirty minutes away."

"I'm glad you didn't say Incline Village. Could you imagine what my mother would say if she saw me right now? And my dad?" Addie looked at her phone. "Two missed calls. They are not going to be happy with me."

"Or me, but if they look at your location in the morning, they'll see that you're miles from them. That'll help."

"You said Mt. Rose? The name sounds perfect. I can drive if you need a break."

"I'm good," Mason said. "Let me run in for a minute."

Mason went inside the gas station. When he returned, Indy was in the driver's seat.

"You think you're going to drive now?" Mason waved M&Ms and bottled water. "I got some late-night fuel for us."

"And nothing for Indy?" Addie teased.

He produced a bag of beef jerky from his back pocket. "Her favorite!" Mason said, scooting Indy over and climbing in the driver's seat.

"Thanks for driving," Addie said. "I don't think I could have handled it if we stayed in Valterra."

"Me either," Mason said.

They headed up Mt. Rose Highway, and Indy stood on the center console, sniffing the air.

"Do you smell the pine?" Addie asked. "That is so much better than the dust of Nevada."

"You might want to rephrase that ... we're still in Nevada," Mason said, as the Jeep twisted and turned up the mountain.

Addie grabbed Mason's hand and brought it to her lips.

# CHAPTER 45

"Wake up, sleepyhead," Addie whispered in Mason's ear. "I brought you coffee."

"Now I know I'm dreaming," Mason said without opening his eyes. "You never wake up before me. And where would you get coffee?"

Addie kissed his eyelids, the tip of his nose, his ear.

"Oh, I definitely like this dream," Mason said with a moan.

"Goof!" Addie swatted Mason's stomach.

Mason opened his eyes, and a mug of coffee hovered above him.

"From our neighbors," Addie said in response to his raised eyebrow. "I met them when I took Indy for a walk. How did the birds not wake you? They're so annoying."

Mason sat up and tried to smooth his hair. "Am I in an alternate universe?"

"Can you smell the air?" Addie said. "I love it."

"I can only smell this wonderful coffee." Mason propped himself up on an elbow and sipped. "Is your hair wet?"

"There are no showers, so don't get excited. But there is running water. I sort of showered in the sink. It's ice cold. Be prepared."

"What time is it?" he asked.

"Just after nine," Addie said. "I woke around eight. Those darn birds. I wanted to let you sleep longer, but, well, my dad has had enough of our road trip. Plus, I think my mom is excited for me to see the house."

Addie started to roll her sleeping bag.

"You know, you're getting to be a pro at that," Mason said.

"Don't get too excited. I still like my Harlan Hotels."

Mason put his hand on Addie's to stop her from packing up. "How are you today? I mean, you know ... that was a lot last night."

Addie straddled her partially rolled sleeping bag. "I'm thankful it's over, especially for Kenna," she said. "But I know that it won't ever be over for her, will it? Or for us."

"You should really, at the very least, talk to your mom about what happened," Mason said. "I mean, not about the vision or us stalking Guy, but you know."

"Can we talk about this later? I really want you to meet our neighbors."

Mason knew this was false cheer, that Addie was trying to pretend like everything was fine, but he didn't want to push her. He followed her out of the tent and stretched his arms into the air. As he did, he leaned back and looked at the towering pine trees.

"Wow!" he said.

"I know," Addie said. "They looked amazing against the stars last night, but this morning, the green of the trees against the blue of the sky. Stunning."

"It might not suck living here," Mason said.

"Remember, I'm upset about the people I'm leaving, not the scenery."

The reality of her move had disappeared from his mind when they were trying to find Kenna, and now it rushed back. Today, they would meet up with her parents. Actually, in a matter of hours, they'd be with her parents. There would be no more curling up in the tent with Addie. He would be in a separate hotel room, probably on a whole different floor, than Addie.

Mason grabbed his toiletries and washed up the best he could in the bathroom sink. Addie had been right, the water felt like snowmelt, but it was much better than the twenty-four hours' worth of dirt and dust that coated his skin.

Mason rejoined Addie, who chatted with the couple at the next campsite. "You must be the owners of this mug. Thank you. I cleaned it out."

"Late night of driving for you two, huh?" the man asked.

"Yes, but we made it." Mason didn't know what Addie had told them, so he said very little.

"This is Jenni and Jeff." Addie motioned to the couple. "I told them about my dad's transfer and the move."

"And we told her that she'll love it out here," Jeff said. "It's a different pace than Chicago—I should know, I used to live in Wheeling —but it's the perfect pace."

"You made the same change?" Mason asked.

"I moved out here to be with this beautiful woman twelve years ago, and I've been happy ever since."

"Don't let him fool you," Jenni said. "He moved out here to ski. I was just a bonus."

Addie raised an eyebrow at Mason. "Another bonus. Imagine that."

The kettle on their camping stove started to whistle. "Would you like more coffee?" Jenni scratched Indy's belly, who was lying down next to her.

"No, thank you," Mason said. "It looks like you have a new friend."

"They camp all the time, Mason. You'd totally get along."

Mason poked Addie in the side. "Did she tell you that she's more of a five-star girl?"

"Living out here, you'll get over that," Jenni said. "One of these days, we'll build a deck on our house that has a pull-out bed, then we can sleep outside on something more comfortable than a foam pad."

"And still have electricity and a shower," Jeff added.

"What a cool idea." Mason nudged Addie. "A cross between camping and a Harlan."

"Sounds like a perfect combination," Addie said, laughing and wrapping her arms around Mason's waist. "Thanks again for the coffee. I guess we better pack up. We sort of crashed this campsite, and I don't want to get anyone mad."

"No worries," Jenni said. "Welcome to Tahoe."

"Look at that," Mason said when they crawled back into their tent. "You're making friends. Just like Indy."

"Don't tell my parents."

"I like your choice of T-shirt." Mason pointed at *Everyone in this town is high*.

She looked down and smiled. "You said it would be funny if I arrived in Incline Village wearing it. I still plan to torture my parents some more for this move."

"Speaking of your parents ... what do we tell them?" Mason started to roll up his sleeping bag.

"I'm not in that big of a hurry," Addie said, reaching out and stopping his arm.

"Oh." Mason stopped rolling. "Me either."

She leaned her pillow on his partially rolled sleeping bag. "How was the drive last night? Sorry I totally fell asleep on you. Was the road okay?"

"That's the funny thing," Mason said, folding his pillow in half and leaning back on it. "I didn't see any visions."

"What?" Addie propped herself up to look at him. "There weren't any skid marks?"

"No. I mean, there were skid marks. It's just, I didn't have any visions."

"What?" Addie sat up completely. "Are you sure?"

"I purposely drove over marks and saw nothing."

"Are you telling me that you've had this cool superpower your whole life, and now it's gone?"

Mason couldn't tell if she was disappointed. "I don't know what happened, but I can't see visions anymore."

The jeering sound of the mountain blue jays interrupted their discussion.

"See, I told you they were annoying," Addie said as she slid next to Mason and rested her head on his chest. "We need to talk through this. I can't believe they disappeared."

Mason intertwined his fingers with hers. The tent fluttered in the breeze. "I know. It seems like too much to hope for, but it felt great driving without the visions last night. I needed that, especially after everything that happened."

"I hope they're gone, for your sake. Then you can drive to visit me whenever you want." She squeezed his waist.

"Oh, I'm flying when I visit you. Trust me," he said. "How about you? Really, how're you doing?"

"Better," she said. "I get these images that pop into my mind, you know, and I can still hear Kenna scream. But I guess that'll fade."

"It was a terrible sight."

"But she's safe now. That's good. I just remind myself of that."

Mason ran his finger along her arm, weaving between her freckles. "You know, we should really tell your parents what happened."

"No," Addie snapped. "I don't want to tell them anything about it."

"Nothing about Kenna?"

Addie shook her head, and Mason pulled her in for a hug.

"I know Deputy Burke said he was going to say it was an anonymous tip that led them to Guy's, but someone might call you," Mason said. "They might need more information. Your parents would lose it if they found out what happened months from now."

Addie shook her head again, and he felt her tears through his T-shirt.

"That's a lot to keep to yourself," he said, keeping his voice soft. "You should at least talk to your mom. She would listen."

"Parents don't always understand. You should know that."

Addie's comment had its intended effect—it stung.

Addie looked at him and rested a hand on his chest. "I'm sorry," she said. "I shouldn't have said that. It was an unprovoked attack. It's just, I know my mom. She'll totally overreact. I don't think I could handle it. She'll lose her mind if she found out what I saw."

"I get it." Mason held Addie close.

"What about you? Are you okay keeping it from your parents? 'Cause if you told yours, then..."

"I don't want to think about it, let alone explain it to someone," Mason said. "And I think I have a pretty good history of keeping things to myself."

"Let's make a deal: if I need to talk about it, I'll call you." Addie kissed him softly on the cheek. "And if you need to talk, you call me."

Mason thought about the news articles that would come out, the ones he searched for but never found, proclaiming Kenna Cook had been found. He could only hope that Addie's parents were too absorbed in their move to pay attention to the news.

"But if you change your mind and tell your folks, or if they ask and you have to tell, that's cool," Mason said. "Just give me a heads up, so I can talk to my mom. If she hears about it from yours, she'd probably drive straight to my dorm room in Champaign to yell at me in person."

"Deal." Addie leaned back on her pillow. "Do you think your visions are really gone?"

"I don't know," Mason said. "I guess I can only hope."

"How will you be a super crime-fighter now?" she asked.

"I'm not convinced they're gone, but it's kinda weird. I've lived with them as long as I can remember. They became part of who I was."

"Here's an idea." Addie ran her hand down his back. "We'll Face-time everyday when you go back home. Then neither of us will ever be lonely."

"I like that idea. But..." He wasn't sure if he should ask his next question. "What about us? You said you didn't want to deal with a long-distance relationship. We'd be about as long-distance as it gets."

Addie's mouth dropped open. "Are you kidding? I didn't want a long-distance relationship with Declan. You're a whole different story."

"But you need time," Mason said. "You were with Declan for a while. I don't want to be a rebound guy."

Even as Mason said it, he knew how true it was. He was the truest definition of a rebound guy.

"No. Goof." Addie messed up his hair. "I don't know what you are. But I don't think 'Rebound Guy' fits."

"How about the incredibly hot boy next door who'd drive across the country for you?" Mason leaned in to kiss Addie, but before he could, Indy nuzzled her head between them. "This dog really is a spy for your dad."

"It's okay, girl." Addie scratched Indy's head, and the dog lay down between them.

"Oh no you don't. Go on, girl." Mason tried to push the dog out of the way, but Indy only licked Mason's chin.

"She just wants some love too," Addie teased

"I want to snuggle with you. Not this hairy beast."

Addie's hands, cool on his neck, made his body prickle with goose bumps that tingled to his toes.

Mason pulled back to see Addie in the morning light. Every freckle and birthmark that dotted her face and neck was beautiful. He wanted to make constellations of them all. He kissed her neck and escaped—for the moment—the reality before them.

"Definitely the incredibly hot boy next door," she murmured into his hair.

# CHAPTER 46

The campsite was only twenty minutes from Addie's new house, but they still left later than they should've.

With the Jeep top down, the smell of pine saturated everything. Mason drove to let Addie get a better look at her new surroundings. Azure-blue glints of the lake shone through the green pines as they wound down the mountain toward Incline Village. What they saw hinted at the beauty of the lake, but they didn't fully grasp it until they rounded a curve and the length of the lake, stretching for miles, appeared before them.

"Wow!"

Mason squeezed the Jeep into a parking spot at the lookout area so they could take it in. "It's beautiful," he said.

They got out and left Indy standing on the center console, sniffing the air. A stone wall, tall enough to sit on, ran along the viewing edge. They leaned against it and looked out over the lake. The brilliant blue reflected the sky, contrasted only with the deep green of the pine trees. On the far shore, mountains were capped with snow.

"You know," Mason said. "You might decide to stay here longer than a year."

A boat cut across the lake, inviting all the possibility of summer.

"It's beautiful, but no way. You need friends to enjoy all that." Addie looked up and down the shoreline. "Where do you think the Harlan Hotel is from here? Dad said our house is only a few miles from it."

Mason pointed toward the left. "I think it's that way."

"Maybe you can come out this winter to ski. I can be the bonus." She leaned into him, and he wrapped his arms around her waist.

"And how am I not going to kiss you when we're with your parents?" he asked.

"Oh don't worry. I'll find a way to kiss you." Addie stood on her toes and kissed the tip of Mason's nose.

Indy barked, and people came and went, taking pictures of the lake.

Mason took a deep breath and exhaled all the stress of the drive and his fears about Addie. This ending was only the beginning of the rest of their relationship.

"Hey," Addie said, hopping up to sit on the stone wall. "You never told me what you wished for on the first star. Or the shooting star. I'm keeping track."

"I won't tell. I'm still hoping my wishes will come true. I'll let you know when they do."

"Intriguing," she said. "I made a wish, too, remember?"

"What was it?"

"We'll compare notes later," Addie said, wrapping a foot behind his leg and tugging him closer.

"I like how that sounds."

"Let's take a picture before we go." She held her phone up, and they posed with the lake behind them, heads together, smiling.

Mason kissed her. "After the last few days, I think we can handle anything."

"I know I can definitely handle a hot shower," Addie said. "And a comfy bed."

"Don't bash camping so soon," he insisted.

"What did Jenni say? A pull-out bed on the porch? That's my style of camping."

Mason brought Addie's hand to his lips and kissed her fingers.

"You promised me a favor for going on this trip with you, remember?" he said.

"I was hoping you'd forgotten about that."

"Fat chance." He looked out toward the lake before turning back to her. "Ms. Adelaide Jean Lynmar."

She straightened her back at the formality of her full name.

"The favor, which you promised to grant me, is this: You are not to tread water until you go to college. Give this new place a chance. Have fun. Meet people—girls, not boys." He kissed her lips softly. "But meet people and have fun."

Addie's hand went to her heart. "That's so sweet."

"And maybe, before I fly back to Chicago, we can start giving this place a chance together. School got out last week, so I'm sure kids will be hanging around."

"Wait. How do you know school just got out? Did you research that too?" She hit him playfully on the chest.

"Let's just say that my haircut," he flipped his hair over his eyes, "would fit in fine at Village High."

"You even looked at photos? You're too cute." Addie ran her fingers through his hair, brushing it from his eyes. "I grant your favor."

She kissed him.

---

THEY WOUND THEIR WAY DOWN THE REST OF THE mountain into Incline Village.

"No visions?" Addie asked as the Jeep came around a curve and drove over several skid marks.

"None. Maybe they're gone for good," Mason said.

"Thank goodness they didn't disappear before we found Kenna," Addie said. "Wait, you don't think they disappeared *because* we found Kenna, do you?"

Mason shook his head. "I can't go there, not yet."

"You're right," Addie said. "Hey, we never came up with a name for this move. Remember, Ta-hoax? Tahoe-pocalypse? Tahoe-nado?"

Indy still stood on the center console with her head out the top of the Jeep.

"I think you should go simple—just call it Tahoe," Mason said.

Addie stuck her tongue out. "Boring."

"You know, I'm glad your dad got transferred."

She narrowed her eyes. "What—"

"Let me explain," Mason said, putting a hand up to silence Addie. "If your parents didn't decide to move, we wouldn't have been able to help Kenna."

Addie nodded. "Facts."

"And you'd still be dating Declan." Mason waved at a passing Jeep. "I'm totally getting into this Jeep-wave thing."

"I don't think I'd have dated Declan much longer, even if I stayed." Addie looked out the passenger window. "I really hope Kenna'll be alright."

"Me too." Mason focused on a skid mark in the road, reflexively bracing for a vision that never came. "And Lieutenant Wallace. If the other woman was his daughter."

"It's terrible to think about," Addie sighed.

Mason rubbed the back of Addie's neck. "I meant what I said," he said. "You should talk to your mom. She won't freak, like you think."

Addie tilted her head and raised an eyebrow.

"Maybe she'll freak out a little," Mason conceded. "But she'll listen. And it's better to talk about it than to keep it hidden. Trust me, I know."

Addie squeezed Mason's hand. "Thanks."

He squeezed her hand back before pulling it to his lips. "Need to sneak another one in before we get there. What road are we looking for again?"

She read the text from her mom. "Lakeshore Boulevard. Ha. Funny. Sounds like Chicago."

"Just like home. Sort of. Hey! Maybe that's the word for this move —Ta-home."

"Don't push it," Addie said, smiling.

"You never showed me the photo album the girls made for you," Mason said. "I didn't get to write in it."

"I have it. You can. I wasn't ready to look at it earlier, but I think I am now. Thanks to you."

# CHAPTER 47

Mason turned down a side street lined with pine trees. Four days ago, he sat in his bedroom looking down at Addie's Jeep unable to fathom how he'd make it through 2,000 miles of visions to get here. He'd done it, thanks to Addie, and now his visions seemed to have disappeared.

Addie squinted at the house numbers and pointed. "There. That's it!"

He slowed to a stop before the stone house. Shimmers of light danced off the lake behind it. "I think this won't suck," Mason said.

The moving truck wouldn't be there for a couple of days, and he was glad that Addie's first impression of Incline Village was of her new home, not the hotel.

Addie jumped out of the Jeep and ran to her mom, who was already coming down the front steps, arms open to give her a hug.

Mason let Indy out to explore the yard and hung back, giving Addie and her mom a moment together. After everything that happened in the last two days, Mason figured Addie could use a good long hug from her mom.

Indy chased chipmunks and sniffed around the trees, while Mason snuck a quick picture of Addie and her mom in front of their new home, embracing.

"What do you have there?" Mason asked, when Indy trotted up with something bright green in her mouth. "Is that a little kid's shoe?"

Mason thought about his lost slide, somewhere on Byrne Mountain, where it fell off in the panic to get Addie back to the Jeep. He hadn't cared one bit about losing that shoe, but someone was probably looking for this toddler-sized lost shoe.

"Drop it," Mason said and bent to pick up the green Croc that fell from Indy's mouth, hoping to put it where someone could easily find it.

"Come join us, Mason," Addie called from the front door.

As Mason grabbed the shoe, a vision of a small blond-haired boy dangling his feet off the back of a red wagon flooded his mind.

Mason instantly dropped the shoe and looked at Addie, panic once again welling in his chest.

"Are you feeling okay, Mason?" Mrs. Lynmar asked, her eyebrows knitted together. "You look like you've seen a ghost."

Addie raced to Mason's side. "What happened?" she asked.

Mason retrieved the shoe, and the vision returned of the boy, wrapped in a shark towel, probably going home from the beach. He sat in the wagon, and the Croc flew off his foot and landed in the grass. The parents, unaware that the shoe was gone, continued walking, pulling the wagon behind them.

Mason handed the shoe to Addie, and the vision immediately disappeared.

With a sheepish smile, he mouthed, "They're not gone."

Addie looked at the shoe then back at Mason, her left eye squinting almost imperceptibly.

Mason turned to Addie's mom and smiled. "I'm good, Mrs. Lynmar," he called, once again pretending. "Sorry about that. Your house is beautiful!"

"Look." Addie raised the bright green Croc to show her mom. "Some little person lost this."

Mason looked down the block, following the path of the couple in his vision, and pointed to the red wagon in a driveway. "I'm guessing they have kids. We can ask if it's theirs." He winked at Addie.

"What a great idea," Mrs. Lynmar said, crossing the yard toward them. "And Addie, you can introduce yourself. I bet they need a babysitter this summer! But not now. I have to show you the house. You are going to love the view from your bedroom, Addie."

Addie set the shoe on the sidewalk, and she and Mason followed Mrs. Lynmar who'd already turned back to the house.

"Shoes?" Addie whispered. She slipped one of her sandals off and handed it to Mason. "Hold this."

"Gross," Mason joked, but he took the shoe.

Nothing. He shook his head.

Mrs. Lynmar stood at the front door, smiling. "Well, I can't wait to hear all about your trip. Mason, you were so kind to drive with her all this way."

"We had a great time, Mrs. Lynmar," Mason said. "I'm glad I could do it."

Mrs. Lynmar's smile faded as she eyed her daughter's T-shirt. "Where did you get that shirt, honey? And what does that mean? *Everyone is high*?"

"Colorado." Addie laughed. "Let's see the house, Mom."

"Oh yes! Go check out the view!" Mrs. Lynmar opened the door for them.

"It was a lost shoe," Mason whispered to Addie as they entered. "Maybe the shoe has to be missing for me to see a vision."

Addie's eyes grew wide as she looked at Mason.

"I know," said Mrs. Lynmar. "The view is stunning."

THURSDAY, JUNE 20, 2019

*Reno Gazette*
Reno, Nevada

**Missing California Woman Found Alive; Unidentified Remains of Two Bodies Discovered; Local Man Involved**

Kenna Cook, 24, of Daly City, Calif., who was reported missing on May 23 was found alive yesterday. The Valterra police followed an anonymous tip that led to the residence of Robert Lantieren, known in Valterra as Guy Smith.

Police discovered Cook locked in a dwelling dug into the mountainside near the Lantieren residence. A similar-but-collapsed space discovered nearby appears to have been used as a makeshift grave. It contained the remains of two bodies, one of which is thought to be Kat Wallace, a Valterra teen missing since 2009, the same year Lantieren moved to Valterra. The coroner will release a report after DNA testing.

Lantieren was armed, according to Valterra County Police, and was fatally shot at the scene. He was wanted in South Dakota for sexual assault, assault with a deadly weapon, and attempted murder.

Cook is in stable condition, according to hospital personnel, and should be released shortly.

# Our Monarch Collection

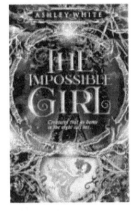

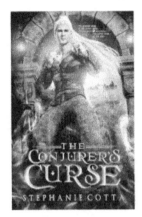

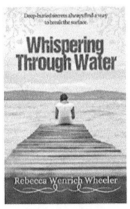

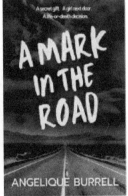

www.monarcheducationalservices.com

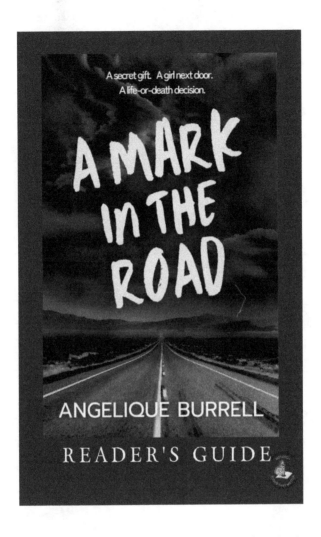

Are you ready for more of A Mark in the Road? Check out the Monarch website www.monarcheducationalservices.com for the Mark in the Road Reader's Guide. This free educational resource is perfect for educators, librarians, homeschools, small groups, and readers who want more of Mason's story.

# ACKNOWLEDGMENTS

Thank you to all the people who have encouraged, supported, and helped me along the way. This book is as much yours as it is mine.

Thank you Jen Lowry of Monarch for believing in Mason and his story. Your positive and supportive nature have been a blessing. You are an amazing champion for all of your authors, and I am honored to be a Monarch. Thank you Kelly Martin and Kayleigh Merritt for the developmental edits that guided the story in the right direction. Your ideas combined with your encouraging words were exactly what I needed. Thank you Jessica Abiatta for your keen eye during copy edits. Haley Hwang—wow! Thank you for making the story shine through your line edits and for convincing me to leave a door open. To all the Monarch authors, thank you for your positivity and humor and for promoting and supporting each other.

To my agent Bonnie Swanson of The Purcell Agency—thank you for finding the perfect home for this book and for your writing advice. Your pointers now live in my head. Thank you Joel Brigham for forcing me to face the demons I pretended didn't exist. To Tina P. Schwartz, owner of TPA—thank you for taking me on as an author. Your drive and energy are boundless, and I am forever thankful for you.

Thank you to my Jackson Avenue neighbors, especially Jeff and Eli Mathews, for taking time from your own road trip to take pictures of U.S. Route 50 for the cover of Mason's road trip.

To Sylvia Gordon, thank you for teaching me the world of social media. Your patience with my repeated questions and mess-ups is impressive and appreciated.

Thank you to the teenagers I've taught and those I haven't. Your lives are rich and busy and complicated. Continue reading fiction—it helps you do the hard work of figuring out who you are, so you can build up others.

To the educators who encourage students to fall in love with reading, thank you. A special thank you to the remarkably intelligent and compassionate teachers of the H.C. English Department. It is a privilege to work with you every day.

To all my friends who encouraged my writing, whether you knew it or not, thank you. Special thanks to Jackie and Mike Palmquist—you have always lifted me up and helped me find balance so I can be a better human. Thank you Kymmy Butts, Kate Saunders, Heather Fehrman, Lauren Otahal, Stephanie Hiffman, Kim Williams, Erin Palmer, Debbie LaDeur, and Jen Kennedy for bringing laughter to my days and always being there to lean on. Jared Friebel, thank you for organizing the group that started me writing again; you encouraged my words, along with Myles Laffey and Robyn Corelitz, and pushed me to move the story from notes on my phone to a document.

Thank you Chris and David Clement and Kari and Ed Taylor for sharing the Burrell family love of Tahoe with me, and for making it not just a destination but a piece of my heart.

Thank you Mom and Dad—Roberta and Jack Wiesemes—for your unconditional love and for teaching me the power and joy of language. You've always made me feel like everything is possible. Mom, you've taught me to be independent and your confidence in me has given me the strength to go after my dreams. Dad, you've taught me to be passionate and that there is courage in being vulnerable for what you love. Thank you, both of you, for being my foundation. Rochelle Pokorn, you are a rockstar of a sister; you are strong and witty and generous, and I admire you. You and Jim have challenged me to write from the first Fairytales, Inc. story of Jeffrey to countless others, and I'm thankful for your belief in me.

Thank you to my husband Walt for making sure there's a fire in the fireplace when I'm writing, and for taking care of everything when I disappear behind a computer screen for hours. I could not have written this book without you. When doubts crept in, you banished them with your humor and love. You boost my confidence and your love makes me a stronger person. Thank you to my children, Hadyn and Chase, for being my inspiration and for teaching me how to be brave in the face of challenge. Hadyn, I love that you were the very first reader of this story. Thank you for loving it, even as a rough-rough draft. Chase, thank you for letting me into your runner's mind, so I could develop Mason's. And thank you Harley, our dog, for being the reason our family started driving to Tahoe. Walt, Hadyn, and Chase–I love you. You are my world.

And thank you to my readers for spending time with Mason and Addie. Thank you for buying, borrowing, or sharing this book, and for supporting authors. Your actions make creative endeavors like this possible.

Above all, thank you God for planting the seeds of stories in my mind and giving me the opportunity and community necessary to make them grow.

# ABOUT THE AUTHOR

With an English teacher as a father and a librarian as a mother, it's no surprise that Angelique grew up loving to read. Now, she teaches high school English and creative writing in a suburb of Chicago, working to bring her love of reading and writing to high school students.

She is blessed to have a supportive husband, daughter, and son, who don't mind her binge writing, an extended family who always encourage her creativity, and a dog who keeps her company late into the night.

Angelique and her husband Walt love their home in Illinois, but their hearts are forever hiking in Lake Tahoe, California.

# NATIONAL SUICIDE PREVENTION LIFELINE

If you know someone is hurting or if that person is you, please reach out. Talk to school staff, family, and/or a friend, and reach out for professional help if needed. Know you are not alone. You are loved.

National Suicide Prevention Lifeline: 988

Crisis Text Line: Text "Hello" to 741741

National Alliance on Mental Illness (NAMI)

www.nami.org

National Center for PTSD:

www.ptsd.va.gov/